# LIFE'S RICH MIX

## THE WORKING LIFE OF A CHEMICAL ENGINEER IN THE SIXTIES AND SEVENTIES

## BY

## VINSON CHARD

 **New Generation Publishing**

*This book is dedicated to my wonderful, long- suffering wife Christine who has had to endure long periods of isolation while I immersed myself in the computer.*

*Thank you for your love and support, I could not have done it without you.*

# ACKNOWLEDGEMENTS

The author wishes to thank all those who have helped
and encouraged during the production of this book,
especially literary agent Darin Jewell, for having faith
and his invaluable guidance in getting this story
published.

The author would also like to thank New Generation
Publishing for physically getting the story onto the
bookshelves.

# CHAPTER 1

As the words in the song express it so aptly and succinctly, '*Life's A Roller Coaster, You Just Have to Ride it*!' Recalling incidents, events and people throughout my life, that statement corroborates my sentiment exactly concerning its vagaries and rich mix. There have been so many interesting events and characters experienced during this journey we call life, I felt compelled to immortalize them in print. It is a journey which, at times, seems like a hundred lives and in which I have been married three times, had one long standing relationship, together with a few sexual dalliances and adventures along the way for good measure. It is a journey where I have been: Student, Steelworker, Civil Servant, Bus Driver, Shift Manager, Process Engineer, Plant Chemist, Quality Manager, Toxic Waste and Effluent Engineer, Barman and even a Debt Collector.

Invariably it has been a life filled with the usual gamut of deeply conflicting emotions, with feelings of: joy, sorrow, rejection, acceptance, exhilaration, and despair, yet, always mixed with excitement, surprise and a sense of adventure, never knowing what lurks around the next corner.

I have also experienced love with its peaks of euphoria and its deep chasms of heartbreak, having been both vanquished and victor on that particular emotional roller coaster.

My journey begins in a small South Wales valley town called Ebbw Vale. Ever since my earliest childhood, the first recollections I have are those involving industry. The images catalysed and generated in my mind during those important formative years, living, as I did, in the shadows of a medium sized steelworks, with its brown plumes of elemental oxides, belching and spewing in voluminous clouds, having been conceived in the seething cauldrons of the blast furnaces, Open Hearth and LD. Convertors during the oxidation processes. Strange aromatic, coal tar and chemical odours, in conjunction with black smoke and water vapour emanated from the coke ovens located just up the road from my parents' home and in close proximity to a housing complex incongruously named Garden City.

All these images instilled a wondrous fascination in the mind of an impressionable young boy. In retrospect, hindsight and knowledge acquired throughout the years, the amount of pollution emanating from the steelworks at that time must have been totally horrendous and completely uncontrolled. The River Ebbw exhibited a rainbow of colours as a result of the numerous toxic chemical concoctions being discharged into it. Columns of steam rose from the river as a consequence of the complex, exothermic, chemical reactions taking place within the swirling eddies and currents.

At the beginning of the fifties, throughout my very early childhood, Bill Haley and the Comets reigned supreme. Elvis Presley, with his suggestively gyrating hips, was about to emerge on the scene and shock the older generation. In charge of the country, with the exception of a few enlightened individuals, the country possessed an establishment and hierarchy, insulated and completely out of touch with the common individual. Words such as ecology, environment and green had no place in the everyday vocabulary of the time, awaiting their calling and political elevation towards the end of the sixties, in the wake of that momentous flight to the moon by Apollo VIII at the twilight of 1968. That auspicious first orbital moon mission giving us all an insight from a quarter of a million miles away into the fragility of this planet we christened Earth and its need of nurturing and protection.

One of the first houses in which I lived with my parents happened to be located just a few yards from the boundary fence of this fully integrated steelworks and one of the few fully integrated steelworks in the country. Fully integrated steelworks meant it started with raw iron ore at one end, with the completed product of tin coils or galvanised steel at the other.

During the night, the incandescence of the furnaces and ladles lit up the darkness of the evening sky, giving the appearance of an artificial day with the orange glow being encapsulated between the steep slopes of the glacial valley, trapping the beautiful, angry hue, enhancing the glorious lighting effects being generated by this manufacturing village.

In addition to the industrialised, man-made pyrotechnics, the gentle, almost soporific humming of the generators and turbines could be heard, particularly during the stillness of the night. The incessant movement of the trains together with their attendant rolling stock, moving hypnotically along making the familiar gentle, rhythmic, mellifluous 'clickety, click' sound as the bogies on the wagons slowly traversed the expansion joints in the railway tracks. All these images enhanced and magnified my fascination, which this industrial conurbation had awakened in me. Even when young, I had decided to be part of this industrial world upon reaching adulthood.

In later years, during my teens, I had the good fortune to attend the local Grammar School, which, upon reflection and hindsight, happened to be an excellent institution, where I discovered my penchant for the sciences; particularly Chemistry and Physics, even acquiring the nickname, '*Prof*' from my peers. These attributes, quickly helped consolidate my belief a career in industry would most definitely be my vocation. The path which I intended to follow clearly set out in my mind's eye and choosing an Applied Science course at college, believing perhaps, with the naiveté and ignorance of youth, by pursuing this line of study, I could do something to alleviate the damage which industry continually subjected the environment to and hopefully improve the world.

During my infant years my mother contracted tuberculosis, from which, thankfully, she later recovered but only after being forced to spend a year in a sanatorium. I later believed the toxic gasses spewing in vast clouds from the steelworks exacerbated her ill-health at the time. By my teens I became convinced by studying Chemical Engineering I could help diminish the effects which the manufacturing industry had been inflicting upon the environment throughout the centuries. Or alternatively, perhaps my subconscious remembered Steve McQueen as Hiltz in the 'Great Escape' informing Ives while both had been subjected to the '*cooler*' he had studied chemical engineering back in the States and, perhaps, I wanted to emulate him… who knows?

Eventually, after attending one of the local red brick universities located in Swansea, after three years I graduated in Chemical Engineering, discovering I may have been educated in Chemistry and Engineering but not in the '*University of Life*'. Only during my time in industry did that form of education fully present itself. Experiences I will never forget, a complete insight and revelation of the industrialised world, never the less thoroughly enjoyable.

My first encounter with the industrial world

occurred during the summer months prior to commencing my studies at The University College of Swansea and in the world which had fascinated me so during my formative years; namely Ebbw Vale steelworks.

My parents did not have a lot of money, so, after sitting my 'A' level examinations in the summer of 1969, it became necessary for me to find a summer job and earn some serious money in order to supplement my meagre grant, helping sustain me through the forthcoming academic year. With the proviso my 'A' level results would be sufficient to help me gain a place in my chosen university.

By 1969, the Beatles had reached their zenith and were on the point of disbanding forever. The ubiquitous hippies introduced psychedelic into the everyday vocabulary, together with their seductively tempting promise of free love.

In complete contradiction to the hippy ethos, during the evenings, the Vietnam War monopolised our television screens generating images of Vietnamese children after they had been subjected to napalm, together with South Vietnamese soldiers shooting suspected Vietcong captives through the head, in the streets and in broad daylight, totally unconcerned with world opinion.

On the positive side, Neil Armstrong made,' *One small step for man; one giant leap for mankind.*' And the beautifully sleek, elegant, futuristic Concorde embarked on its maiden flight.

Another major redeeming factor of the late sixties being, they were the halcyon days of full employment, with most people in a job. My father worked in the steelworks, the very steelworks which had galvanized my imagination (no pun intended). The concomitant result being he was able to pull a few strings for me to get temporary employment at the works. Many of my school friends obtained employment there by the same means, a fact which helped mitigate any pangs of conscience I experienced concerning nepotism. The interview with the Personnel Manager Morris Whinge was just a formality. Within a week I commenced employment in my first real job. Apart that is from a Sunday paper round, which cannot be put into the category of employment.

Thus in late June 1969, shortly after completing my 'A' level examinations, I entered the steelworks of Richard Thomas & Baldwin, embarking upon my first real employment, working in the Open Hearth. Health and Safety did not have the high priority it richly deserves today. I reflect with horror at the cavalier attitude which the men working in steel works had for their own safety. Unfortunately, I have to include myself in this reprehensible statement.

The place resembled Dante's Inferno; molten metal appeared to be free flowing everywhere with a permanent red and orange aura about the place. Metallic sparks and cinders projected into the air, existing for a short time before eventually dying, then falling to the ground. The doors of the furnaces continually opened, traversing up and down, allowing an unrestricted view of the molten metal, bubbling angrily inside. The instant the doors opened an intense heat emanated from within the furnace core, enveloping anyone in the near vicinity. The molten steel trapped inside the body of the furnace bubbled away appearing to be an enraged living being, fully intent upon escaping from its place of incarceration. One could not look directly at this seething mass for too long with the naked eye. To do so would most certainly result in irreparable damage to one's retinas. The furnace operators could only look at this molten metal cauldron through highly tinted glasses. By looking into the furnace through these tinted glasses, the senior operator knew the exact moment to tap the furnace, permitting the angry mass to escape, and flow freely into the ladles below, then from the ladles into the moulds, which stood waiting by the teeming landing. There the metal became more passive, slowly solidifying in preparation for the rolling mills, where it underwent yet another metamorphosis, changing into coils of steel.

The men employed in the steelworks were as tough as the steel they made; genuine, hard-working, hard playing, individuals, but also, possessing, warm hearts, and willing to endure these puny students who had the temerity to encroach into their world every summer vacation and whom they were obliged to work alongside, tolerating them in silence. The conditions in which the steelworkers toiled aged them prematurely, making most appear much older than their actual years and, in all probability, terminating their lives well before the biblically allocated three score years and ten.

During my time in the Open Hearth, I first experienced comradeship and teamwork with each member of the team helping the other and everyone taking pride in the quality of their work. This instilled an *esprit de corps* within each shift team. The statistical process controls, Ishikawa diagrams, cusums, pie charts, or at that time, even basic computers,(unless one happened to be involved in the NASA space programme), belonged to the emerging, future breed of Quality Analysts, with very few of the aforementioned analytical process aids existing at that time. Yet, somehow, the steelworkers' experience saw them through and very rarely did they produce sub-standard product. The Ebbw Vale steelworkers were the epitome of true craftsmen and artisans; skills, alas, now lost forever to the town of my birth.

I did not get involved in the actual steel making process, being employed as a 'general labourer,' spending most of my time '*slinging*,' a term used to describe the simple task of putting and removing crane hooks into the lugs of twenty feet long metal containers, which resembled giant metal canoes and which were used for shipping the scrap steel. There were normally four students employed on this particular operation, working in teams of two, with each person of the team at either end of the metal container. The one team involved in unloading the containers from the vehicle beneath, the other team on the landing above removing the hooks from the lugs. The Open Hearth furnaces were perched on a stage, sometimes referred to as *the landing* and approximately thirty feet above ground level. The rigid, flat-bed vehicles arrived loaded with the containers filled to the brim with the scrap steel. The vehicles parked as near to the edge of the stage as possible allowing the containers to be winched or lifted with ease onto the stage. Two students located the hooks on the vehicle itself; the other two students removed the hooks once the containers had been placed on the landing. The empty containers already on the landing were then themselves hooked up to be put onto the vehicle for the return journey. This operation would be repeated until all full containers were on the landing, all empty ones put back onto the vehicle.

One particular day, I had been teamed up with another student, Andy, who everyone considered to be an arrogant, self-opinionated, obnoxious, supercilious braggart and not very well liked, either by myself or my fellow student labourers.

A scrap container had just been placed with pinpoint accuracy and precision by the crane driver onto the landing. Andy and I were in the process of removing the hooks from the container lugs and then placing them inside the container body, allowing the crane driver to lift them clear. Unfortunately, on this specific occasion, the crane driver was just a bit too quick off the mark in lifting the hooks, allowing Andy insufficient time to perform his required task. This resulted in him leaving one of the hooks outside the container. The containers had overhangs, on the outside, which created quite a protuberance, and the reason the hooks went inside the container, where there were no overhangs for them to catch on. The itinerant hook caught the overhang and started to lift the container on the one side during its upward journey. Ultimately, the hook broke free, violently parting company with the container, causing the latter to drop noisily back onto the platform at an acute angle due to the other hooks holding onto the other lugs. The hook then rose vertically into the air with a tremendous force and momentum, taking the attendant umbilical chain with it, travelling for what seemed an interminable amount of time.

Finally, the force of gravity equalled the inertial and tensile forces, which had caused the hook and chain to elevate in such a dramatic and forceful manner. At that instant the hook appeared to hang in the air for a considerable period of time before spiralling downwards, accelerating as it did so, ably assisted by the force of gravity. The hook and its connecting concatenation appeared to slither in a snakelike manner as it commenced this downward journey with an uncertainty as to which route it intended to take. Unfortunately for Andy, he was still underneath and in the vicinity of this, by now, lethal projectile with its increasing velocity. He decided perhaps it was time he hastily vacated the area. But no matter which direction he went, the hook, together with its umbilical chain connecting it to the crane arm, appeared to follow him, firstly to the right, then to the left, seemingly to possess a mind of its own and apparently, fully intent on inflicting injury on this risible student below.

I looked on, totally mesmerised, viewing the spectacle from a safe distance in an almost hypnotic trance, observing this ballet between a human being and an inanimate object, completely fascinating to watch. At last, the inevitable happened, the hook, with its considerable weight, connected with Andy's tin safety helmet, firstly making a tremendously hollow sound; a sound which reverberated around the building. Also, as it was metal connecting with metal, sparks began to fly; and the force of the impact generated an extremely large indentation in poor, unfortunate Andy's safety helmet. Almost at the instant of the aforementioned impact, Andy let out a loud, blood curdling scream and immediately began staggering around, appearing to be drunk, after having been very slightly dazed by the impact. He fell to the floor, but rose almost immediately, discovering much to his chagrin and embarrassment, the safety helmet had become tightly wedged onto his not inconsiderable cranium.

By now, quite a gathering of students and steelworkers had formed, to investigate all the noise and commotion. Upon observing this fiasco taking place in front of them, exhibiting a complete absence of sympathy, began laughing at the spectacle being performed in front of them. Andy desperately tried to extricate the safety helmet from his rather large cranium, where it had now become firmly lodged. He appeared to be using tremendous force with both hands in this endeavour to prize it off. In retrospect, we should not have laughed at Andy's predicament, but it did appear humorous at the time and his personality, or rather, lack of it, added to the hilarity of the situation. There is no denying the tin safety helmet had saved Andy from receiving crippling, or even possible fatal injuries, but I believe his pride took even more of a dent than the helmet. Andy did not like being the butt of anyone's jokes, although he did it to others and often in a black, sarcastic vitriolic manner. He later appeared to be fine, surviving his experience and living for many decades after the incident.

One of the other jobs I had to do during my time in the Open Hearth was that of safety man on one of the cranes were used for moving the ladles inside the huge building or doing heavy lifting work. The normal safety man had a vacation and so a replacement was required. This particular day it happened to be me. The job was not arduous, in fact it was very easy, and my main task involved ensuring the crane did not collide with another crane which was further along on the same gantry. If they were getting too close to each other, then I had to inform the crane driver. Most of the time I appeared to be superfluous to requirements as the driver, who had been doing the job for quite a number of years, remained forever vigilant. I must also mention it was a time prior to the sophisticated electronics which we have today with proximity switches sensor alarms etc.

The most difficult part of the job necessitated climbing a metal ladder with hoops in order to gain access to the cab of the crane. The cab being located virtually in the lap of the gods near the roof of the building, I estimate about one hundred feet, or possibly more, above the ground, involving quite an effort ascending that vertical ladder; however the climb was well worth it just for the spectacular view. From the cab one could see the whole length of the building. The men working beneath going about their designated tasks looked like little moving model robots, appearing minute as they did to my eyes, just as the Lilliputians must have appeared to Gulliver.

What a spectacle the Lilliputians beneath me created, tapping the furnace containing the newly made steel, completely enthralling, mesmerising and utterly fascinating to watch. The hot, molten steel flowed with ease down the refractory lined chute into the ladle waiting beneath. When full, the steelworkers push the chute to the next ladle waiting to be filled. Metal sparks and cinders projected everywhere. Each Lilliputian knew exactly what they had to do and their required part in the hazardous operation. I watched intently as they scurried about beneath my elevated perch, each man concentrating on his specific job. The tint of the glass in the cab, allowed me to watch the spectacle below without causing damage to my eyes. I was completely hypnotised by the show going on beneath me. My respect and admiration grew for the steelworkers who did this dangerous, physically draining, hot, sweaty, work, day in, day out. Frequently one of the Lilliputians would take the small towel worn around his neck and mop the salt liquid from his hot, sweaty brow, preventing the saline solution from irritating his eyes.

Finally, the time arrived for the crane to pick up the ladle containing the thirty tonnes of molten steel and transport it halfway down the huge building. Then carefully place it in a concrete plinth for collection by the other crane. The second crane would then take it to the teeming landing located at the other end of the huge complex. The crane driver putting the huge grabs of the crane under the two giant lugs of the ladle with pinpoint accuracy then gently lifted the huge 'beaker.' It was hugely impressive and exhilarating to watch the driver at his highly skilled task, as he lifted the giant ladle containing its molten hot, lethal cargo. Once he had attained sufficient height the driver traversed the huge leviathan and its cargo down the length of the building. There could be no sudden jerks, or accelerated movements, for to do so would cause the molten steel to spill over the brim of the ladle resulting in fires, explosions or, heaven forbid, possibly spill onto someone who may be in the vicinity and inevitably maiming or killing them. This particular operation was performed a number of times during the shift and not once did the driver spill even a gram of the lethal molten contents.

Most other times during the shift, the driver tended to be involved in lifting cold empty ladle for relining in the bricklaying section or lifting heavy pieces of equipment with hooks. The shift went by without any mishaps or problems.

I never performed the task of safety man on a crane ever again, much to my disappointment. However it was an experience never to be forgotten and I am grateful to have at least done it the once.

The Open Hearth indeed tended to be an extremely dangerous place to work; I had been working the day shift from six in the morning until two in the afternoon. It was my customary habit to head towards the changing rooms and shower before going home. This particular day, I slowly made my way along the hearth platform; I could not believe my eyes, for there in front of me lay a sea of molten steel which appeared to be heading slowly in my direction. The molten metal flowed inexorably along the floor of the platform like some malevolent reptile. The living being had escaped from number two furnace where it had been incarcerated and now slowly moved outwards in various directions. Steelworkers scurried and rushed about and at the same time shouting incoherent instructions, incoherent to me at least, but each man understood the other.

In an instant, I decided I could do absolutely nothing to alleviate the situation, coupled with the fact heroism is one of the many virtues I do not possess, being a devout coward. I therefore walked briskly in the other direction, the one I had just come from, but on the way, informing my fellow students in the mess hut of the impending disaster looming upon them. All to no avail, as to a man, they all thought it was a wind up on my part, this despite all my fervent protestations. I walked back out of the mess cabin and back onto the landing to view one of the most incredible sights of my life. Fred Rhimes, the shift charge hand, and our immediate boss, went hurtling past me, heading in the direction of the slow moving, fluid mass, running on a section of the metal which had slowly and partially solidified on top of the molten metal. He then raced towards the back of the furnace, the cause of all this mayhem. This particular section of the malevolent reptile had formed a thin, solid crust on the top of the steel and sufficiently thick to prevent Fred from sinking into the molten part of the steel which lay beneath it. The special clogs he wore contained metal studs on the soles, preventing the shoes from melting with the intense heat.

Fred was by no stretch of the imagination a young man, but at that instant he appeared to exhibit the agility and speed of an Olympic athlete. His feet appeared to barely touch the hot, solid, mass below him, as he propelled himself along. The whole incident suddenly presented itself to me in slow motion. The adrenaline now coursing through my veins induced my brain to slow everything down. It was totally bizarre and had never happened to me before this incident and it has only happened once since, whilst observing a car crash from a safe distance.

Fred achieved his desired goal, reaching the back of the offending furnace, mercifully and thankfully, without any mishaps. For undoubtedly, had he fallen over, or tripped, he would have burnt to death where he fell and in the most excruciating pain imaginable.

Meanwhile, on the landing immediately in front of the furnace, a driver remained in his '*charger*,' continually manoeuvring the arm of the vehicle into the gaping mouth of the furnace. Located at the end of charger arm was an empty scrap container, which substituted as a battering-ram. The container, by now, had become thoroughly burnt and charred from the intense heat of the furnace. The driver completely surrounded by the molten steel.

Suddenly a loud cheer en masse could be heard from behind the furnace. At last, the obstinate, obdurate clay plug relented, becoming dislodged, allowing the molten steel to flow freely and uninhibited into the desired destination, namely, the empty ladle waiting below.

Gradually, the flow of steel from the front of the furnace abated as the level inside the furnace slowly dropped. The danger had passed but to this day, I still shudder when recollecting the actions of Fred and his colleagues and possible consequences had they failed in their endeavours, particularly the consequences had Fred, God forbid, lost his footing and fallen onto the hot metal beneath him!

The following weeks passed without any further major incidents. A year indelibly etched into my memory, purely from a sense of history. Just as I am able to recall where I was the night Lee Harvey Oswald assassinated President Kennedy, I can also recall the historic night Neil Armstrong and Buzz Aldrin landed and ultimately walked on the moon. That particular evening I happened to be working the night shift in the

Open Hearth and rushed home as fast as I could to observe the momentous event live on television. The first men to walk on the inhospitable satellite. Upon arriving home at about six thirty in the morning imagine my disappointed on discovering the two intrepid astronauts had re-entered the Lunar module following their short excursion on that inhospitable surface. I had missed the live historical event, something I have always regretted to this day.

During those concluding weeks working in the Open Hearth, some of my time was spent in the company of George, whose duties consisted mainly of haunting the cellars beneath the furnaces, cleaning out clinker. George seemed to be older than Methuselah; with his haggard, wrinkled features, although he was most probably much younger than his outward appearance. During one of our many breaks, George decided to enquire about his young new assistant. His questions being asked in one of the strongest Eastern Valley accents I have ever encountered.

'Student is you butty?'

I answered to confirm he was indeed correct in his assumption.

'I've worked with a fair amount of students in my time butty,' he continued. 'I've even worked with that red haired student. You know the one who became the MP for Bedwellty. What was his name now?' he asked of himself and of me.

I must admit, at that time, I had not the foggiest inkling of the person George was talking about. There was a prolonged silence between us while he thought strenuously to remember the name of the minor celebrity with whom he had worked. George suddenly shouted the name of the MP in victorious re-collection.

'Kinnock ... Neil Kinnock that was the name of the bastard. Do you know him?'

I answered that I did not know him and had, in fact, never even heard of him. George once again went silent, obviously reminiscing about his time with Neil Kinnock, while puffing thoughtfully on his pipe which must have been filled with the cheapest, most vile smelling shag it was possible to purchase at the time. Once again George's strong Ebbw Vale, Welsh Valley accent broke the silence between us.

'He was a lazy bastard, I could never find the fucker and when I did he was always sleeping.' This last comment was not uttered with any form of hatred, or even in the form of recrimination, but in a matter of fact way, with what appeared to be, a hint of admiration. If anything, as if to say,

*'Good luck to him for getting away with it*!'

The statement concerning Neil Kinnock's horizontal hobby having been made, George continued puffing pensively on his old pipe, obviously savouring every inhalation of the cheap shag, deep in his own secret, enigmatic thoughts.

A few years would go by before I heard the name of Neil Kinnock being mentioned again and occurred during his rise to political power and aspirations in becoming leader of the Labour Party. When I did hear his name, the recollections of old George puffing on his old, dilapidated pipe came flooding back, with those words reverberating in my head,

'*He was a lazy bastard*!!' With those recollections, a wry smile came to my, by now, older features. Was there a chance this '*lazy bastard*!' could one day possibly become Prime Minister of Britain?

I always enjoyed collecting my pay packet on the Thursday evenings; pay night involved a special journey by bus from the new council estate where I now lived with my parents at the north end of the valley to the south end of the steel works, necessitating a journey of quite a few miles in distance. That is unless I happened to be in work at the time.

It was always a thrill to queue outside the pay booth, and to be handed the packet bulging with notes and coins. To feel it in your hands containing wages for the previous week's efforts. In today's society, most people have their wages/salary paid directly into the bank and do not physically come into contact with their earnings. There is absolutely nothing which beats the physical touch of the new, crisp, unblemished, smooth notes in their sealed envelope, take them out and begin counting. There was also the distinctive smell of the crisp, newly printed notes of the realm. To actually see the tangible, perceptible evidence of the reward being paid for one's toil.

The indigenous workforce would get annoyed when peeking at the students' payslips indicating, nil tax, despite them having worked a large amount of overtime and having a fairly substantial wage for the week. As long as our earnings were below a certain limit, we were not taxed.

We worked what was known as the continental system which went like this:

| | |
|---|---|
| Monday, Tuesday days | 06:00 – 14:00 |
| Wednesday, Thursday Nights | 22:00 – 06:00 |
| Friday, Saturday, Sunday Afternoons | 14:00 – 22:00 |
| Monday, Tuesday | Days off |

Which meant the shifts would then rotate during the weeks. As they did so, every few Thursdays resulted in working the day shift and having to collect my pay in the evening and not working until the following night. The other week I could collect my wages after working the afternoon shift with the following day as my day of rest. On both those Thursdays, after collecting my wages, I travelled, by bus, directly to *The Level*, a newly opened pub. My fellow student workers and colleagues usually accompanied me and we all headed for the pub after we had all collected our pay packets. *The Level* became extremely popular with my peers and school friends. On those particular Thursdays mentioned, because I did not have to get up early the following morning, quite a few beers would invariably be consumed, by me and my friends, before wending our slightly inebriated ways home. With most people flush after having collected their wages, the pubs invariably became packed with customers of my age group. Oh yes, during the sixties and early seventies, Thursdays in Ebbw Vale indeed tended to be very sociable, convivial evenings and most pubs packed to capacity, unlike the new millennium with pubs closing by the dozen every week.

The final weeks passed and my first experience of working in industry drew slowly to a close.

My last shift happened to be a night shift. Stan one of the regular steel workers insisted I left early, about three thirty in the morning, promising me he would clock me out, a practice which was and is illegal, and tantamount to fraud. Discipline was lax and clocking other people out, although illegal, was rife. I still feel, guilty about being party in such fraud by agreeing to Stan's offer.

I later discovered from one of the other students, Stan had offered to clock out eight other workers that morning, which he did, unfortunately, he forgot to clock himself out and had great difficulty in persuading his immediate supervisor to sign his clocking card.

With my sojourn in the Open Hearth coming to an end, it only remained for me to await the results of my 'A' Levels, which, I must admit, I was not at all confident about, awaiting my letter with great apprehension. Fortunately I was successful in my attempt to gain entry to the University College of Swansea, commencing my course in Chemical Engineering September 1969, much to my relief.

The following summer, once again, I obtained temporary employment in the steelworks, but in a different section. Nevertheless, it would prove to be just as interesting and as dangerous, if not more so, as my time spent in the Open Hearth.

# CHAPTER 2

The following summer, after completing my first year at the University College of Swansea, I once again applied for temporary employment in the steelworks. As hoped, my application was accepted without question. By now my physical appearance had changed somewhat, having made a complete metamorphosis into the stereotypical student of the sixties and seventies, with the obligatory long hair, unshaven and unkempt appearance, totally resembling a hippy, no longer encumbered with the discipline, rules and regulations of a schoolboy. Notwithstanding my appearance, the fact that I had worked in the steelworks the previous summer helped me attain employment, there once again, together with the numerous strings being pulled on my behalf by my father.

I went through the usual formality of the interview with Morris Whinge, the Personnel Manager who informed me this particular summer I would be working in the Convertor Shop, a more updated steelmaking process. The Convertor Shop being situated in the building right alongside the open hearth. The interview, if it could be described as that, was held on a beautifully, clear, hot summer's day. Following my short meeting with Morris Whinge, it was then necessary for me to walk to the Converter Shop and obtain the Convertor Manager's approval and final confirmation of my acceptance for employment during the summer months. The walk meant negotiating through the steelworks, a distance of about two miles. Because of the beautiful weather, I had no objection to this leisurely stroll through this industrial conurbation, which had enthralled and fascinated me throughout my short life.

Prior to the interview with Personnel Manager, I had indulged in conversation with one of the other students. He had been given a job in the *'Forty Five Yard,'* a large stores, located a mere two hundred yards from the Personnel Office.

Following my stroll and receiving the Convertor Manager's approbation, the next stage in my itinerary required returning the two miles back to the top end of the steelworks for a brief medical examination. This ensured I would not have a heart attack or such like during my forthcoming spell in the Convertor Shop. Imagine my incredulity upon finally reaching the medical centre only to discover my new friend still there; being fully convinced he would have long gone by this time.

'How long have you been here?' I enquired, making polite conversation.

'About an hour and six cans of Coke,' was his somewhat dejected, melancholy reply. It transpired he had become completely dehydrated because of the heat of the day and as a consequence completely incapable of producing the obligatory urine sample required for determining the presence, or absence, of diabetes. He was still there twenty minutes later, following the completion of my medical examination. I never met my fellow student again to enquire how long he eventually took to produce the required sample.

The next week my employment began in the convertor shop. The convertors worked on the Bessemer principle, but a more updated version, whereby instead of air being blown into the molten pig iron, pure oxygen was used, blown through a lance. This resulted in a much more efficient process, producing better quality steel. The full name of the process was LD Convertors, named after the places where the process had been perfected, the letters LD, an abbreviation of Linz & Donawitz, the names of the two towns in Austria. Ebbw Vale had very small convertors, approximately eighty tonnes, quite small when put alongside the gargantuan convertors being used in the seventies, eighties and nineties, located in Newport and Port Talbot. Despite this variation in size, the equipment and whole operation still appeared awesome and impressive to a young nineteen year old student.

One of the first tasks I was given along with three other students involved cleaning the landings above the converters. Unfortunately during our stint on the landings the convertor began to blow, generating copious amounts of brown smoke, making it virtually impossible to see where you were going, necessitating all of us standing still, otherwise we could have fallen into one of the numerous holes festooned about the upper landing. I recalled, years earlier, watching the smoke from a safe distance of my house when young wondering at the copious volume of brown smoke effusing from the buildings in the distance. Now, years later, here I was in the middle of that polluting, brown smoke.

When compared to the Convertor Shop, the Open Hearth was a veritable haven of safety. During my short time employed in the Convertor shop, I nearly met an early demise on a number of occasions. The workforce in the convertor shop tended to be predominantly, younger than those employed in the Open Hearth and consequently more irresponsible, prone to horseplay and forever indulging in childish pranks, getting into all sorts of mischief and trouble.

On one occasion upon entering the mess cabin, used for taking meal breaks and drinking cups of tea, I discovered some of the younger members of the shift had set a pile of newspapers alight. The bundles of paper had been strategically placed underneath a slatted bench upon which one of my fellow students blissfully slept, completely oblivious to the flames now licking around his torso.

When I arrived upon the scene, the flames had well and truly established themselves around the comatose body. Suddenly, the slumbering student awoke, screamed and immediately shot up, evidently aroused by the heat generated by the now completely vibrant flames. He immediately ran to a safe distance and stared back in disbelief at the flames, which had now positioned themselves in the void, which he had so recently, hastily vacated. Fortunately he had been wearing flame-retardant clothing supplied by the steelworks, otherwise by this time he would have been a human torch.

The perpetrators of this prank thought the whole episode highly amusing, bursting out in childish laughter at their victim's obvious displeasure and embarrassment at being on the receiving end of their practical joke. The rudely awakened student immediately left in disgust. After visualising this spectacle, I made certain I never fell asleep in the cabin, fearing there would be a repeat performance, this time with myself as the improvised entertainment. The Convertor Shop was a dangerous enough place without having to be alert to the pranks of the young, high-spirited, somewhat dangerous, indigenous workforce.

The hazards and dangers of the place, as with the Open Hearth, tended to be varied and numerous. Frequently sirens emitted loud, wailing sounds informing the workforce of a 'running stopper.' We were told to stay well away from the ladle. A 'running stopper' was, putting it simply, a leaking ladle except the leaking fluid happened to be molten steel with temperatures well in excess of a thousand degrees centigrade. The ceramic stopper in the ladle was used to control the flow of molten steel from the ladle into the moulds having becoming dislodged for one reason or another with loss in controlling the flowing molten mass. Often, the molten steel gushed out of the ladle.

The colossal arms of the crane embraced the full ladle and elevate it as fast as possible once it became apparent the ladle was a '*running stopper*'. The crane then transported at breakneck velocity through the building, as high a speed as was possible without causing the lethal cargo to cascade over the rim of the container.

Upon reaching the teeming landing, the steelworkers directed the gushing molten steel as quickly as possible into the moulds now under the ladle. Anyone directly in the path of the effusing ladle now being transported at such high velocity was forced to dive for cover as the container spewing its lethal contents whilst hurtled through the building. There was absolutely no way the crane driver could suddenly arrest the traversing of his mechanical charger once it had attained its terminal velocity.

If anyone had been unfortunate enough to be caught in the cascade of this red-hot liquid, undoubtedly their demise would be instantaneous. It was more by luck than judgement no-one was ever injured by a *'running stopper'*, well at least not during my time there. From a safe distance, a *'running stopper,'* appeared an awesome, impressive, frighteningly, spectacular sight. The red hot molten discharge, would, upon contact with any combustible material, immediately cause it to burst into flames. Contact with pools of water resulted in a loud, ear-shattering explosions, the intense heat instantaneously and violently vaporising the liquid. Clouds and dust formed above the once existent, but now extinct water, the fumes adding to the already highly polluted atmosphere of the building, the explosions adding to the cacophony of noise already being generated in the building.

Running stoppers happened to be just one of the many hazards. Pig iron from the blast furnaces was stored in giant vessel known as 'mixers' prior to its conversion into steel by the converters with air being continually blown through the molten iron to maintain the temperature and keep the iron molten and fluid. Just like keeping the cinders alight in a fire by using bellows, but on a much, much larger scale.

Periodically the hatchway through which the molten pig iron entered the mixer became contaminated with metal clinker. This build-up of metal clinker prevented the hatchway from closing tightly, resulting in terrific heat loss from the mixer. I was given the task one shift of assisting two, experienced steelworkers in removing the offending clinker, which had solidified around the mixer hatchway on the top. So we climbed to the top of the huge vessel, the airflow into the mixer had been stopped, allowing us to perform our task, the hatchway lid was opened and we were presented with the spectacular sight, six hundred tonnes of molten iron right there beneath us. 'Right!' bellowed the man in charge as he handed me a giant, flat edged bar. He shouted his instructions, not in temper or anger or any form of belligerency on his part, but mostly in an attempt to be understood above the cacophony of noise emanating from inside the building and in the vicinity of the mixer. He continued shouting his instructions,

'Put the blade under the clinker while I knock the fuck out of it with the sledgehammer. We'll push the clinker into the mixer... got it?'

I nodded my head indicating my understanding of the instructions, then immediately positioned the flat edge of the bar into the base of the clinker. Our leader began bludgeoning, or using the technical term, *'knocking the fuck'* out of the bar with the sledgehammer. He did it in a steady rhythm, gradually, bit by bit, the bar inexorably infiltrated into the offending clinker, rupturing any affinity it had with the casing of the mixer. The bits of clinker were then contemptuously projected into the inferno below by the third member of our party. We continued in this manner for about a quarter of an hour, taking breaks periodically to escape the intense heat emanating from the mixer. Finally, only a small amount of the offending clinker remained.

'Nearly finished!' bellowed our illustrious leader. I carefully positioned the blade of the bar into a small orifice in the small piece of clinker remaining, our leader re-commenced bludgeoning, or *'knocking fuck out of it'* as before, except this time the blade became dislodged from its position, skidding off the metal and, because of the force with which it had been hit the bar hurtled towards the gaping mouth of the mixer and the inferno below, taking me with it. In an instant, the third member of our party grabbed hold of the collar on my flame retardant jacket and pulled me back with a sharp jerk. My heart began pounding like a navvy's jackhammer realising the dire consequences had he not performed that particular action.

'Nearly lost you there son!' shouted our leader with a matter of fact attitude as if it were a slight fall he was referring to and not my certain demise. The way in which he uttered the sentence belying the seriousness of the situation yet, strangely, re-assuring me, making the possible outcome appear not so final. The two workers told me to sit down while they finished the job. It was an instruction I gratefully accepted, without any argument.

There were other instances which nearly terminated

my rather short life, taking the temperature of the molten steel in the converters for instance. This was a manual operation performed to ensure the molten steel had reached the optimum temperature for oxidizing the elemental impurities in the steel, generating them as gasses. It was a manual, archaic, almost primitive operation, requiring the operator to plunge a lance containing a thermocouple into the molten mass whilst the convertor was tilted at an angle of approximately forty five degrees and holding the thermocouple there for a period of ten seconds. The heat radiating from the vessel was intense and holding the thermocouple there for ten seconds seemed more like ten hours and sheer purgatory. Occasionally, it was my task during the shift to perform this onerous task and it was a task I detested immensely. Invariably, it usually necessitated three or four attempts on my part to obtain the required register on the circular, graphical readout pulling the thermocouple out much too early. I would always begin my arithmetic countdown at the correct pace 'one.... two..... three.... four.... five.'

By this stage the searing heat emanating from the molten mass would begin to take effect, becoming unbearable, causing my tin safety helmet to become uncomfortably hot. My counting became less precise and less protracted. 'Six.... seven.... eight.... nine.... ten!' Those few counts lasting barely two seconds and not the obligatory five. I would quickly retract the thermocouple from the seething mass. I do not know why I always speeded up the count, being fully cognizant from past experience the readout would have to be performed again until the process temperature had been registered on the graph. It was nothing more than self-preservation. The dreaded words would be heard, uttered by the senior operator following my pathetic effort,

'You did it too fucking quickly, the temperature didn't fucking register. Fucking do it again!'

This particular shift, I was about to perform my third or fourth attempt at taking the blasted temperature. Perspiration effused from every imaginable pore which my puny body possessed, and my face had the appearance of a thoroughly boiled lobster ready for consumption. By this stage in the proceedings, I had decided this was most definitely going to be my final attempt, come hell or high water and it did most definitely seemed like hell. Holding the long lance containing the thermocouple, I bravely walked towards the cavernous mouth of the converter with its lethal mass of molten steel, continuing relentlessly, my face pointing towards the floor endeavouring to gain what little protection I could obtain from the intense heating radiating towards me, a soldier marching through no-man's land to hell during a conflagration. My resolve in performing the task correctly overriding all other considerations, with my powers of concentration intent only upon getting the damn temperature, to such an extent, I failed to notice some of the molten steel pouring over the lip of the converter and landing upon the ground floor of the building some twenty feet below the platform upon which I was walking. As the molten liquid cascaded downwards, it landed upon some combustible material strewn about below, causing the material to spontaneously ignite. In the process generating a fireball of flames rising with tremendous velocity, licking around the platform upon which I continued my relentless march towards the converter mouth. Gazing straight down at the floor, I failed to perceive this fireball holocaust ahead. Once again a redeeming hand pulled me back sharply from the swinging scythe of the Grim Reaper. Within a fraction of a second, flames were licking around the place where I once stood.

'You would have burnt to fucking death!' uttered my human angel of mercy, stating the obvious. The fireball necessitated waiting a few moments for them to abate. Thankfully, my next attempt was at last successful without any more incidents.

In addition to the dangers, the work in the Convertor Shop did tend to be more arduous and physically exhausting than in the Open Hearth and in hindsight my whole working life. In fact the physical exertion encouraged a dramatic metamorphosis in my physique. Prior to my employment I was the original nine stone weaklings, with no muscles to speak of. It was a different story following my time there, having filled out, developing my muscles, biceps and solar plexus quite dramatically.

One night shift probably did more to enhance this metamorphosis than any of the others. It involved a job called stripping and before the reader jumps to erroneous conclusions assuming sexual deviations perpetrated by the workforce. The aforementioned task was normally performed by one of the regular workers, namely Stan, and involved stripping the refractory lining from the ladles, each of the ladles being stripped on a rotational basis. The main implement used for carrying out this operation being a pneumatic jackhammer. Once Stan had stripped the ladle, it was re-lined with new refractory bricks, once again allowing the shell of the ladle to withstand the extreme temperatures of the molten steel and iron.

One would have thought Stan or *'Stan the Stripper,'* as he was colloquially known, with the rigours of his job, would be built like the proverbial brick shithouse, weighing in at about twenty stones, possessing rippling biceps. This is an erroneous impression, not a bit of it, Stan was a middle aged man about five feet ten inches

36

tall, weighing approximately eleven and a half stones, with not an ounce of fat on him. A person seeing him for the first time would be totally misled into believing a puff of wind could blow him over without much effort. Not in the case of Stan, he was what could only be described as wiry

This particular night shift I was given the onerous task of covering for Stan. With the audacity and self-confidence of youth, it was my opinion if Stan could strip three ladles in a shift, so could I. Oh, the naïveté, innocence and self-confidence of youth, attributes of my life which have all now long since disappeared with the knocks my life has received throughout the years, inexorably eroded, bit by bit.

Once Reg, the Shift Foreman, had delegated all the tasks for the night, he took me to the ladles requiring stripping; I was being led like a lamb being led to the slaughter. Reg was the total antithesis of Stan, weighing at least twenty stones, with simian like appearance, complimented by his slow, lumbering gait. Once he was knocked down by one of the hooks used for lifting the fifty tonne ladles, resulting in him suffering a heavy blow requiring a two hour respite in the surgery, after which, Reg was back at work. Had any other individual suffered the same accident they probably would have been killed, not Reg, apparently the knock had little effect upon him.

But once again, I digress. Reg led me to the waiting ladle which had been dropped into a pit inside the ladle was a ladder allowing access to the bottom of the molten steel receptacle. At the bottom of the lair, the sleeping monster, my adversary with which I was about to do battle lay dormant awaiting revival with compressed air. I entered the lair, oblivious to the task ahead and slowly descended the ladder. Upon entering the lair of the ladle, imagine my chagrin at discovering the ladle was still quite warm , this, despite the copious amounts of water which had been projected at the lair by means of huge fire hoses, for at least twenty four hours. Ambient temperature had not been reached by quite a few degrees, so one can imagine the temperature of the ladle prior to this bombardment of water.

Upon reaching the base of the ladle, I casually picked up the pneumatic jackhammer discovering, much to my consternation, I could barely lift it. This was the implement with which I was supposed to remove the now redundant brickwork?

'*Heaven help me*!!' or words to that effect, went shooting through my brain. For hours I tried in vain to dislodge the refractory bricks heavily coated with solid steel. At each attempt, the drill head kept bouncing off the steel coated brickwork, causing me to point the reverberating jackhammer aimlessly into the hot, humid air of the ladle, with gravity quickly taking over, causing me to drop the heavy implement on to the floor and taking me with it. The whole action only took a few seconds, allowing me insufficient time to take my index finger off the trigger only performing this action when the implement was on the floor. With that the reverberation would cease, together with the cacophony of noise also being generated and echoing inside.

Time and time again, this pointless exercise would be repeated. Infrequently, I would have a small amount of good fortune and the drill would occasionally burrow into the brickwork of the hot ladle.

When the brickwork did eventually condescend to break away and relinquish any affinity with the body of the ladle, I became enveloped in clouds of steam, the penalty for allowing me this minor victory. The steam billowed out from the voids, where, in the form of water, it had been hiding, the intense heat of the brickwork transforming it into steam. My tribulations were not helped by Reg, who periodically came to inspect my handiwork and scrutinise the progress, or rather lack of it, which I had made. He would then complain vociferously about my ineptitude at performing the task and tell me in no uncertain terms that the Holy Grail of the schedule was not being adhered to, and then the sting in the tail, continually telling me how Stan could quite easily strip three ladles in about half a shift.

By that stage in my shift I had managed to extricate a puny one third of the bricks from the ladle. Reg began instilling in me a feeling of guilt at my pathetic ineptitude, to such an extent, I even gave up my meal breaks in an effort to make amends for my ineptitude and tries to finish this insurmountable task ahead of me. The sweat was gushing out of all my pores; the fine dust caked my face. During the operation, I had worn goggles to protect my eyes from the fine dust being generated. Upon removing the goggles, there I had two huge white patches around my eye where the goggles had once been; at least proving they were effective in their chosen task. This gave me the appearance of a human panda and I must have looked quite ridiculous to my colleagues.

Finally and much to my relief, the night shift came to an end and despite all my, heroic and valiant efforts, I had only managed to strip about three quarters of a ladle. I was thoroughly exhausted, or as my fellow students would say ' totally bolloxed.' Reg was not amused at this abysmal effort and continued to tell me so in no uncertain terms. I arrived home at six thirty in the morning. I did not realize the scale of my physical exhaustion until reaching the haven of my bed. The next time I attained consciousness, my mother was calling me. I can still hear her calling me to this day as she rudely awakened me.

'Vinson, it's time to get up or you'll be late for work!'

The first thought I had being *'But I've only just come to bed*!'

I shouted back, 'What time is it?' only to be informed it was nine o'clock in the evening, with my next night shift about to begin start at ten o'clock. I was still exhausted, horrified and filled with trepidation at having to repeat the purgatory of the previous night shift, even contemplating pulling a 'sicky,' but I desperately needed the money.

My pessimism was totally unfounded, for upon arriving at work, I discovered Stan back in work. He had only taken the one shift off. I have never been so relieved and so happy in my life to see a person in work, as I was to see Stan the stripper that particular night shift in the knowledge I would not be required to strip out any ladles that evening. My respect and admiration for Stan following that infamous night shift knew no bounds. Thankfully, I was never told to do stripping again. To this day I am convinced Reg considered it more prudent to give the job to someone else when the need arose, not wishing to go through the same stress again at not reaching the quota of stripped ladles. My physique gradually altered following my night of hell. As previously mentioned, I began to develop muscles.

The human reflex of self-preservation is a wondrous thing to behold. One particular shift, I was performing my task of 'sample boy' basically taking the sample slugs of red hot steel from small mould using a pair of tongs, cooling the red hot slug in a bucket of water prior to dispatching to the metallurgical laboratory via an overhead conveyor system much like the system used in the old Victorian stores. As I was about to perform the aforementioned task, there was a tremendous explosion emanating from the direction of the convertors. Prior to this explosion, I had observed one of the regular steelworkers, a young boy about the same age as myself standing approximately twenty feet away from the monstrous piece of manufacturing equipment. He was leaning on the railings, oblivious to everything around, daydreaming quite content in his mental aberration.

It was at this juncture, the cacophony of the explosion reverberated throughout the edifice of the Convertor Shop. Before I had time to blink, the young steelworker had managed to project himself in my direction, a distance of approximately seventy five yards, included in that distance was a flight of steep stairs. His feet appeared to barely touch the ground, as he ran past the landing where I stood with my colleagues, not arresting his momentum until reaching, what he evidently considered to be a safe distance from the source of the explosion. It was only at this stage, did he turn around to survey what had transpired and what he had left behind. When he did so, he did not have the spectacle of a holocaust; instead all he saw was the spectacle of his workmates standing smiling at him, much to his discomfort and embarrassment.

'Gave you a bit of a fright did it son?' Enquired one of the older men rhetorically, who had seen about virtually everything during his time in this man made hell.

The young boy smiled back sheepishly, obviously trying to hide his humiliation and embarrassment.

'What the fuck was that?' he shouted with the obvious terror in his voice.

'Oxy lance in the converter snapped causing the oxy to explode!' came the nonchalant reply from the teeming landing Charge Hand. 'No harm done,' he added as an afterthought to the young steelworker whose pallor had assumed the colour of white chalk. The young steelworker was conspicuous by his absence for the remainder of the shift, obviously hiding in some secret place, of which there were many, to recover from his fright and humiliation.

Disaster appeared to follow me in whatever task I had to perform during my stint in the Convertor Shop and one such incident happened concerning an electrical tram. Basically it was a small flat cart used for conveying two skips. The controls for the tram were located at the both ends of the tram at which the operator stood. The controls were simply a lever for forward and reverse and the amount the lever extended determined the velocity at which the tram propelled itself along the rails. Each skip on the tram had the capability of holding approximately one to two tonnes of solid material. One skip was used for containing lime, the other held dolomite, both materials being added to the iron in the convertor during the steel making process. The containers were filled from the base two giant silos in which each of the materials were stored. The bases were cones which ensured the materials funnelled into the container below. The flow was generated by turning a switch for an electrically operated valve. Once the containers were full, they were then on the tram a hundred yards just below the converters. The operator would put the chains onto each container as they were about to be lifted. The chains were located so that the crane diver could lift the skips and when they were over the seething cauldron of the converters, lift one of the chains allowing the base to open. The solid material would then fall into the steel making vessel.

The particular day in question, I happened to be operating the electric tram. There were a few problems, one of which being the silo containing the lime happened to be empty. Eventually word arrived the silo was being filled and contained sufficient to start filling the skip. But we had to hurry as the steel making was running behind schedule and they were awaiting the addition of the lime. My instructions from Reg were to get the lime to the converter as quickly as possible. Three container loads were required. Once the skip was filled I pushed the lever on the controls of the tram to forward full throttle in order to attain the maximum speed as quickly as possible. Unfortunately in my haste, I misjudged when to put the lever onto stop, having been told never put it directly into reverse. The tram hit the end of the track with a sickening thud, causing it to lift in the air, de-railing immediately. Unable to find Reg, I ran to the Shift Manager who appeared not to understand the gravity of the situation which I was trying to convey to him. In the end, good old Anglo Saxon expletives were required.

'The electric tram for the lime is fucked and it's impossible to get the fucking lime into number one convertor!!' I had to shout in order to be heard above the din of the building.

It is surprising the effect a few well-directed expletives can have. And my Anglo-Saxon utterances and expletives most certainly did have the desired effect. Immediately, everyone sprang into action. The crane driver was told to lift the tram and relocate it onto the tracks after expert hands had located the chains on specific points. Within a short space of time the tram was back on the tracks. Reg was found and took control of the tram with me as passenger. Thankfully, not much production time was lost. My fellow students thought the whole incident highly amusing

As my time spent in the Convertor Shop drew to a close, mercifully, the tasks I was asked to perform became progressively easier, probably instigated by the shift foreman, who, after witnessing my abysmal attempts at performing previous tasks which could affect production, decided it would perhaps be safer for everybody on the shift, for me to indulge in non-hazardous duties and which could not interfere with production. There were no more taking temperatures, exorcising clinker, stripping out ladles or skimming. Instead I was given the mundane task of opening and closing the huge sliding doors at the end of the gargantuan building, allowing access for the trains and preventing draughts permeating throughout the building the remainder of the time. Eventually, I had this particular task pinned down to a fine art, knowing the exact times the trains arrived during the shifts to bring in and take out the filled moulds. This was the early seventies when, I must confess, the industry was grossly over-manned. Today, that image has reversed with people having to take on more duties and are stretched to the limit. There appears to be no happy medium. The supervisors in the seventies had an impossible task maintaining control of the workforce, or have full knowledge of the workforce's whereabouts. The concomitant result being, members of the workforce would abscond for hours at a time. I too was guilty of participating in this 'disappearing act' being led astray by my fellow students who would persuade me to imbibe at a local hostelry, The Park Hotel at the beginning of each night shift. After clocking in at ten pm and being allocated our duties for the night and provided none of us had the unenviable task of Stripping, we would all make our way to the Park Hotel, which I must confess, in those days was, what could only be described as a spit and saw dust hotel, frequented by the local reprobates, hardened drinkers and travelling contractors, so I felt quite at home and fitted in quite well. After sinking a couple of pints we would all return to our allocated duties at about eleven thirty

During my stint on the doors, I indulged in this practice quite frequently and as previously stated, had the timing of the trains down to a fine art, safe in the knowledge the first train would not arrive until about twelve midnights to collect the moulds, allowing me ample time to have a couple of drinks and return to work with time to spare. One particular evening following our drinking excursion, one of the regular steelworkers informed me the Shift foreman had noticed my absence and had been searching for this itinerant student since ten thirty. Unfortunately for me the shift foreman happened to be my friend Reg who had a very low opinion of me at the best of times since the stripping episode and still harboured a grudge against me. The remainder of that particular shift, I maintained an extremely low profile, trying to keep out of Reg's way, but always having an alibi where I was. Fearing he would ask questions concerning my whereabouts for the first hour of the shift and for which I had no obvious excuse. It was only at the end of the shift did I discover I had been the victim of a wind-up and I was relieve at discovering Reg was not after my blood to feel any animosity or anger towards the perpetrators of the joke. It did however dissuade me from making any more excursions to the local hostelry.

The last shift for any student in the converter shop always resulted horse-play and high jinks by the indigenous, young workforce; taking great delight in the fact the students were the butt end of the joke. Apart from the wind-up previously mentioned, I had been fortunate to escape any indignities, which the young workforce was capable of dreaming up in their fertile young, mischievous minds. It was with this knowledge of what young workforce were capable I had deliberately kept my leaving day a firm secret, keeping it only to myself and hoping the managers would also not divulge the date. Unfortunately for me, the workforce discovered my final terminating day. The source of their information never came to light, but it did have dire consequences for me.

With about two hours of the shift remaining and I began experiencing a feeling of smug satisfaction at having duped my colleagues in evading any humility, which the sadists were capable of conjuring up. So there I stood on the teeming landing waiting to get the sample of steel. Suddenly, and without warning about half a dozen of the workforce pounced, pinning me to the floor, pulling down my flameproof trousers, together with trunks and then began inexplicably slapping green swarfega all over my wedding tackle. Once this nefarious deed had been completed, they told me the sample was ready for sending to the metallurgy laboratory and being the sampler, I had better get on with it. With this task to perform and after pulling my clothing back up to my waist, with a feeling of total humiliation began the task of getting the hot metal sample out of the mould, not realising the ramifications of the deed, which had just been perpetrated. I did however get the distinct feeling of being observed and watched. I began extricating the small slug of hot steel from the small metal mould in which it was incarcerated, using the metal tongs to shake and bludgeon the mould to release the hot metal trapped inside, still bemused by the whole episode, wondering what the point was of putting swarfega on my bollocks, they weren't that dirty surely and how would they know anyway? Almost immediately my bemusement, puzzlement and questions were answered as a tingling sensation slowly began affecting my genitalia. The sensation was slight at first. The intensity gradually increased and after a short period of time; my testicles began to feel as if a thousand needles were stabbing them at the same time. As the pain increased, I was still struggling with the mould trying to get the sample out almost on the point of desperation. By now the pain was becoming excruciatingly unbearable and still the damn sample would not come out of the mould! The pain was now agonizing and the sample was quickly forgotten; there was now just one thing on my mind. I had to wash the swarfega off my bollocks and the sooner, the better. Throwing down the tongs, sample and mould, I ran as fast as my legs would carry me and my stinging testicles allow, to the changing rooms, which, unfortunately for me, happened to be quite a considerable distance away. Observing the pain I was experiencing, my sadistic perpetrators began laughing obviously fully cognizant of the pain I was experiencing. This is the spectacle they had been waiting for, having carried out this prank many times previously.

Upon reaching the changing rooms, the procedure of divesting my flame retardant clothing began in haste, removing my apparel as quickly as possible from my puny body, while at the same time immediately heading directly for the shower cubicles. Strewn clothing indicated my course and direction. The bathhouse attendant looked on incredulously at this maniac running towards the showers virtually tearing his clothing off in the process.

The instant I entered the shower cubicle, I immediately turned the cold water tap on. There was absolutely no time to mess about with the luxury of obtaining the optimum water temperature. It had to be a cold shower to expunge the offending gel from my wedding tackle as quickly as possible. Oh, the relief as inexorably the offending gel slowly began to dissolve in the cascading water. As it dissolved so too did the excruciating pain in my testicles. There I remained for a considerable period of time ensuring all of the offending material had been eradicated from my person and in particular, my bollocks! Because of the pain being initially experienced, the coldness of the water was not noticed by my body's nervous system, having all its attention concentrated on my testicles.

When totally satisfied the offending material had been completely removed, the task of drying began. I was shivering intensely due to the coldness of the water. Once dry, it was necessary for me to retrace my steps and collect the hastily discarded attire in order to dress. After dressing, I returned to my hastily neglected duties, whereupon my assailants gave me a loud round of applause.

'Enjoy your shower?' One of them enquired, with more than a hint of sarcasm in his voice.

I immediately glared back at him, and upon seeing my expression, he came over to me.

'Don't take it to heart, it's only a joke and it being your last day, it's traditional.'

My scowl slowly turned into a smile. In retrospect, my testicles probably had the best clean ever.

In all fairness to my assailants, they told me to spend the remainder of the shift in the canteen while they covered my duties. That was the last time I ever worked in the converter shop. Sadly, a few years later the entire steel-making or heavy end as it was known of the works was shut down and dismantled. The slow decline of the steelworks had begun and the loss of steel making from the valley, sadly it was the end the end of an era. The whole steelworks finally closed their gates during the summer of two thousand and two with the entire workforce being made redundant or forced to relocate. The steelworks could not make the volumes required and in the eyes of the accountants not cost effective and so the plant had to go with thousands losing their jobs and a knock on effect for other industries and suppliers in the neighbouring valleys.

# CHAPTER 3

The following summer, my next period of temporary employment was spent working in, of all places, the DHSS. After completing my second year at College, for some unknown reason, when I signed on at the unemployment office, as it was then known, the Social Security department offered me employment for a couple of months throughout the summer vacation. Never having worked in an office environment before, I jumped at the opportunity, mainly to gain the experience, despite the low remuneration being offered, especially when compared with the earnings which could be made working in the steelworks, with the overtime permitted to work being virtually unlimited.

One obvious and distinct advantage of working in an office environment being, the work was nowhere near as dangerous as working in the steelworks, that is, apart from a wonderful lady called Myfanwy Morgan with whom I shared an office. Myfanwy, I discovered, was quite a character. Although a mature lady in her early fifties, because of my time spent with her in that small office, I fell in love with her. She was remarkably attractive for her age and must have been a real stunner in her youth. It was not entirely her physical beauty which attracted me to her, but her personality, vitality, intelligence, exuberance, sense of humour, and most importantly, her '*Joie De Vivre*.' I hoped to have her vitality and energy when I eventually attained that age.

Myfanwy was a spinster, or as she preferred to be called, a '*Bachelor Girl*.' A status and situation she enjoyed immensely, always telling me she had become far too set in her ways to now settle down with anyone, having lived on her own for a number of years. Lonely most certainly did not have a place in her vocabulary. I lost count of the number of men who avidly pursued her during my stint at the DHSS. There appeared to be a new consort virtually every day of the week and I think every one of them asked for her hand in marriage, only to be met with a firm, but polite rejection.

Being alone with Myfanwy in our little office meant we had plenty of time in which to become acquainted. She frequently reminisced about her time working at one of the munitions factory during the Second World War, located somewhere near Swindon in Wiltshire. A time and place which generated fond, evocative memories in her sharp, intelligent, active mind. Myfanwy recollected her time there with obvious affection, her favourite phrase being,

'It was a good war for some!' The implication being, she most certainly did not have a bad war. For her it had indubitably been a very good and memorable one. Her articulate, well pronounced, extensive vocabulary belied her political affiliations. She did have quite a posh, anglicised accent, unusual for the valleys, but she was a Welsh valleys girl through and through and extremely proud of it. When I first became acquainted with her, my initial thoughts were, *'Now there's an out and out Tory!'* an anathema to my socialist background and upbringing. So one can imagine how pleasantly surprised I was upon discovering my pre-conceived belief to be totally erroneous. As our friendship grew, Myfanwy proudly proclaimed of her friendship with Aneurin Bevan, the founding father of the National Health Service. He had been our local Member of Parliament and someone whom I had seen making a speech during his last General Election campaign when my parents took me to hear him speak. It was probably one of the last public speeches he made in his life. What a wonderful orator he was. Even as youngster at the tender age of nine or ten, I acknowledged there was something special about the man. Observing the people present as they listened in awe, silence and reverence to the great man, who, at one time, ran two ministries at the same time, being both Minister of Housing and Minister of Health. The people present obviously worshiped him, for not only was he in charge of the two ministries at the same time, but he did more to improve the health of the nation and also had more new housing built after the Second World War in a small period of time than any other minister up until that time. He was in fact that rare breed of Parliamentarian, one who delivered on his promises.

The family had a legend concerning Aneurin Bevan involving an Aunt (My mother's sister-in-law). During his youth, my Aunt's father became heavily involved with the miner's union. It had been decided by the local union committee, one person should be sent to college in order to advance their career and education with all fees to be paid for by the Union. The final choice for this sponsorship came down to two individuals. One of the candidates being my Aunt's father, the other being the late, great Aneurin Bevan or Neu Bevan as he was, and still is, affectionately known in the valleys. The final decision, being so close, came down to the toss of the coin which the young Aneurin Bevan won. My aunt said she was glad it happened that way, considering the effect it would have had on the country. For in all probability, there would not now be a National Health Service had the coin flipped the other way. It is quite a sobering thought, history being determined by the flip of a coin.

It soon became evident; Myfanwy was a staunch socialist and one of her pet phrases expounded with total conviction, belief and sincerity.

'Jesus Christ was the first true socialist!'

I used to get goose pimples at her complete sincerity and conviction in that phrase. My newfound work colleague was also a friend of Michael Foot who succeeded the late Neu Bevan as the local MP for the Blaenau Gwent constituency. Myfanwy showed me newspaper photographs of her accompanying Michael Foot at the front of one of the many CND marches held during the early liberating sixties. There was definitely more to this remarkable woman than my early impressions indicated. With each additional piece of information imparted by her, so my admiration for this remarkable woman increased.

One of Myfanwy's failings was her addiction to the dreaded weed. Not marijuana, I hasten to add, although it would not have surprised me to find she indulged in that too, but the common and legal cigarette tobacco. She virtually chained smoked her way through the day. This was prior to non-smoking in offices when it was still a tolerated habit and smokers were not considered to be social outcasts or pariahs they are today and being forced to accommodate and indulge their dreaded cravings by having to smoke outside and at the mercy of the elements. Not possessing a cigarette lighter, Myfanwy regularly used Swan matches or England's Glory to light the white stick containing the toxic chemical mix. She had the proclivity of projecting the discarded match into the waste paper bin. Unfortunately, the matches did not always extinguish themselves during their rather short trajectory. Invariably the waste paper bin always contained waste paper, a fairly combustible material, particularly when allowed to come into contact with naked flames at the head of a lighted match. Because of this idiosyncrasy on Myfanwy's part, it often became necessary for me to indulge in a bit of, *'Fire Fighting for Dummies'* and extinguish the concomitant fire.

Before finally leaving and returning to my studies at Swansea, I gave Myfanwy my final parting gift, a cigarette lighter. This gift had a dual purpose, firstly to remind her of our short time together confined in, what could easily have passed as a broom cupboard, and secondly, and the most important reason of all, for her own safety and well-being.

My duties at the DHSS tended to be fairly mundane and pretty boring, consisting mainly of punching out pension and supplementary benefit books. I must confess, not a particularly mentally stimulating function, but the income supplemented my grant. Occasionally, there were the brief interludes which helped pass the hours, such as my practical, on the job training with basic fire fighting skills, and my enlightening conversations with Myfanwy. But I wanted more excitement such as attending 'the clients' at the front desk. It was to this end; I generally pestered, cajoled, barracked, harassed and made a total nuisance of myself. Until eventually, I thought my pestering had paid off, when Gerald, one of the senior clerical officers suddenly walked into our broom cupboard and asked if I would like to present a cheque to one of the clients waiting in the reception area. Jumping out of the chair, I immediately grabbed the cheque from Gerald's hand, asking him the name of the client, and what was needed, then proceeded to make my way with total exuberance and unabashed enthusiasm to the reception desk. In those days the desks did not have a protective glass screen, unlike the offices of today.

Upon reaching the reception area, I observed  only one male sitting there. He was slightly dishevelled in appearance, about forty years of age, short and heavily built. The main feature I noticed about him was his broken nose, which looked as if it had been broken more than once and quite extensively on each occasion. Being still relatively naive, I thought nothing of it, which, as I recollect the story, is just as well. I must admit to exuding an air of total friendliness and boyish charm, which I had been told was one of my attributes. Thus I approached the '*client*,' asking him for the obligatory signature as proof of receipt, which he did fairly obligingly and without any form of rancour. With the formalities completed, I handed him the cheque, whereupon he went on his merry way.

With the task accomplished I had sense of having helped a fellow human being with an accompanying sense of wellbeing with a self-satisfied form of altruism. I returned to the broom cupboard which Myfanwy and I called our office. During the walk back I had to negotiate the labyrinth of corridors which permeated throughout the building. Gerald was still there talking or to be more precise, laughing and joking with Myfanwy.

'Everything go smoothly?'

Gerald enquired with an unerringly smug expression, on his youthful face, a face which belied his actual age. Gerald could barely contain his obvious desire to burst out laughing.

'Nothing to it,' I replied, in a matter of fact way, slightly exhilarated at what I considered to my benevolent deed of the day.

Gerald replied in his educated, Welsh Valleys accent and unable to contain his laughter anymore, 'That chap has just come out of prison, and you'll never guess the reason?'

My smile dropped and I shook my head indicating I had no idea, and afraid of the answer I was about to receive.

'Pulling a gun on a DHSS officer and then beating him up.'

My mouth gaped open in absolute horror and disbelief with the realisation of what could have happened, contemplating an alternative bloodier scenario to what had just transpired in the reception area and having just escaped the possibility of spending numerous weeks in a hospital ward. With these thoughts, my colour changed.

Observing the instantaneous change in my expression and pallor brought more of a smile to Gerald's face. Initially I had believed it had been a magnanimous gesture on his part in allowing me to present the cheque to the client, now I was fully cognizant of the fact, it became obvious, Gerald had self-preservation in mind, coupled with a sadistic sense of humour. From that moment on, I refrained from ever asking again to be allowed into the reception area to meet the clients and he never offered again.

It was shortly after that experience, my time working as a Civil Servant came to an end.

The next time I went there, it would be as a client. It had been yet another episode in my career, but not the sort of place or environment I would like to work in all my life. Enjoyable, nevertheless.

My final year at The University College of Swansea beckoned, with one more summer of temporary employment left to go through the following year.

# CHAPTER 4

Eventually, my studies at college came to an end after having completed my final year. At the time of leaving, I still did not know if I had obtained a degree, experiencing, once again, the purgatory of having to wait a few more weeks for the result.

Meanwhile, I had been frantically sending off applications for permanent career jobs but while the selection process with the various companies took its course, I needed to earn some money and quickly at that. Hopefully, this would be my final year of temporary summer employment as a student, not this time in the DHSS but back in the steelworks, with the opportunity of earning a fair amount of money before embarking on my first steps up the career ladder.

Firstly, the usual formalities had to be followed by applying to Morris Whinge, the Personnel Manager at Richard Thomas & Baldwin for the temporary employment and the obligatory '*Interview*' before I could start work.

For my final year, working in the steelworks, Morris gave me a job in the Hot Mill, the next stage up in the manufacturing process from the steelmaking operations of the Open Hearth and Convertor Shop. Here the ingots of red hot steel became transformed by means of rollers into thin strips of steel coils later to be used in the making of: cars, refrigerators, washing machines and numerous other consumer products. The remainder of the steel had other uses in the voracious, consumer society, such as tin cans or galvanized steel, which involved further rolling and electroplating processes at the Ebbw Vale steelworks.

At that time in the early seventies, the Ebbw Vale steelworks still employed quite a few students during the summer months, and once again I enjoyed working with my fellow students and peers, unlike the previous year when I had been put into a totally alien environment with an assortment of people not having the same interests as myself. Not that my time at the DHSS had been miserable, or unedifying, only for this my final summer as a temporary employee I relished, once again, working alongside fellow students, about the same age and mentality as myself with the same warped and somewhat juvenile sense of humour and the interests of the young. Interests mostly associated with sport, pop music, drinking and members of the opposite sex, but not necessarily in that order, generally mixing with people of my same age which had been absent from the working environment of the previous summer.

For the first few weeks of my stint at the Hot Mill my fellow students and I generally spent cleaning with the aid of sweeping brushes and shovels and not getting involved with the production process. The hard work lay ahead of us during the two week shut down period, when the heavy duty cleaning and maintenance of the machinery came into play during the last week in July, first week of August, known in South Wales as the 'Miner's Holiday' because of the huge amount of miners employed in the south Wales valleys in the first half of the twentieth century. To this day, in the new millennium, the name has stuck notwithstanding the fact there are no deep mines remaining in the South Wales coalfields and hardly any miners.

The heavy bottom end of Blast Furnaces, Open Hearth and Convertors did not have a shutdown, maintaining continuous process throughout the year because of the impracticability of leaving the furnaces to cool down. Only from the Hot Mill upwards did the steelworks shut down for those two weeks. Those first few weeks in the Hot Mill, tended to be fairly mundane, tedious and boring with the workload in no way ascribing to the description of being excessive.

In the Hot Mill, as with the Open Hearth and Convertors, there were inherent dangers. In the case of the Hot Mill this tended to be the bloomer. The bloomer can only be described as a hugely enormous piece of mechanical equipment which converted the red hot ingots of steel into thin slabs or monoliths, the process not unlike a baker rolling dough into thin pastry with wooden rolling pins. However, the bloomer invariably happened to be a much, much larger tool, with giant rams operated by pneumatics and hydraulics. The operators sat in a giant air conditioned control room, usually two of them working together to carry out the operation. It can only be described a fascinating piece of equipment. Observing the operation from a distance, it appeared very impressive.

The red hot ingots arrived from the soaking pits, a name given to kilns in which the ingots were re-heated following their short journey from the Open Hearth or Convertor Shop. Despite being a short journey, the ingots lost a lot of their residual heat which dissolved to the surrounding air. The soaking pits restored the lost heat necessary prior to the squeezing operation performed by the bloomer, an operation impossible to perform on cold steel. Only red hot steel possessed the optimum malleability permitting this process to be carried out. The five tons of red hot metal ingot after being placed carefully and with precision onto the conveyers by the overhead cranes, moved inexorably towards the bloomer. There the giant rams flipped it over as if it was a light cardboard box, then pushing it through the huge rollers which gently squeezed and extruded the metal, flipping it over once again, now making the base the top and vice versa, then once again repeating the extrusion operation.

This process continued for some time, visibly altering the shape of the ingot, gradually changing it from a metal obelisk like structure into a long thin slab of metal. Once the operator(s) deemed the slab to be sufficiently thin, they then mechanically jolted it onto the rollers beyond the bloomer whereupon the slab became further mechanically abused on hundreds of small rollers, each awaiting their turn at squeezing the slab beyond recognition. As the slab progressed through this never ending sequence of rollers, the shape became thinner and thinner and what originally began life as a five feet wide, twenty feet long and two feet thick piece of hot metal now became one continuous strip of metal, five feet in width and now hundreds of feet in length, and a couple of millimetres thick. The metamorphosis began taking place before one's very eyes. On one side of the rollers, the parent slab gradually disappeared, as the rollers slowly enveloped it, only to be reborn on the other side as a thin strip of metal, growing in length, transforming into a slithering serpent as more and more it extruded along the conveyer system.

The length, now bearing no resemblance to the slab from which it had been born. To accommodate this increasing length, the velocity at which this serpent traversed the rollers also increased mathematically. Eventually the fast travelling metal became just a blur to the human eye. This extrusion of the metal had another side effect, with the increasing speed; the building experienced a tremendous increase in noise level, which can only be described as the cacophony of numerous express trains within close proximity. At the other end of the building and hundreds of feet away, the 'coiler' waited patiently to arrest and curtail the momentum of this lethal serpent as it slithered in its direction, trapping and holding forming a neat, tight coil of thin steel. Following eight hours of this constant bombardment of incessant noise, the human ears experienced a ringing sensation accompanied by a reduction in one's hearing ability.

In those days it was not deemed necessary to issue the workforce with ear defenders, and probably considered an extravagant indulgence, and would not be tolerated in today's manufacturing industry. Fortunately, this ringing in one's ears and impaired hearing lasted for only a short time and disappeared within a short time. As for the long term consequences to my hearing, only time will tell.

Prior to my rather boring monologue describing the operation of the bloomer, I made the statement that the bloomer was yet another dangerous place in which to be employed, and is not necessarily directed at the noise level but to other factors. Frequently, the ingots often had protuberances emanating from the base, caused by incorrect placement of the moulds onto their plinths, and as the molten metal poured into the receptacle, the initial flow of metal invariably percolated through this breach between the mould and the plinth until temperature reduction eventually caused it to solidify.

Upon removal of the mould from its base, there would be the concomitant outgrowth, disfiguring the symmetrical features of the enclosed structure. As the disfigured obelisk gently squeezed between the giant rollers belonging to the bloomer for the first time, the immense compression forces exerted induced the offending protuberance to project itself with great celerity in numerous parts in various directions and elevations. A loud bang also accompanied the physical projectile at the instant the protuberance wrenched from the main body of steel in a form of protestation, as thunder accompanies lightning. Frequently, large chunks of this surplus steel landed in the vicinity where I absent-mindedly swept the floor, deep in my own personal thoughts. Undoubtedly had the red hot projectile connected with my body, at the least I would have been hospitalised and at worst killed outright.

Because of this period in the Hot Mill, I began to obtain first hand practical experience of the cause and effect of shellshock or, as it is known today, post-traumatic stress, with the fear of being hit by a random projectile from the bloomer every time there was a loud noise. I began to experience a common empathy with soldiers from the wars, in not knowing if the next noise would result in your possible demise. Fortunately, I ended my days in the Hot Mill relatively unscathed; apart from possible impaired hearing and an aversion to loud bangs.

Work for the student workforce began in earnest during the two week shutdown when the annual preventative maintenance programme began. Our first designated task to clean out the channels or 'cellars,' which lay beneath the numerous conveyor rollers. Throughout the previous year, metal scale accumulated after being discarded by the fast moving, hot metal above. The first day of the shutdown, the foreman guided his ramshackle workforce which consisted mostly of long haired students, including myself, to the Hot Mill rollers, which now lay dormant and unerringly quiet a distinct antithesis to the normal noise we had become accustomed to.

'Right!' said our leader, 'I want you all to remove the shale from the channel, and tip it into the pit at the far end of the building using shovels and wheel barrows.'

'How far does the shale go down?' asked one of the more inquisitive students.

'About twelve feet,' replied our leader in a nonchalant tone. At this unexpected and unwelcome reply we all looked at each other in utter disbelief, unable to comprehend the mammoth task which obviously lay ahead of us. The mill rollers had a length, of one hundred feet, with a width of six feet and a depth of twelve feet and in that volume shale which had to be cleared in two weeks, a totally unbelievable and horrendous prospect.

'Oh fuck!' exclaimed my inquisitive colleague, now wishing he had not asked the question, rapidly becoming a convert to the belief, '*Ignorance is sometimes bliss*'.

So for the first week, we laboured incessantly, our previous week's easy time now at an end. Transporting the offending shale to the pit, working overtime to cope with the immense task and volume of shale involved. Fortunately, the shale being loosely distributed and not compacted made our task to extirpate it slightly easier. Teams of the indigenous workforce also toiled in the other sections of the channel. Gradually, our efforts began to pay dividends and we began to make visible inroads into the shale, literally beginning to 'See light at the end of the tunnel.' At last we reached to within a couple of feet, reaching a hole at the end of the channel, leading directly into the depository, thus enabling us to move the wheel barrows along the channel, twelve feet below the rollers, speeding up the work immensely. Once the shale had been consigned to the pit, a giant grab periodically emptied the pit transferring it to waiting trucks, the shale then transported to the open hearth for recycling, consisting mostly of steel it could be re-used. As we emptied the wheel barrows into the pit, a causeway slowly began to develop.

The pit can only be described as a reception area or concrete tank about fifteen feet deep and thirty feet square. The crane driver, unable to view into the depository from his cab, relied upon the assistance of a safety man, who guided him from the wall perimeter at the top of the pit allowing him to view anything happening below where we worked. This particular day, the safety man was late returning from his break period and the crane driver, being the impatient sort, took it upon himself to remove the shale from the pit without the aid of his colleague. Unfortunately, at this time one of my fellow students happened to be in the process of emptying a wheelbarrow filled with shale. By this stage our man-made causeway of shale had extended itself into the middle of the pit. Suddenly, the unmistakable sound of the umbilical chains connecting the grab to the crane could be heard making a clanking sound as it descended at high velocity into the pit. The steelworker heard this noise, realising the possible horrendous outcome, ran onto the causeway instantly grabbing the student, pulling him into the safe haven of the tunnel. A split second later, the grab descended onto the stranded wheelbarrow, generating the sound of metal scraping against metal, the wheel barrow coming off worse in this altercation, being completely squashed like a grape. The crane driver in fact received a reprimanded for this action of dropping the grab without a safety-man which so nearly ended in the death of a student.

At last, the cellars became clear of the offending silt and we were then given another onerous task to perform, which involved a piece of equipment called *'the deep piler.'* To this day I do not know the actual function of the 'deep piler,' all I can recollect is this particular piece of machinery had a defective grease seal in need of urgent repair before the mill resumed production. This defective seal resulted in one horrendous, disgusting, black, viscous, greasy mess being deposited into the sump below the machinery. Before the maintenance department could repair this imperfection, in the equipment, the accumulation of grease had to be removed from the sump of the deep piler immediately below the rollers. The offending grease was a thick, heavy, viscous sludge, totally immobile and difficult to remove from one's clothing.

The task of removing the grease necessitated squatting in the five feet cube chamber. Invariably this disgusting job fell upon us students. In truth, the foreman tended to be quite equitable in attributing the task to us students, utilising a rota system. Each student worked in the confined space for one shift at a time, with each of us taking our turn. I had served my time performing the aforementioned task, bearing it with fortitude, getting my overalls completely covered in the offending material in the process. The contamination on my overalls was present to such an extent it became necessary to totally discard them at the end of the shift. We all accepted the situation stoically; after all, one eight hour cleaning stint once in a while seemed reasonable.

I make the statement that we all accepted the situation stoically, but that is not entirely true. There is always the exception to the rule and in this particular case the exception happened to be a fellow student named Craig Seaward. Craig belonged to his college's Socialist Society being a staunch socialist himself, almost bordering on communist and a practicing political activist. He considered himself to be a socialist warrior, a fighter for the rights of the proletariat, the Che Guevara of the valleys. We consider him to be more like Citizen Smith, which meant he was averse to indulging in hard work, having expended most of his energy fighting for the common man or proletariat (referred to as 'Proles' by the Conservative hierarchy).

Craig spent his first acquaintance of the deep piler working in the grease and grime for almost two hours. However, after this period of time, he had had enough then absolutely refused to continue for the remainder of the shift, complaining vociferously and bitterly to the Foreman, all to no avail. Once having failed to persuade the foreman about the conditions in which he had to work, Craig resorted to complaining in person to the Hot Mill Manager. The Hot Mill Manager remained unsympathetic to Craig's fulminations, informing him without any form of ambiguity that he had better get back to work in the deep piler or collect his P45.

Being a temporary employee, Craig had no rights whatsoever and could be dismissed immediately. Forced to swallow his pride he had to acquiesce to this ultimatum and return to the dreaded deep piler, working there without any more recourse to complaining and whinging. Unfortunately, reporting the Shift Foreman to the Hot Mill Manager happened to be the worst possible thing he could have done, generating an antagonism in the Foreman towards himself. The next day Craig was, once again, instructed to dig out the grease from the sump of the deep piler and the next day and again the next day. Each time Craig protested to the Foreman, the latter, became totally intransigent in his attitude towards the unfortunate Craig. The more Craig complained, the more he exacerbated this antagonism from the Foreman. Of course, all the students yet to work in the deep piler encouraged and actively egged Craig on; fully aware the more Craig complained the less likelihood there was of them having to carry out the objectionable task. One day a fellow student caught Craig intently studying the Health & Safety Board. He unsympathetically stood behind him and sarcastically remarked, 'It's under D for Deep Piler.'

I must confess, towards the end, I experienced immense sympathy for Craig. As each day passed, his spirits sank to new depths. He could be seen shuffling along after a day's work in the Deep Piler, a pitiful, broken, dejected individual, whose working clothes had by now become totally impregnated with the offending grease. The rest of us at least learned from Craig's experience, never complain to the Shift Foreman and most certainly never go above him to the Hot Mill Manager. Craig continued to be allocated the task of working in the Deep Piler throughout the remainder of his time in the Hot Mill, much to his chagrin, but selfishly, much to the relief of his fellow students.

The indigenous workforce in the Hot Mill exhibited similar traits to those of the Convertor Shop, or for that matter any working environment, and were certainly not averse to indulging in practical jokes and generally winding people up.

Two workers decided one day to 'set up' one of their colleagues. The victim was an inquisitive type with total self-belief in his ability to perform feats anyone else could perform. The reader has undoubtedly come across this type of person in their journey through life. The two pranksters found a building brick which had been broken almost centrally into two pieces, with the fracture running almost down the centre. Fitting the two pieces together, they placed the damaged brick on two supports and waited patiently for their unsuspecting victim to walk by. The instant he came within earshot, the one prankster indulged in conversation with his mate and immediately began demonstrating his prowess at karate, learnt purportedly at evening classes. Their victim approached like a lamb to the slaughter, his inquisitive nature by now running out of control, just in time to witness the edge of the lethal karate hand descending upon the fractured brick. The hand appeared to connect with great force and the brick parted into two separate sections, apparently breaking it with ease.

The fly approached the spider's web, totally succumbing to the subterfuge, informing his 'friends' he too had the capability of performing the same feat they had performed. The two practical jokers assisted in locating a whole brick ensuring its solidity before handing it to their unsuspecting victim. Carefully placing it on the supports, they waited for the demonstration. The victim raised his karate hand with great aplomb ready to show his prowess at karate. The hand came down with great force, style and panache in typical karate style. The edge of his hand connected with the totally solid brick. The instant this happened, we heard the blood curdling scream. It was not the scream of a man exhilarated at performing a superhuman feat, but that of a man in agony and excruciating pain, following the breaking of his right hand. We all ran to investigate the source of the scream, only to find the victim of the prank writhing about in agony on the floor, the pranksters by him apologising profusely for what they had just perpetrated and their stupidity. Despite the victim's heroic effort, the brick remained intact. The management suspended the two perpetrators and the victim ended up on sick leave for a considerable period of time. There is a post script to this story, with poetic justice prevailing.

A few months later, one of the practical jokers happened to be in the vicinity of a runaway ten ton coil of steel which then rolled over his foot. Had he been wearing protective safety shoes, he would probably have only sustained bruised toes. Unfortunately for him, he happened to be wearing trainers, giving totally inadequate protection, particularly when involved in an altercation with ten tons of itinerant steel. The practical joker writhed about in agony for some considerable period of time, his colleagues thoroughly acquainted with his proclivity for horseplay and winding up, believing this being one of those occasions. For at least half an hour, everyone kept walking around him, oblivious to his protestations and cries for help. Eventually, one of his mates thought he had better investigate, only to discover the truth; the joker had sustained a broken foot during the altercation with the coil of steel, immediately rushing him to hospital.

There happened to be quite a few accidents during my time spent working in the Hot Mill, and ironically, more than occurred during my time spent in the Convertor Shop and Open Hearth, where one would have thought they were more likely to occur, although there were indeed a few near misses. Two men were working on a guillotine, one pushing the sheets of metal under the blades, which cut the sheets to the desired size, the second operative stacking the sheets as they emerged on the other side of the blades. The question of Health and Safety, or rather the lack of it, keeps re-occurring during my early days in the steel industry. The guillotine had no guard to prevent the first operative from pushing his fingers too far and placing them under the lethal and dangerous blades of the guillotine. On this particular day, the inevitable happened. The operative, possibly through lack of concentration, pushed his hand too far up the sheet of metal with the concomitant result being the tops of his two middle fingers were sliced off along with the sheets of metal as the guillotine descended. The operative felt the searing pain in his fingers, but could not bring himself to look down, afraid of what he would see and the injury which he had sustained; instead he kept his head up looking at the roof, his whole being succumbing to a state of shock.

'Dave, I've had an accident!' he squeaked, in a voice an octave or two higher than normal, then adding, 'I think I'll have to go to the surgery.' Almost immediately Dave observed the sheets of cut metal tumbling out of the guillotine accompanied by the tops of his colleague's fingers, at which point Dave immediately fainted. Other steelworkers nearby heard the shouting and looking over, observed Allan, the operative with his fingers cut off, staring into space and Dave lying comatose on the floor.

The outcome to this whole sorry episode resulted in Allan, the injured party, walking to the surgery, while Dave, who was in fact perfectly healthy, ended up being carried on a stretcher.

Sadly, Allan lost the ends of his two middle fingers. The next day a guard was hurriedly fitted to the offending guillotine.

I learned many lessons during my early days working in industry, one of the most important being, never discuss events, circumstances, or personal history with people you are not fully acquainted with and do not know.

Being a large conurbation, the steelworks, tended to not only employ a fair amount of men mostly from the Ebbw Vale area, but also a large percentage from the neighbouring valleys. Ebbw Vale has always been and, still is to this day, a typical Welsh Valley town, with a close knit community. There is always the distinct possibility any person you may be discussing or criticising to another individual could be related or friendly with that person you are holding the conversation with.

I learnt this lesson one day in the changing rooms, when two steelworkers whilst sharing a communal shower, and indulging in friendly conversation as you normally did. These two workers obviously did not know each other but began indulging in a friendly conversation. The one steelworker began discussing his sexual adventures with a married woman with whom he had recently become acquainted; a typical male chauvinist discussion about women and their attributes. The second steelworker became genuinely interested in the sexual exploits of his newly found showering companion, finding the story compelling, entertaining, fascinating and amusing. Eventually, the recipient of the storytelling asked the raconteur for the name of this adulterous woman, probably hoping, he too, could have carnal knowledge of this female who appeared to be so free with her sexual favours, particularly after being informed by his new friend the promiscuous woman lived in the same area of the town as himself. Foolishly, the raconteur willingly divulged this information, without any hesitation whatsoever.

'Ceinwen Morgan,' he obligingly replied. Suddenly, all hell broke loose as the listener hurled himself at the by now bemused raconteur.

'You fucking bastard!' the listener shouted, whilst at the same time subjecting the raconteur to a fusillade of punches. 'That's my wife!' he added in explanation for this sudden and unexpected change in his temperament and demeanour, now totally lacking any humour concerning the raconteur's sexual adventures.

Total mayhem ensued as other steelworkers dived into the shower, endeavouring to pull the two pugilists apart. Bodies appeared to be everywhere with copious amounts of water cascading from the showers and meandering along the floor of the changing rooms. Fortunately, one of the managers appeared during the melee, attracted by all the noise and commotion. His appearance resulted in the immediate termination of the proceedings. The two protagonists received explicit instructions to stay apart or be sacked immediately.

Both obeyed leaving the changing rooms separately after getting attired. Whether they continued with the altercation outside work, I do not know, never having seen or met them again. The morale is, 'be careful what you say to people you do not know.'

My last recollection of working in the Hot Mill involved a drunken Saturday night out on the town. Prior to commencing my last week of working there before terminating my employment, some of my fellow students had decided to finish slightly earlier before me, wishing to make the most of their remaining summer vacation before resuming their studies, having earned their permitted tax free allowance.

The rest of us who continued to work had completed our time at college and wanted to make as much money as possible before commencing our full time employment and still awaiting replies to our numerous job applications. Their final Saturday night the students terminating their summer employment had decided to have a celebratory night out in one of the local student haunts and my favourite watering hole, the Level, to which all and sundry were cordially invited. As with any normal student activity and as one can imagine, the beer flowed like water and a thoroughly good time was had by all, including myself. Also, as I later discovered, those students lucky enough not to be returning to work at the Hot Mill on the Sunday morning, had decided to get those of us who unfortunately had to work the next morning as inebriated as possible, a feat which they achieved with resounding success by spiking our drinks.

At the end of the evening, one of my fellow students, Ioan Edwards arranged for his elder sister to collect him in her car, he then kindly offered for her to also give me a lift home, much to her annoyance. From the first time I clapped eyes on her. I was immediately attracted to her. Due to the excess of alcohol consumed that evening, I tried to arrange a date with her, alas all to no avail. She had no intention of spending an evening with this drunk, ex-student, and reprobate, fully cognizant of how the general male student population behave; after all, she had a brother who also happened to be a degenerate student. In addition during the journey, both Ioan and I displayed excessive exuberance in exercising our vocal chords, much to her annoyance and irritation, so much so, even threatening to evict both of us from her vehicle.

She is one of the many, many females I have alienated on my journey through this life. I asked her for a date on other occasions following that evening, all to no avail, having thoroughly disgusted her that evening with my reprehensible behaviour.

Unfortunately, as well as her, I antagonized another female that particular evening, this time it happened to be my mother. Upon getting out of her car, I discovered my parents had returned home following a two weeks' vacation in mainland Spain, Alicante, as I recall. My mother, upon discovering the state of the house, lost her sense of humour and became angry upon discovering unwashed dishes together with clothes strewn over the bedroom. Her temperament further deteriorated when her one and only son arrived home in an extremely advanced state of intoxication, looking distinctly the worse for wear. That was the last straw, almost immediately she blew like Krakatoa and began reading the riot act. I retired to bed as early as possible trying to consider whether it had been a good night or not, my contemplation did not last long, for almost immediately, I fell into an alcoholic-induced deep sleep.

The following morning somehow I went to work at the Hot Mill, very decidedly the worse for wear, ashen faced and nurturing one monumental hangover. Throughout the bus journey I experienced great discomfort, trying to prevent all my meals of the previous day erupting from the pit of my stomach and discharging over the floor of the bus. How my fellow students made I made it through the day is beyond my recall, I do however recollect one incident when one of my fellow student colleagues was subjected to a torrent of icy cold water from the fire hydrant in an attempt to revive him, the task being performed with relish by members of the regular workforce. The poor unfortunate student ended up being subjected to a deluge of freezing cold water for at least half an hour before eventually returning to the land of the living, wet, shivering and absolutely freezing...

That following Saturday, the remainder of the students, including myself, terminated our employment at Richard Thomas & Baldwin as per the instructions of the management, our services no longer required and our duties at an end.

An era had come to an end; I still harbour distinctly fond memories of those early days working in the Open Hearth, Convertor Shop, DHSS and Hot Mill. Perhaps the memories are clouded because they occurred during my youth; memories always seem better from the perspective of one's youth, with few cares at the time and everything an adventure, or perhaps it was purely due to the fact we were young naive and innocent, insulated from the rat race of the working environment, where unfortunately, whether we like it or not people are in conflict in an effort to get to the top, ultimately resorting to stabbing each other in the back along the way. For whatever reason, memories from those decades ago will be with me until my dying day.

Alas all those monuments to the days of steel making at Ebbw Vale have all sadly disappeared, victims caught in the name of profit and viability, a sacrificial lamb to the accountants, the men in blue suits, the bean counters. The land later became transformed and reclaimed for the Garden Festival of 1992, resulting in a complete metamorphosis to the Ebbw Valley. The final, remaining part of the Ebbw Vale works, the tinning lines, sadly finally closed in 2002 costing thousands of steelworkers their jobs.

I have ambivalent feelings concerning the demise of the steel industry in the Welsh valleys. On the one hand it did pollute, contaminate and scar the landscape and indeed it was an extremely dangerous place to work, causing quite a number of fatalities and serious injuries throughout its existence. However, on the other hand, it did bring employment and prosperity to the region and, after all, it will always be a part of my life with enduring, fond memories.

The big, bad world now beckoned, with adventure and characters galore. My chosen subject in Chemical Engineering allowing me access into an eclectic range of industries from Hi-Tech to Waste Management, from Cardboard Manufacturing to Cosmetics, from Oil Recovery to Electroplating.

# CHAPTER 5

Within a few weeks following the termination of my summer employment at the Hot Mill, I began my first full time employment and the initiation of my working career in the service of a company called Birchwater Containers. Birchwater happened to be one of the major global manufacturers of cardboard boxes, with a huge manufacturing facility situated near the docks at Newport, Gwent, a medium-sized Welsh coastal town, fortuitously situated about twenty miles directly south of my home town.

I considered it prudent and wise to accept the first position offered, having received numerous *'Dear John'* letters of rejection throughout those summer months of 1973. Birchwater happened to be the first major company offering me a position, which I jumped at. The company or at least, the division where I was to be based manufactured cardboard boxes. To me, a totally new manufacturing field. At the time I erroneously believed working for Birchwater would be my first step on the career ladder, working my way up within the company before finally retiring at sixty five after having worked for the company forty odd years. It was, as it transpired, a totally naïve and overly optimistic assumption, on my life in the manufacturing industry.

My position within Birchwater had the grand title of *'Trainee Manager'* or as I was to discover a better title would have been GDB, General Dog's Body or Gofer...... 'Go for this, go for that.' The contract promised the earth with the assurance of receiving full and comprehensive training in all departments during my first twelve months and then promotion to a fully-fledged Manager in charge of my own department. The prospect was enticing to a young graduate in his early twenties. The catch to the whole scenario, being, as, there is always a catch; my initial salary would reflect that of a trainee and a pittance, before aspiring to the position of a fully-fledged manager, whereupon I would eventually receive the salary representative of that position.

The first, and as it transpired, only department, where my training began, happened to be the Customer Liaison Department, where I received a training, of sorts. The job consisted mainly of answering the phones and mostly placating irate and often verbally abusive customers. Other duties included arranging production schedules for regular orders, maintaining stock levels, organizing deliveries, expediting orders for customers and generally being a point of contact, duties which could have been performed by a person with a modicum of intelligence and common sense and most certainly not requiring a degree in Chemical Engineering.

All the promises Birchwater had made were basically only a ploy to lure a well-educated person to perform general tasks for an absolute pittance. All enquiries concerning previous Trainee Managers indicated they had all terminated their employment of their own volition, after becoming disillusioned at not attaining full managerial status and after spending a considerable amount of time in that position. The incumbent managers were there to stay and fully intended to maintain the status quo. Being at that time a reasonably self-assured and yet naive individual, I believed an opportunity would become available to me within the company. I was, however, mistaken, and would eventually leave some months later for exactly the same reason as my predecessors, although other factors also played a part in my decision.

In truth, my days with Birchwater were actually

numbered within two weeks of commencing employment after indulging in a head to head altercation with Customer Liaison Manager in front of the whole office.

It was 1973, at that particular time industry happened to be going through a terrific boom period, and the demand for cardboard boxes was un-abating to meet consumer demand in the high streets. As with most companies, Birchwater had over-committed themselves, finding it difficult to adhere to promised delivery schedules. Everyone was under pressure and tempers became frayed. The office was chaotic, and as far as the customers were concerned it became basically a case of, *'He who shouts the loudest.'* It was a totally anarchistic way to run a business and sowing the seeds for disaster.

From my first day, in the Customer Liaison department, there was the constant clatter of typewriters, accompanied by the incessant cacophony of ringing phones, answered by who ever happened to be available. Staff talked on the phones, or rather, shouted, to be heard above the din; it was complete mayhem and confusion. My initial training amounted to, 'Answer that phone!' and having to pick everything up as I went along, *'winging it'* as they say. Never having experienced such a working environment, I had been well and truly thrown in at the deep end and was drowning rapidly.

I had been enveloped and suffocated for about two weeks of this total mayhem and madness when this one particular morning a number of circumstances came together to cause the head to head argument with Dean Crabbe, the Office Manager. Dean tended to be full of his own self-importance, but as I soon discovered, totally incapable of carrying out the simple tasks which his subordinates performed with relative ease. One of

Birchwater's major customers, Girlings, had been enquiring about a consignment of cardboard boxes which were well overdue. The boxes were required to ship out a load of electrical components and if the boxes were not forthcoming, Girlings would have to stop production, not having the facilities to store any more of the electrical components. Fred McCartney, the account manager happened to be away on vacation and his unfortunate female assistant was left trying to fend off and mollify his irate customers, one of which was Girlings. The assistant eventually discovered the whereabouts of the boxes in the scheme of things, only to discover much to her dismay and chagrin they had not yet been manufactured and would only be ready for delivery in approximately two weeks' time. At being told this, the buyer for Girlings became understandably angry as the boxes were already four weeks overdue and now he would have to wait another two weeks. He demanded to speak to the most senior person on site. Circumstances had conspired against me that day. Dean Crabbe, although fairly low down in the pecking order in the scheme of things as far as the plant was concerned, just happened to be the most senior person on site this particular day. The assistant went to Dean Crabbe to explain the situation and request the buyer for Girlings be put through to him.

I was the innocent observer and had absolutely nothing to do with the whole affair, but suddenly and inexplicably became embroiled in the whole situation, through no fault of my own. Dean Crabbe's phone rang and for some unknown reason he shouted out to me from his office…. Why he chose me is beyond my comprehension, I was situated the furthest from his office, with other members of the staff in closer proximity to him, probably because I happened to be the new guy on the block.

'Vinson!' He bellowed from within the confines of his office, 'Phone the switchboard and tell them I'm not in my office!' Not a hint of please, or thank you in his demand.

Being the obedient employee, I did as instructed and told the switchboard in all innocence and being totally unaware of the circumstances, informing them Dean Crabbe was too busy to take the call. Within a matter of seconds, he came charging out of his office heading straight for my desk. 'I told you to tell the switchboard I was not in my office... not that I was too busy to take the call. Next time do as you're instructed. Understood?'

This vehement, and what I considered, unprovoked, unnecessary, unjust verbal attack, caught me unawares and bemused me for a few seconds. Suddenly, I could feel the anger welling up inside me, this arrogant bastard appeared to be victimizing me for no apparent reason. A person can only take so much.

'Oh come on!' I retorted, 'the switchboard know you are in your office!' standing up at the same time as I spoke. Dean was shorter than me and this now gave me a distinct height advantage, and I needed every ploy in the forthcoming argument which I knew was about to erupt.

'That's not the point!' he retaliated. 'I'm the Office Manager and when I tell you to do something, you obey it to the letter, understood?'

I could not comprehend why he refused to answer the phone and as he walked away, I followed him tenaciously.'Why won't you answer the phone?' I enquired.

Dean turned around, the intense irritation and anger, almost bordering on loathing and hatred toward me becoming blatantly obvious.

'I haven't got the time to talk to every tuppenny

ha'penny customer who's got a problem and chasing delivery dates!' he replied, with venom in his voice and shouting as he made this totally unprofessional statement.

At that instant I knew he was on the ropes. I was not about to let the opportunity slip away the words came to me instantly and almost naturally.

'If it wasn't for those tuppenny ha'penny customers like Girlings, we would all be out of a job!' I shouted back. It was at this instant I looked around and suddenly realised the office had assumed a deadly hush. All conversations on phones, the incessant tapping of the typewriter keys, no longer evident, have ceased. All eyes focused intently on the two of us.

'If you feel so strongly about it,' Dean retorted, whilst trying to walk away at the same time, 'why don't you talk to him?'

'Right, I will!' was my defiant, impertinent reply. After having said this and not having the foggiest idea what I was about to say, I walked toward the assistant, right hand outstretched, indicating my willingness to take the phone call and talk to the irate buyer. The assistant looked firstly at me and then Dean, a sheepish expression evident on her face.

'He doesn't want to talk to you; he wants to speak with Dean or the most senior manager on site.'

'There you are!' I continued, pressing home my advantage. 'He doesn't wish to talk to me, he wants to talk to you!'

I was fully aware I held the moral high ground, and the fact Dean Crabbe had a professional duty and obligation to converse with the customer gave me the impetus to continue the argument. Dean then continued walking towards the safety of his office. Shouting back 'I'm too busy!' whereupon he slammed the office door behind him, and sought the refuge of his inner sanctum.

I looked around the office to observe a load of open-mouthed customer liaison personnel looking up at me, and staring in utter amazement in complete disbelief at what had just occurred resembling goldfish gulping for air. Despite the altercation which had just occurred, I could not help but smile to myself, as the whole scene I surveyed as it looked so farcical. Frank's assistant was the first to break the unreal silence, to simply report.

'He's hung up.'

Almost immediately my phone rang. It was Pat Cooper the receptionist.

'The buyer from Girlings heard every word of that.' She also added with a hint of mischief in her voice, 'I deliberately kept the line open so he could hear what a pig of a man Dean Crabbe is. The buyer also asked me to thank you for trying to help him and said he is very sorry if he has got you into any trouble. He also wanted me to tell you he will be reporting Dean Crabbe's attitude to the plant manager and that your attempt at trying to help will be mentioned.'

Talking to Pat calmed me down and it also gave me warm feeling, I at least had not upset the customer, knowing the moral high ground was on my side during our contretemps.

The buyer from Girlings was true to his word, the following week; Dean received a reprimand from the plant manager which did nothing to help my situation in the office or from that point onwards did nothing to ingratiate me in the eyes of my immediate boss. That argument led to a distinct animosity between us until the day I finished, but I always had the smug satisfaction of knowing Dean had been totally in the wrong. I believe he was afraid to talk to the customer and be shouted at by them.

Apart from Dean's animosity towards me, my time spent at Birchwater was reasonably pleasant and enjoyable, being the first place of employment where the women outnumbered the men. The women on the shop floor completely shocked me and to be quite honest intimidated me slightly, with their indiscriminate use of *'Anglo-Saxon'* and ribald, lascivious, sexual behaviour.

Some of the girls I knew in college swore, being selective in their choice of vocabulary. The women working at Birchwater had a totally different philosophy, forever using expletives as adjectives, adverbs or nouns, being totally indifferent and unconcerned as where they should be used. I may appear to be snobbish and pretentious in making the above statement, but it is a statement made with slight admiration at their honest and uninhibited approach to life.

Believing I was the only person to be intimidated, it came as a complete shock upon discovering one of the managers, Don Peters, the Assistant Sales Manager had also been intimidated and as a result had a phobia about going down onto the shop floor, a fear he had held for nigh on ten years, almost the instant he started work at the facility, as a young teenager straight from school embarking on his first job. He still had this phobia, some ten years after, this fact only coming to light by accident.

Don was forever asking me to go down to the production area to expedite production orders for his main customers and to evaluate how far the pressing orders were along in the actual process. The fact is Don never actually went down to the area intrigued me, after all he was a senior manager with the authority to push orders through, whereas I was basically the new kid on the block , an office junior with no real authority.

Fred McCartney was the person who enlightened myself as to why Don Peters, our illustrious Assistant

Sales Manager never actually ventured down to the production area. Fred was a wonderful story teller and loved divulging stories concerning his time spent at Birchwater. He would have made a wonderful after dinner speaker and raconteur. Not only were his stories interesting, but he also had a thoroughly entertaining way of imparting the information to his listener(s) and the sort of person one could listen to for hours.

'When Don first joined Birchwater as a young man,' Fred began his story, 'he was a fresh, faced, young, nice-looking boy and girls used to virtually drool after him, their mouths gaping open as he passed by. There was no doubt about it, they found him attractive. I only wish I had that effect on the fairer sex,' Fred added as he wistfully stared into space.

Following a brief pause, Fred continued with his story about the Assistant Sales Manager. 'After about three months of being employed by Birchwater, Don had to go down into the production area. The girls in the area decided they wanted to get near his body and took it upon themselves to pounce onto the unsuspecting youth. Unfortunately they did get carried away and ended up stripping Don down to his underwear, a task they performed with unmitigated relish and enjoyment.'

Fred ended his story with a smile.

'There you have it; ever since that day, Don has attempted to keep away from the shop floor, and rarely ventures into the area.'

'They never pounce on me!' I added, with an obvious unhidden, envious air in my voice and demeanour.

'Well let's face it Vinson, you are an ugly looking bastard.' Fred replied, a huge smile beaming from his slightly rotund face. His observation and statement unfortunately appeared to be substantiated that following Christmas, my first at Birchwater.

It was a memorable Yuletide, my first Christmas working full time in industry. It was a complete revelation to me how the workforce suddenly embraced the Christmas spirit, both metaphorically and literally.

The season began very well for me, I was fortunate enough to take phone call from a businessman from Cardigan whom I discovered later happened to be The High Sheriff Of Cardigan. He was in desperate need of high density boxes in which to put his turkeys ready for shipping. As previously mentioned, it was a period of boom and it would have been impossible for him to order and get the boxes manufactured and delivered before Christmas season. After taking the enquiry and listening to this distraught business man, I did some searching and discovered to my amazement there was a flatbed loaded with over two thousand reject boxes and just about the size the Sheriff required. It just got better and better, the boxes were in good condition and were just an over-make on an order. The designated customer did not require these additional boxes and therefore had not paid for them. They were in fact destined to be scrapped. I explained to the High Sheriff the circumstances and sizes of the boxes. He nearly bit my hand off down the phone and said he would take them. He even asked if he could come and pick up about a hundred in a day or so the next day. I rapidly made arrangements; Birchwater agreed to deliver the rest and charged him a nominal amount for the cases plus transport.

The businessman arrived true to his word next day, paying Birchwater in cash for the boxes plus transport. He also gave me one hundred pounds plus a huge fifteen pound frozen turkey plus a turkey for Dean Crabbe, which helped relieved the animosity between us for short while. Everybody was happy. Birchwater were happy, they had sold some surplus boxes. The High Sheriff was happy. He managed to get his turkeys delivered in time for the festive season. Dean was happy he had a huge turkey for Christmas and took the credit for getting rid of the boxes. I was happy getting 100 quid and my parents had a huge turkey for Christmas. So all in all it started off very well. Also, there were numerous functions and parties to attend and I had been accepted by other members of the customer Liaison department; ah yes: Christmas 1973 was a very good time.

The last day of working, prior to the Christmas break, Pat on the Switchboard was intoxicated and inebriated by about eleven in the morning, obviously slurring her words as she spoke after having consumed numerous martinis that morning. We had all been told we could finish at noon and there was no concern about people drinking on plant, unlike today.

I had been informed no male was safe in number three factory, where the female workforce was on the rampage in search of some sort of sexual excitement after drinking alcohol. At hearing this news, I decided perhaps it would be a good time to walk around number three factory.

After walking around number three factory for about half an hour, no female approached me and I ended up being unmolested, much to my chagrin. Fred's words haunted me.

'Well you are an ugly looking bastard!' My ego received quite a jolt that day.

That lunchtime I headed to the pub with the other members of the Customer liaison Department in an attempt to massage my bruised and decidedly battered ego. Clutching my frozen turkey which I had collected from the canteen, where it had been stored. On the way to the pub I dropped the solidly frozen turkey, cracking a paving stone in the process, irreparably damaging it and probably causing a hazard to pedestrians in the process.

Not having a car, I used public transport to travel home to my parents thirty miles up the valley and so I was able to consume quite a few drinks before taking my leave. Desperately clutching my precious frozen fifteen pound turkey, I staggered precariously out of the pub, heading in the general direction of my bed-sit to collect my ready packed case before heading to my parent's for the Christmas season and anticipating a thoroughly enjoyable, time meeting up with my old friends, hopefully indulging in debauched evenings during the holidays.

The holidays came and went, far too quickly for my liking, and then I returned to the rigors of Birchwater and unfortunately, the mutual animosity between Don Crabbe and myself.

As I have mentioned, Birchwater did have a lot of females working there, with the sexual harassment working both ways, apart from the episode with Don Peters, there was another incident which Fred imparted to me during one of his storytelling episodes, concerning a young boy called David Morgan. He worked on one of the machines for used for making Heavy duty boxes, known in the trade as Tri-Wall and the machine he worked on was called the Bar Beam Bender, used for making creases in the heavy duty cardboard. Dave worked alongside three women, who in truth gave him a really rough time, the main protagonist being a woman called Pearl.

Dave was in his mid to late twenties and would be described today as having learning difficulties. In those days he would have been described as something else, and a much more cruel description. As if that was not enough, nature had been even crueller, inflicting more humiliation on the poor unfortunate Dave, making him unappealing and unattractive to members of the opposite sex. His female colleagues were fully cognizant of this fact, teasing him mercilessly and being totally unrelenting in heaping humiliation upon the poor man.

Pearl was a woman in her mid-thirties, fairly attractive and putting it bluntly, well acquainted with the facts of life, no doubt having experienced it to the full probably with numerous males and possibly even females. Indeed, she was a woman of the world and street wise.

Virtually day after day, Dave was subjected to the same humiliation and torment, mainly from Pearl.

'Did you have it in last night Dave?'

'When did you last have it Dave?'

'Are you still a virgin Dave?'

One day Pearl really pushed him over the edge, by rubbing her not insubstantial breasts against his back and speaking in a loud voice for the benefit of her friends.

'If you came out with me Dave, I could show you a thing or two. I love sex and can give terrific blow jobs. Do you think I have nice tits?'

With all this sexual talk and suggestive remarks from Pearl, Dave's passions, not surprisingly, became aroused and before a surprised and startled Pearl could do anything, Dave had her pinned against the wall with one hand, desperately trying to loosen his trousers with the other.

Pearl screamed, her friends looked on, static and frozen with astonishment at the spectacle in being enacted in front of them. Dave now, sporting a giant erection, with every intention of inserting it into Pearl's unwilling vaginal orifice.

Then, men working on one of the other machines

ran over to separate the two before having a chance of performing coitus on the, by now, hysterical Pearl, which they eventually managed to do.

Later that day, after the situation had calmed, somewhat, the two of them had to go before the Works Manager, and following much deliberation, no action was taken against Dave by reason of Pearl acting highly provocatively towards him. The eventual solution was to put them in different sections of the factory. Fred reckoned Pearl did try to press charges for attempted rape, although he did not know if that was true and if it had proceeded.

# CHAPTER 6

After working in the customer liaison department for a few months, it was decided, by the powers that be, I should be given extra responsibilities for specialized products and, as part of the deal, I was given a young female assistant named Bronwen to do all my typing, paperwork, filing etc.. The reader must remember, this was 1974 and prior to the inception of the now ubiquitous PC's, laptops and word processors with companies employing a large number of typists of which Bronwen happened to be one.

Following a period of time, our working relationship developed into something more. I was unattached and Bronwen was in the process of going through a divorce and estranged from her husband. So technically we were young, free and single, she nineteen and I twenty two. She first came to my attention during the first week in the office when I first started working there. She was attractive, five feet six inches, with medium length blonde hair and a figure to die for. She always wore miniskirts in order to show off her fantastic legs which appeared to extend forever. Unfortunately the way Bronwen dressed did draw attention to her, frequently getting her into trouble. One day after missing the company bus from the centre of Newport, as it was a beautiful summer's day, she decided to walk down the docks where the plant happened to be situated, her tight fitting top exaggerating her ample breasts. She also wore one of her many miniskirts, exhibiting her long legs to great effect. As she walked the one and a half miles to the site, down the dockland road, daydreaming and soaking up the warm sun, the docklands police suddenly pulled up next to her then bundled her into the car after which they took her to the police station for suspected soliciting. It was only after frantic phone calls to the Birchwater's office did they eventually release her. Bronwen was not a happy bunny and when she eventually appeared in work at about ten that morning, she complained bitterly about the supposed guardians of the peace accusing her of prostitution.

It was sometime after this incident we started going out together, after being brought together by Jackie one of the other girls in the office. We went to see 'The Sting' starring Paul Newman and Robert Redford. After our first date we hit it off with Bronwen frequently staying at my bed-sit in Newport, especially if we had been with the office staff to the local popular nightclub called the Helmaen in Usk. This usually meant we both turned up at work looking like death following some excessive horizontal exercise. By this time, I had also, acquired a little mini estate car and travelled home to Ebbw Vale at the weekends to see my mother who was now terminally ill with cancer. This also allowed my father to go out one night during the weekend, giving him a break from being her Carer.

Bronwen lived in Abertillery a small town situated in the next valley to Ebbw Vale. We would also see each during the weekend. I recall going to a pub quite a few miles from both our home towns. As we were leaving, she casually remarked, 'Did you see a group of lads in the corner of the pub?'

I replied I hadn't noticed. She then casually informed me one of them was her estranged husband. After being told this, my pace quickened somewhat as we headed back to the car, just in case they had noticed us and followed. Bronwen told me they had not noticed us but I still couldn't wait to get away, being the devout coward I am.

As time progressed my antagonism towards Dean

Crabbe increased, feeling continually victimised by him, especially ever since our altercation in the office. It was because of this animosity that one Monday I picked Bronwen up at her home, after having been home for the weekend. We both decided to carry on driving to the Gower peninsular, a place called Llangennith, as I recollect, totally without any feelings of guilt or remorse. Both of us spending a wonderful day on one of the beaches, each of us having phoned in to pull a 'sicky.' It was a gloriously sunny day and both of us ended up sporting effulgent suntans which a professional lifeguard would have been proud of.

The following day, I walked into the office pretending to have recovered from some sort of exotic and rare stomach bug. Dean called me into his office for some intensive cross-questioning concerning my previous day's absence. It was extremely difficult keeping a straight face and refraining from smiling, I had ostensibly been agonizingly ill and at death's door the previous day and here I was looking disgustingly healthy, exhibiting a radiant suntan and sunburned nose.

'Where were you yesterday?' he enquired belligerently.

I think I should have been awarded an Oscar in giving my reply and maintaining my composure. 'I had a stomach bug and unable to make it to work.'

'Bronwen was ill yesterday as well.' Was his questioning indicating he suspected there had been a conspiracy between us?

'Was she?' I rhetorically replied with a slightly incredulous manner, feigning ignorance, knowing full well she had been with me most of the day, enjoying time off together and indulging in extremely passionate lovemaking in the dunes around Llangennith beach and enjoying each other's bodies.

'Don't let it happen again!' he barked, probably knowing we had been together, but having no real proof or evidence.

I did have quite a responsible job while at Birchwater maintaining stocks and production scheduling. This somewhat disconcerting fact hit home following an incident concerning a company called BDA (British Domestic Appliances). The company included quite eminent and reputable companies such as Hotpoint and Murphy Richards and at the time was one of Birchwater's major customers

During my time in the customer Liaison department my responsibilities included maintaining minimum stocks levels of boxes and components, arrange production schedules and arrange delivery schedules. The deliveries were made mainly on forty foot length flatbeds, the vehicles then delivered the components to Peterborough, the main warehousing for the company.

A large delivery of cardboard boxes had been arranged for the Wednesday of one particular week together with various internal fitments for a particular model of Hotpoint washing machine. The internal fitments were required to safely package the machines and stop them moving loosely about in the heavy outer carton. Production schedules had been put into place weeks earlier for boxes and miscellaneous associated internal components that made up the total packaging. The main outer boxes were large, comprising of quite a few pallets. The smaller internal fitments such as corner pieces, top sections etc. did not usually amount volume, taking up a small amount of space on the vehicle.

On the day of the delivery, I received a phone call from Kevin, the chief buyer from BDA, informing me of the fact the larger outer boxes had been delivered but there were no internal corner pieces on the vehicle. If they did not receive them within a couple of days, they would not be able to pack the washing machines being manufactured at their facility.

After making somewhat frantic enquiries, I discovered the corner pieces had been delayed in the production schedule and had not been ready for the vehicle that morning missing the delivery and not put onto the vehicle. Kevin was not amused in the slightest after being informed of the fact. The washing machines were being manufactured a fast rate at their facility and they were rapidly running out of the corner pieces, despite searching the warehouse at Peterborough for any spare ones which may be hanging around from previous over deliveries.

Kevin and I had a long telephone discussion and between us came up with a solution. I suggested we could deliver a pallet of the corner pieces on a small vehicle. However this was rejected immediately by our Transport Department as being too costly and they would not budge on the issue in accepting my suggestion. I wracked my brains but came up with another solution. Programmed for the following Wednesday was a delivery for another load of cases for another model of washing machine which Hotpoint manufactured. I proposed to our transport department they bring the delivery of the load forward ensuring the required corner pieces be put on it. Eventually, they reluctantly agreed to.

However, I needed to get Kevin's agreement before re-scheduling delivery. After Kevin held discussions with his directors, it was agreed the cases and fitments for the other model be delivered on the Thursday together with the missing corner pieces from the other model. Following further discussions with the transport department, it was all agreed. BDA agreed to this although they did not actually need the cases for the other model and were in fact about to put the original delivery back a few more days.

Just to cover myself, I wrote a memo, which Bronwen typed with her fair hands, stating the agreement, making it abundantly clear the priority was the delivery of the corner pieces and it was imperative that the corner pieces were put onto the vehicle. Copies of the memo were sent to the production and transport departments and every man and his dog. A copy was also reluctantly sent to Dean Crabbe, control freak extraordinaire.

Thursday morning arrived. That night I did not sleep much, lying awake in my pokey little bedsit and went into work early that morning. My first visit was to the transport office only to be met by the Transport Supervisor with whom I had been liaising, only to be informed the large boxes which BDA did not actually require until the following week had been sent. Unfortunately, the corner pieces, the main reason for re-scheduling the delivery, were still at the Newport site. My heart sank and my stomach churned over with my first thought being.

'Ah well, hello again P45.' I asked the Transport Supervisor, not mincing my words, 'What the fuck happened?'

He then informed me, with a somewhat dejected and forlorn look on his face, the night shift had not loaded the corner pieces as requested and it had not been his shift which had been responsible for the unmitigated cock up. He had quickly passed the oversight out to the wing as they say.

It was time for me to inform Kevin at BDA, a task which filled me with dread, but a task which could not be delayed. Upon receiving the bad news, there was a pregnant pause before he hit the roof, swearing profusely, generating a verbal tirade down the phone, a perfectly understandable reaction, considering the circumstances. He tried explaining between expletives the reason for his outburst. It appeared the plant at Peterborough would shortly be on stop, as they were now unable to pack the washing machines which had recently been manufactured. The BDA directors would also have to be told. With that he slammed the phone down.

Within the hour, Dean Crabbe came bounding up to me demanding to be put in the picture after he had received an irate call from the site Plant Manager. I knew I would invariably be held responsible in Dean's eyes. I tried to keep the obnoxious manager out of it, but unfortunately, there was no way this could be done and he had to be involved. Upon being told the story we went to Dave Holmes, the Commercial Manager who was more reasonable and understanding. I showed him the memo which had been sent to every man and his dog.

We then all had to troop down to the Plant Manager, who asked me why I had not arranged for a small delivery. When informed the Transport Department were unwilling to organise it, he immediately picked up the phone and instructed them to do exactly that. While he talked to the transport manager, it became clear the Managing Director of BDA had actually contacted the MD of Birchwater, with the plant at Peterborough indeed being put on stop. Kevin had not been exaggerating. Within a short space of time, a small vehicle had been ordered and the pallet of corner fitments loaded and shipped to Peterborough.

Thus, indirectly, I had been involved in the shutdown of a large manufacturing facility in Peterborough. During the dark days of the Second World War, the BDA facility had manufactured vital aircraft components for the war industry. Even Hitler, Goering and the Luftwaffe were unable to shut it down, yet somehow the transport department at Birchwater and I had managed to do what they had failed to accomplish.

I knew I should have informed Dean Crabbe of the situation before it got that far, but he was such a martinet and control freak and thus not easily approachable and after my first couple of weeks at Birchwater, I was not one of his favourite people in the office and so I tried to handle the situation without involving him.

It was annoying when my initial suggestion of sending a much smaller vehicle proved to be the final solution to the problem.

I was warned about keeping managers out of the loop and receiving a verbal warning as a consequence. One of the supervisors in the transport department also had a verbal warning. If I had not written the memo, then possibly I would have indeed had my P45, finishing with Birchwater much earlier than I eventually did.

It was only because of Bronwen I remained so long at Birchwater. She dissuaded me from leaving on a couple of occasions. Once, even after I had actually handed in my resignation. It was only after she terminated our relationship that I eventually did leave, thinking it was time to move on.

During August 1974, Bronwen informed me she had decided to renew her relationship with her previous boyfriend who had dumped her and now he wanted her back. She now, as a consequence, wished to end our relationship. I was utterly devastated and heartbroken. The next few months were torment as we still had to work together, and I still had feelings for her.

We were not the only ones having a relationship in the office, there were others, one of which was Dean Crabbe's own son, David, who despite being married was having a relationship with one of the other typists, namely Jackie, the same person who brought Bronwen and me together.

Another one was Denzil Jeffries who was also having an extra marital relationship with one of the girls from the office. Having seen his wife I could well sympathise with his philandering. His wife was domineering, overbearing and an out-and-out snob.

One particular Saturday, Denzil had been involved in an automobile accident whilst on his way to the office to do some overtime. Fortuitously, neither he nor his passengers were seriously injured, escaping virtually unscathed. Denzil travelled the same stretch of road day in and day out to work, unfortunately it is a case of *'familiarity breeds contempt'*. This particular Saturday, the right of way had been altered. Denzil had not read the signs and failed to see the new Give Way sign at the junction, which the previous day had not been there. At the same time as he crossed the junction, a bus unfortunately happened to be approaching from the left. The bus carried on, as it now having the right of way. Denzil also carried on, and with the misapprehension he too had the right of way. The inevitable happened, with a metallic and mechanical altercation between the bus and Denzil's ill matched automobile, which, being the more diminutive of the two, came off the worse before finally ending up in the glass front of the British Home Store's shop window. Denzil and his three passengers were badly shaken up and dazed by the whole experience. They all managed to get to work after the police had informed Denzil he would be prosecuted for driving without due care and attention.

Within an hour or so of Denzil arriving at the office, after having been picked up buy another colleague, a tremendous commotion was heard in the uncarpeted corridors of the building. The lack of padding exacerbating the cacophony of noise from and the unmistakable sound of Anne, Denzil's wife, as she came along the corridor  virtually hysterical, screaming and shouting, uttering oaths and profanities in a deluge.

'Where is that fucking bastard? I'll kill the stupid twat. He's lost us our no-claims bonus. It'll cost a fortune to repair the fucking car!'

It was touching to observe the care, consternation and worry that Anne exhibited concerning the welfare and well-being of her husband, following his almost near death experience incurring  possible injuries from his slightly one sided altercation with a bus.

Upon hearing the gentle dulcet tones of his loving wife, he beat a hasty retreat to what he erroneously and mistakenly believed would be the safe sanctuary of the men's toilets. Unfortunately for Denzil, the men's toilets were not the safe haven he had hoped for. Anne managed to track him down, like a lioness after her prey. Upon discovering his lair, Anne berated him mercilessly for a quarter of an hour before eventually vacating the building. Upon returning to the office Denzil made a comment which caused me to smile.

'I think I got off lightly there.'

If that was 'getting off lightly' I dread to think what having a hard time entailed.

During my time at Birchwater, he still continued to have his trysts and assignations with Janet, the other party in the love triangle. The affair remained a secret from Anne. Heaven help him if she had ever found out about it. I don't know if she ever did discover the affair for within the year I had left Birchwater.

The latter part of 1974 was, for me, one of the worst periods of my life. My mother terminally ill with breast cancer and very little time left to live, dying slowly and agonizingly a bit at a time. Life was not good at this time. My mother was dying and I hated my job and my boss and to top it all, the girl I loved Bronwen had terminated our relationship after having rekindled her relationship with her previous boyfriend.

A month before Christmas, I went to see our family doctor on the pretext of suffering from a cold. In truth, my visit was primarily to ask if there was anything more which could done for my ailing mother and reduce the pain she was experiencing, only to be informed she was being given the maximum dose of morphine legally allowed and there was nothing more they could do.

The doctor asked about my alleged ailment, when I told him I was suffering from a cold, he signed gave me a sick note for a month, fully aware I worked away from home and obviously knowing my mother would not be alive at the end of the four weeks. This allowed me to be at home with her during her final weeks alive.

The family doctors in Ebbw Vale were wonderful. On a late Friday night Dr. Selby who had been our GP for a number of years called at the house to see how my mother was. He had been called out on an emergency and took the time and effort to visit my mother on his way home. I thought that was absolutely wonderful.

Whilst Christmas 1973, the previous year had been wonderful, Christmas 1974 was the complete antithesis. My mother gave up her courageous two year battle with cancer and finally succumbed the evening of December 19th 1974 and was cremated December 23rd. She was forty nine years of age.

Christmas Day that year did not exist as far as my father and I was concerned. Neither my father nor I possessed any inclination to celebrate it. He had just lost his partner, wife, lover, friend and confidante of twenty four years. I had lost my mother and friend. We both felt there was nothing to celebrate and be happy about.

So it was with a heavy heart and following the Christmas break, I resumed work at Birchwater, not wishing to return there.

Bronwen and I found it impossible to work together, the atmosphere between us becoming strained and unbearable. She refused to do my typing or any other work, as though the termination of our relationship had been my fault. Transference of guilt I think they call it. Thankfully the other girls in the office shared my typing amongst themselves, being fully aware of the situation and feeling sympathetic towards me. Ultimately, Bronwen was assigned to work with someone else.

Circumstance within industry had turned full circle; the three day week had a tremendous effect during 1974. The final straw was the escalation in the price of oil. I had joined Birchwater during the boom period but within fifteen months it was the flip side. The country was in the grip of a recession. The economy was in deep decline and companies were beginning to '*lay off*' their workforce. Ultimately this economic depression trickled through to Birchwater and a request for voluntary redundancy was eventually put up on the notice boards in the middle of January 1975.

With my circumstances as they were, still employed as trainee manager, being paid a pittance, really beginning to hate my boss and the job, still working in the same office as Bronwen, but still caring for her but knowing she had no feelings for me which was hurting me. So now I had no emotional ties and no female asking me stay. All these factors, acting in unison, helped persuade me it was time to move on. I asked Fred, who was a shop steward, to put my name forward for voluntary redundancy, which he did, with some reluctance on his part.

Following protracted negotiations between unions and management, terms were agreed and lists of people whose employment with the company were to be terminated were drawn up. By the end of January 1975, the employees whose contracts were to be terminated had been given their letters, me included. Some, like me, had volunteered others to whom the termination of their employment came as a complete shock, ironically, one of the reasons for my terminating my employment with Birchwater. Dean Crabbe was given redundancy and instructed to leave the same day he received his letter. His general behaviour and attitude had not endeared him to his superiors, some of whom he had also treated with disrespect. You reap what you sow! As much as I disliked him, I could not help feeling sorry for him. He had worked for the company for nearly twenty years, now he was on the scrap heap at fifty five and unlikely to find alternative employment, being considered too old with no qualifications.

As my particular job had not technically become redundant, I was asked to stay on an extra month to show my replacement from another department the ropes. At the end of February 1975, I finally left Birchwater for the last time, leaving with a mere thousand pounds redundancy.

Working in Birchwater had added to my experience so was not a complete waste of time. Due to my time at the facility, my telephone manner had improved immensely. I had also gained a vast amount of experience in production and transportation scheduling, stock control, stock checks, warehousing together with other things. It had also taught me re-iterate instructions in writing as well as instructing verbally.

My final act before leaving was to get Bronwen alone to say my farewells, explaining I held no hard feelings and perhaps it was for the best, as I was now free to go where I pleased and where fate deemed to lead me, with no ties to encumber me.

I must admit it was with mixed, conflicting feelings and emotions of trepidation, elation, sadness, fear, excitement and wonder as I drove away for the last time, not having the foggiest idea of what I intended to do. Only time would tell. This was to be a feeling I would experience many times in my life caused by various factors with enforced changes and upheavals.

Now perhaps I could selfishly indulge myself and pursue my dreams of travelling around Europe.

# CHAPTER 7

Fate has a terrible habit of throwing a spanner into the works and ridiculing us mere mortals with our pre-conceived aspirations and plans, particularly when it comes to living one's life, destroying all our intentions, throwing them into complete and utter disarray.

Following my departure from Birchwater and with some money bequeathed to me from my recently deceased mother... God bless her, I had fully intended to take at least a year's sabbatical away from the rigours of working life and the hurly burly of the rat race. Take some time out for myself. My first eighteen months in the big, bad world had been a bit of a disaster. My tentative first steps on the career ladder had not been the success for which I had hoped. In addition, *l'amour* had played havoc with my emotions, throwing them into turmoil and confusion. Leaving Birchwater offered a new beginning and an opportunity to take time out from the proverbial rat race and re-assess my life. My intentions lay in purchasing an old van of some description and converting it into a mobile home. Then after completing the modifications, travel around Europe, doing various menial jobs such as grape picking to earn some money.

The years had now slowly moved on to 1975. It was the year America ignominiously vacated South Vietnam, throwing usable helicopters off the sides of their aircraft carriers in order to allow yet more fleeing helicopters to land on the decks. People scrambled and fought with each other to get onto the Hueys landing in the American Embassy compound in order to get out of Saigon before the victorious Vietcong arrived.

The country was in recession and oil prices escalated following the trebling of the crude oil price by the OPEC oil producing countries. There appeared to be little chance of finding employment with my ordinary degree in Chemical Engineering. All job adverts in that field specified "work experience required." Of which, in truth, I possessed none. My idea of going to Europe seemed highly attractive and the best proposition in the circumstances, having convinced myself no employment opportunities existed. Consequently, I did not sign on at the employment exchange straight away, instead choosing to wait a few days before even venturing into that establishment.

By the following Wednesday, I considered it prudent to sign on at the Employment Exchange, driving to the nearest office to where my father lived, now having moved back to Ebbw Vale and using my old home as a base. During my spare time, I fully intended purchasing, then modifying an old van for my intended forthcoming peripatetic adventures across Europe.

Then one of those circumstances which happen to alter one's life transpired. I would experience a number of these events or circumstances during my life. This particular one happened when I casually walked into the Employment Exchange reception area, awaiting my interview with Pam Davies, one of the Employment agency staff. Pam and I had known each other quite a number of years, as I had signed on at that same office a number of times, mainly during my time home from college throughout the vacations, when not employed down the steelworks. We also became better acquainted during my short stint at the DHSS, the offices of which happened to be located in the same office block as the Employment Exchange. We had become friendly as work colleagues and because of this friendship, Pam made every effort in finding employment for me. She knew of my reasons for being unemployed from the previous job but not about my intentions of travelling Europe... well, there are some things best kept secret. Pam began frantically delving through the *'Jobs Vacant'* file. After a few minutes anxiously searching, she suddenly exclaimed euphorically, 'Ah! Here it is West Mercian Oil, they are interviewing here next Monday for a Plant Chemist. Would you be interested?'

'Yes,' I replied, trying to feign enthusiasm, and excitement, not really interested at all. For, after all, my aspirations and plans now lay in other directions, namely travelling and exploring Europe, thoroughly convinced in my own mind there existed no chance whatsoever of ever getting the job on offer. However, I went along with Pam. The non-professional equates Chemical Engineering to pure Chemistry. This is a complete misnomer. They are different fields of the science. A fair analogy would be comparing a General Practitioner to a brain surgeon. Although the GP is conversant with the parts of the body, he would not be able to perform brain surgery without the proper training and experience. Similarly, with Chemical Engineering and Analytical Chemistry. From the job description handed to me by Pam, it became evident the company obviously wished to employ a fully-fledged Analytical Chemist, a field of Chemistry with which I had only a passing acquaintance during my short time at college, with a considerable amount of time have passed since then.

That following Monday, I turned up as instructed at the Employment Exchange, fully attired in my best bib and tucker i.e. my blue interview suite, white shirt, tie etc. thoroughly convinced I had embarked on a fool's errand, a futile gesture and a complete waste of time. This belief was further reinforced by the other candidates present for the interview, discovering they possessed excellent degrees in pure Chemistry, or Analytical Chemistry. Some also possessed M.Sc.'s, LRIC's, PhD's and other miscellaneous letters of the educational alphabet.

Being ambivalent about getting the job, my demeanour must have appeared very relaxed, exuding the impression of being confident and self-assured. In truth, the reality lay far from that. Despite the interview with Dave Jarvis, the Chief Chemist appeared to go extremely well. I believed that would be the last I would hear from West Mercian Oil, apart from the rejection letter.

A week later and much to my surprise, a letter came in the post asking me to attend a second interview, this time with the Deputy Managing Director, to be held at the new refinery being constructed and located at the bottom end of the steelworks. Apparently, I had been short-listed. How that happened was totally beyond my comprehension. All I could think was that I must have come over really well at the interview with the Chief Chemist, Dave Jarvis and really impressed him. I was totally non-plussed and with it, thoughts began permeating through my head.

'*How the hell did I manage to get a second interview? What if they offered me the job, and what about my plans to travel Europe?*'

Once again my lack of self-confidence got the better of me, considering it had been pure luck had got through the first stage and there would be absolutely no chance whatsoever of getting through the second interview and getting the job. I must only be there to make up the numbers.

The following week, once again, I attended the second interview as requested, driving up to the refinery, adhering to the instructions set out in the letter. As I drove my battered, old, sky blue, Mini

Countryman estate through the partially completed gates onto the site, it became blaringly obvious the refinery appeared to be nowhere near completion with no concrete or tarmac around the buildings, all of which appeared to be in the embryonic stage of erection. The concrete bases and a few layers of bricks were cemented together, giving the only indication as to where the perimeters were to be for each individual edifice. That previous weekend it rained incessantly, transforming the ground surrounding the concrete bases into a quagmire. My little blue Mini car slithered completely out of control exhibiting a total absence of any traction on the saturated earth and clay, making guidance of my old car virtually impossible. The site appeared festooned with porta cabins, caravans and all manner of temporary accommodation, which the contractors and employees of West Mercian Oil obviously used as offices, changing rooms and canteens. Experiencing a great deal of difficulty in steering my beloved mini, I thought it prudent to stop at the nearest temporary accommodation and make enquiries concerning the whereabouts of Dave Jarvis and the Deputy Managing Director.

Immediately upon emerging from the mud-splattered mini, my feet sank into the quagmire and my highly polished black shoes became completely covered in mud. I must have looked quite ridiculous stealthily negotiating through the mire, tiptoeing through the muck to my selected porta cabin. The trousers of my one and only reasonable suit became liberally covered with the brown, muddy sludge, this, despite the nimble way I tip-toed along. At last, after what seemed like an eternity, I managed to make it to the relative dryness of the steps to the designated porta cabin and upon reaching the top of the steps, knocked on the flimsy, dirty door.

'Come in!' a male voice from inside bellowed.

Upon entering the porta cabin, it became evident the room only contained one person. He was of average height, dark hair and slim build. I estimated his age to be thirty-something, he was attired in grimy white overalls. The whiteness of his overalls accentuated the dirt and mud which coated them. The stranger appeared to be intently perusing various engineering drawings sprawled before him and strewn haphazardly over a flimsy table.

'Excuse me?' I asked nervously, believing this stranger to be one of the many contractors on site.

'I wonder if you can help me, I'm looking for Dave Jarvis, the Chief Chemist. I have an appointment with him and one of the Directors from West Mercian Oil for a job interview?'

'You must be Vinson Chard?' he asked rhetorically, exhibiting the slight hint of a Brummy accent. 'He is expecting you.' With that, he walked over to another, smaller desk, pressed one of the buttons on an internal intercom machine, and began to speak.

'Dave, I have Vinson Chard here for his interview.' After making this statement, the man in the filthy white overalls released the pressure he was exerting upon the intercom button. Within a few seconds, there was a barely audible, crackling reply over the intercom. This was the mid-seventies with the technology of the day bearing no resemblance to the hi-tech electronic technology of the new millennium with its slim-line mobile phones, Blackberries, laptops, computer iPads and the internet.

'He'll be over in a few minutes,' the stranger imparted to me. Obviously aware I had no idea what the voice on the other end had said.

For a few moments, there was an embarrassing interlude of silence between us. The stranger in the filthy, white overalls resumed his intense perusal of the engineering diagrams liberally sprawled out before him.

Not being one to sit quietly for too long, I decided perhaps I should indulge in some polite conversation and some small talk, putting an end to the embarrassing silence.

'You're the Site Engineer, I presume?' I enquired nervously.

He looked at me with an almost paternalistic smile.

'Nothing so grand,' he replied.

I continued with the polite cross-questioning. It was intriguing ... who was this man who seemed to know all about me? Beginning to consider that perhaps West Mercian Oil was such a small company; everyone knew what was going on.

'You're not a Mechanical, Electrical, Chemical or Civil Engineer? I asked, by now bemused and thoroughly intrigued.

'Nope, 'fraid not, actually I am not all that qualified. Try again,' he replied, a smile beaming from his face. He was obviously enjoying this game of, *'What's my line?'* with this nervous interviewee.

I decided to give it one last shot. This would be my last guess and after that, I would keep my mouth shut.

'Site Foreman?' I blurted out nervously. The instant those pathetic words were uttered, his broad smile immediately changed, into that of a highly amused laugh.

'Wrong again. Actually I'm Craig Theake, the Deputy Managing Director of West Mercian Oil and the person who is going to interview you.'

My mouth dropped as thoughts went through my head, *'Oh Fuck. Ah well, that has well and truly blown it!'* uncertain if I wanted the job anyway, with Europe beckoning seductively.

Mercifully, at that moment, Dave Jarvis entered the porta cabin. I hoped he would extricate me from the hole I had unintentionally excavated for myself. Craig was still laughing, 'Hello Dave.' he said, attempting to speak whilst still laughing, 'I've just been promoted to Site Foreman.'

To my embarrassment, Dave also started laughing. After they had both calmed down somewhat, the interview began in earnest with Craig carefully studying my rather thin CV.

I initially believed there was no point in progressing with the interview any further. For, after all, I had just affronted and insulted the man about to interview me.

Notwithstanding my *faux pas,* the interview proceeded and, to my utter astonishment, appeared to be going very well indeed. Perhaps, as with the first interview, I had become so relaxed, considering the job was out of reach and exuded a certain air of self-confidence.

Dave Jarvis made comments about utilizing my Chemical Engineering knowledge as the refinery became established. After about an hour, Craig Theake looked at me and said in a *'matter of fact'* way, 'Well Dave seems keen to take you on, and that is good enough for me. When can you start?'

For the second time that morning, my mouth gaped open. Events had most certainly not gone as I had expected but, unusually, for the better. For about a millisecond, my dream of travelling Europe went briefly shooting through my thoughts, but then vanished, almost immediately overridden and dispelled by the thought of, at last, utilizing my Chemical Engineering training and job with security.

'Whenever you want me to,' I replied trying to curb my now obvious enthusiasm.

'Right, Dave and I will have a discussion and you

will receive an official acceptance letter by the end of next week setting out start dates and training, pay etc... By the way, would you mind going to Dudley for a week or so for some laboratory training? That wouldn't be a problem would it?'

I shook my head, to indicate it would not be a problem. I was completely amazed; they were actually offering the job at the interview. 'None whatsoever,' I replied.

Craig stood up and extended his right hand, 'Good, welcome to the team,' he said, as he did so, we shook hands.

'Thank you, 'I replied, ' I'm looking forward to it.'

My emotions were mixed, with any aspirations of travelling Europe now put on hold. Finally, I would be working in the chemical and processing industry; this would be my first step as a bona fide Chemical Engineer so there was also the feeling of exuberance and elation.

True to their word, the following week, the official acceptance letter came through the post box of my father's house. After a few weeks, I began my employment and training in the WMO laboratory at Dudley in the West Midlands, where the Head Office was located.

During my first day whilst working at the laboratory bench doing a Schoeniger quantitative test for sulphur content in oil, a man in an expensive suite walked past me on his way to the Office located at the end of the laboratory, where the Technical Director resided. The man walked a fair distance after passing me. He suddenly stopped, turned around, walked back towards me, and began talking to me.

'You must be Vinson Chard, welcome to WMO.' With that he extended his right hand. I shook his hand and thanked him saying I hoped I too would enjoy my stay. There must have been a bemused, quizzical look on my face, because almost immediately, he added. 'Oh, by the way, I'm Phil Meredith, the Managing Director.' To most people it would appear a small gesture, but a small gesture, which went a long way in my eyes. That was the nature of the man, he was a gentleman. I had only been used to dealing with the likes of Dean Crabbe, who was an insignificant individual with a huge ego. Phil Meredith was the head of a large company but possessed common, decent manners; it was something I have never forgotten.

I stayed at Craig Theake mother's house for the two weeks, together with a person who had been employed as the Commercial Manager. He was in his early twenties with aspirations of playing rugby for England as their scrum half. Although a rugby player, I found him unsociable and surly, completely the opposite of most rugby players I have known. This person would turn up periodically throughout my life. At the beginning of the new millennium, he would help shake the Welsh Rugby Union to its foundations and be involved in the '*Mike Ruddock affair.*'

Following my two-week stint at Dudley and my return to the Ebbw Vale refinery, it was a relief in discovering the site had mushroomed, with all of the buildings virtually nearing completion. The former quagmire now covered by tarmac and properly designated parking areas. There were storage tanks with connecting pipe work in bunded areas; a complete metamorphosis had taken place during those few weeks since my interview with Craig Theake. The main refinery building was nearing completion, but still did not have a roof. Manufacturing had begun the operators obliged to monitor the process completely at the mercy of the elements, not an enviable task. It was now March, and the weather bitterly cold and wet. To keep warm, they wore balaclavas and duffle coats or waterproofs, dependent upon how the weather was behaving that particular day, drinking copious amounts of steaming hot soap or coffee from gigantic thermos flasks, the whole scenario reminiscent of a scene from the *'Cruel Sea'* with Jack Hawkins and Donald Sinden.

Those early days in West Mercian Oil were amongst some of the happiest times of my working life. There was a tremendous *esprit de corps* and camaraderie, the likes of which I had not experienced since my days in the steelworks. Unsurprisingly really, as most of the WMO, employees came from the old steelworks heavy end. The steel-making, or heavy end of the works having closed down and the areas where I had worked, receiving my industrial baptism of fire.

The closure of the steelworks was brought about by the prevalent idea of the time that 'Big is beautiful'. With the steel making transferred to the colossal steelworks of Llanwern, Port Talbot and Ravenscraig. The human consequence was many men were made redundant and were eager for employment, hence the ebullient nature of the workforce and their fortitude and forbearance, when asked to work in such austere, difficult and primitive working conditions.

Craig Theake was what I personally considered to be a born leader. Not the type of person one normally envisages as Deputy Managing Director. *'Leading by example'* would be an apt description of his leadership style. On numerous occasions, he helped wherever he could, and even when the need arose, getting into dirty, sludge-laden tankers and cleaning them out. If I had known what he was like during my interview, I would have not been so concerned about my remark elevating him to Site Foreman. The refinery was his project and baby. He was determined to make it a success and ensure it thrived, come hell or high water.

The legend went that he designed the plant during the evenings over a few pints of beer whilst staying at one of the local hotels in the middle of Ebbw Vale. The directors of the main contracting company also stayed there. In the evenings, they used to discuss the layout of the refinery, designing it on the back of discarded cigarette packets. Whichever way it was conceived and designed, it now existed as a wonderful piece of chemical plant. There was another side as well to Craig. He gave the plant the Welsh name for Ebbw Vale. He insisted it was called by the name Glyn Ebwy Refinery, all this from an Englishman, born and bred in the West Midlands. The workforce, including myself, had a tremendous respect and admiration for Craig. Those were the days, no internal politics or squabbling, no intransigent unionism or management, a utopian working environment, with everyone willing the venture along, pure unadulterated teamwork. I recall those days with fondness, wishing all working environments could have the same mind-set. It is something I would experience to a lesser degree later in my working life, but this would be the pinnacle and at that time my first experience of everyone working in unison towards a common goal. However, there would be other situations where it came close.

Working in an environment open to the mercy of elements could a task be fraught with danger, particularly the process landing. One of the operators, Russell Parry, someone I had once worked alongside in the Convertor Shop, discovered himself caught in a sudden strong gust of wind. Russell did not have a big physique and probably only weighed in at eight and a half stones when soaking wet, despite being average height. It is not difficult to imagine how thin he was. Russell's distinct lack of physique presented no obstacle whatsoever to a strong gust of wind intent on blowing anything over which lay in its path. The wind blew at the same time Russell stood in front of the process vessel; suddenly he was unable to fight against the maelstrom, which inevitably lifted him into the air, tossing him over the unprotected side of the incomplete structure, just like a rag doll discarded and hurled aside by its petulant, young owner. Russell was attired in a bulky duffle coat, which generously encompassed Russell's fragile, light frame. He descended the few metres over the side of the refinery building, after projected over by the angry wind, the coat suddenly billowed out, rapidly slowing his rate of descent and preventing him hitting the ground at a possibly injurious velocity. Instead, he gently floated to the ground, like feather caught in a gentle breeze.

The Production Manager happened to be walking alongside the refinery building at the instant Russell's hapless descent manifested itself. All he could perceive apparently was a discarded duffel coat, gently falling to terra firma, with no indication it shrouded a human being in the form of Russell Parry. The Production Manager became suddenly taken aback when after hitting terra firma, the duffle coat suddenly stood up without any apparent assistance. It was only when the coat turned around, did the Manger suddenly realize it enveloped a slightly dazed and slightly bruised Russell. Apart from the minor bruises, Russell came out of the experience relatively unscathed. It was probably the only time Russell became grateful for possessing such a puny anatomy.

# CHAPTER 8

Inexorably, slowly but surely and before my very eyes, the new refinery began manifesting itself. The laboratory too also began taking shape. Expensive, delicate, state of the art pieces of analytical equipment were allocated their specific positions within the laboratory and gingerly put in situ. The purpose for all this equipment was to analyse the recycled oils to high quality standards, standards for which West Mercian Oil had become renowned and respected for within industry, restoring the used oils to the correct specifications making them suitable for re-use. At that time West Mercian Oil, or WMO as we preferred to call it, was in the vanguard of the oil recycling industry, taking old industrial waste oils such as hydraulic, lubricating, cutting, quenching oils, gear oils etc. by reprocessing, or 'laundering' these oils, returning them to the customers as good as new, at a third of the cost of purchasing the virgin product. Oil prices had escalated by up to three hundred per cent in the mid-seventies, initiated by the OPEC oil producing countries. Being entrepreneurs, both Phil Meredith and Craig Theake had seen an opening and seized the opportunity, *carpe diem.* The business had taken off. It was a case of being in the right place at the right time. Phil Meredith desperately needed extra financing in order to expand the company of which building the Glyn Ebwy Refinery was the major part.

Therefore, it became necessary to allow a company called Peshco to acquire WMO, and make it a separate division within its expanding empire.

The volumes reprocessed could be as little as three hundred gallons, or as much as two thousand five hundred gallons. WMO were onto a winner, with the price of new oil, the business proliferated. Craig Theake, apart from being responsible for the Glyn Ebwy refinery, was also The Sales and Marketing Director and he certainly knew how to sell the company. As the saying goes, 'He could sell sand to the Arabs.' He may not have had the technical qualifications but he had the personality and the ability to acquire knowledge quickly with the enthusiasm and belief in selling the business. They also employed a Technical Director who had the expertise to ensure the quality of the recycled oils. With these three directors at the helm, the business just grew from strength to strength and flourished.

The actual reprocessing of the spent oils was simplicity itself. This began by heating the oil to boil off any excess water. Once completed, bleaching agents together with filter aids were then added to the oil. The oil was then filtered through a plate and frame filter press to remove all the solids. Finally, following extensive chemical analysis, additives were then replenished to their correct concentration for the quality standard of that particular product of oil. These additives being such things as Viscosity Index improvers, extreme pressure additives, fats, greases for lubrication and finally base oils, to increase or decrease the viscosity of the oils as required. Once all the reprocessing was completed, the oils were stored and then shipped back to the customers in tankers or drums, whichever they specified. The company had progressed a long way from the days of boiling oils in old railway tankers with heating coils inside them and the heat being supplied by an old boiler.

Somehow, WMO had managed to acquire all the technical quality information necessary for reprocessing the oil and restoring the product to the correct specification for all the oils from the original players in the oil industry such as: Shell, BP, Mobile, Gulf, Texaco, Total and many other smaller companies.

My job entailed performing the quality control analysis on the oils during the production process utilising all the sophisticated analytical equipment at my disposal, which were, at that time, state of the art. After receiving training in the operation of all these pieces of equipment during my time at Dudley, I knew how to operate them. After analysing the results, I was able to calculate how much additive was required to bring the oil back to the correct specification and components to restore the oils to their specifications.

Dave Jarvis was the Chief Chemist at the refinery, while the responsibility for the day-to-day analysis was given to me. Dave concentrated on the technical sales and customer support. He appeared to be forever off site visiting the customers in that role.

To assist me with all this analysis in the laboratory I had Bethany, or as she preferred to be known, Beth. She was an attractive, nubile 19 year old, possessing what I can only describe politely as gigantic mammaries. Beth did not fall into the category of fat. However, she did possess these two gigantic protuberances, which appeared to dominate her whole body. They automatically attracted one's eyes to them whilst one indulged in conversation with her. The fact Beth wore a tightly fitting laboratory coat exacerbated this situation somewhat. Despite all conscious efforts to maintain eye contact, one's eyes would automatically be drawn to those enormous, young, firm, and female attributes; like iron filings to a magnet. They were so compelling! I was a normal, healthy, sexually aware, heterosexual male adult, only twenty-four years of age and not much older than her, so it was only to be expected. The more Beth exhibited her ample cleavage, the worse this situation became. I am convinced she knew the effect she was having and more than likely deliberately exposed her generous breasts.

I was not the only male who succumbed to his primitive, carnal, male obsession with Beth's gigantic breasts. The process operators also exhibited normal, healthy male tendencies. They too were fascinated by her assets. It became almost impossible keeping the operators out of the laboratory and permit Beth to concentrate on her work. The operators continually come into the laboratory on any pretext of talking to her, their ulterior motive being to chat her up openly flirting and ogling her extensive female attributes. Beth was indubitably a constant source of attraction.

During the first few months of production, the internal telephone system had not been installed which meant a reliance upon the infernal intercom as a means of verbal communication between various areas of the refinery. The very same intercom system I had originally observed in operation during my interview with Craig Theake. Operation of the intercom system required a constant pressure on then '*Speak*' button when one spoke, this had to be then released, allowing the person on the other end to reply. There was a downside to this. Every intercom machine on site operated when one pressed the '*Speak*' button, so everybody around the site was privy to the conversations taking place. This could have disastrous effects as a particular episode showed.

Colin Hudson, the Plant Foreman, happened one day to be standing on the process landing indulging in idle banter with the operators. Unbeknownst to Colin, one of the operators, a certain John Smith was standing with the intercom machine behind him, obscuring it from everyone, especially Colin. John surreptitiously depressed the '*Speak*' button on the machine and began indulging in a sexual discussion concerning Beth's female attributes and her protuberances. Deliberately enticing Colin into the conversation, asking him sexually leading questions such as which sexual acts he would like to perpetrate upon Beth, or conversely have her perpetrate upon him. Colin was a garrulous person by nature and required very little prompting; just wind him up with a topic, and off he went. The fact it concerned the female form and his favourite subject of sex happened to be an added bonus, causing him to talk even more than usual. Almost immediately he went into vivid detail concerning the sexual acts he would like to perform upon Beth should she ever condescend to indulge him in his fantasies. This conversation could now be heard throughout the entire refinery where the intercom receivers happened to be installed, particularly the laboratory where the poor unfortunate Beth stood in close proximity to the receiver. Dave Jarvis also happened to be standing close by. Once that '*Speak*' button had been depressed, there was no way, in which the transmission could be stopped or interfered with and Colin carried on with his sexual monologue, blissfully unaware that everyone throughout the refinery, including the highly embarrassed, nubile Beth, was also privy to his sexual proclivities. The plant operators present were fully aware of John's subterfuge, allowing Colin free reign with his sexual fantasies, even actively encouraging or prompting Colin when he seemed to be drawing to a close and helping to prolong the monologue.

By now, Beth's attractive, innocent, young, smooth face was virtually blood red with embarrassment, as she had to listen to this sexual monologue from the Plant Foreman. Suddenly Dave Jarvis, whom I should mention, was a Baptist Lay Preacher, angrily projected himself at high velocity from the laboratory to the process landing. Upon reaching the landing, Dave, made Colin cognizant of the fact his monologue could be heard by the whole refinery, including Beth. The moment Dave appeared on the scene, John removed his offending hand from the '*Speak*' button on the transmitter. Within less than a minute, the intercom in the laboratory went mercifully quiet; obviously, the instant Dave reached the process landing.

For his part in this subterfuge, John received a written warning. Colin also received a warning concerning his sexual remarks. It was a considerable period of time before he was able to speak to Beth, following his little peccadillo. As for Beth, I am not certain whether she had listen intently to any information Colin had imparted during his talk, but it seemed highly coincidental she appeared to acquire a lot more boyfriends who were forever phoning her at work following this incident, so perhaps she made notes, who knows? If the incident happened today, both Colin and John would have received their P45s.

A few months later, another young female assistant began working in the laboratory. She was a dark, slim, attractive eighteen year old called Anne Nelson. Although Anne did not possess the same enormous attributes as Beth, she was nevertheless very attractive and pleasing on the eyes. She also caused the operators to come into the laboratory using the slightest pretext to ogle and flirt with either her or Beth.

Things always seemed to happen or involve Colin, a year or so later, I was carrying out experiments determining sulphur concentrations in oils. Unfortunately, the analysis involved generating bromine, a somewhat toxic, halogenate gas. Bromine is the gaseous form of the chemical bromide and part of the compound potassium bromide, the infamous chemical purportedly used in the armed forces for hampering and suppressing the sexual desires and performance of the Britain's young warriors. Now I was fully aware of the resultant properties of this chemical and made every possible effort to minimise and contain any emissions of the brown fumes being generated during the experiments. I always performed the analysis in the laboratory fume cupboard. Unfortunately, the extraction system for the fume cupboard was not as efficient as it should have been. During the analysis, voluminous clouds of bromine gas were generated, and because of the inefficiencies of the fume cabinet extraction system, invariably and unfortunately for me, not all the gas was completely extracted, with minute amounts of the bromine escaping into the laboratory. We are only talking parts per million. Nevertheless, they appeared to have a disastrous effect on my sexual libido and performance.

By this time, I had become engaged to Cindy, whom I would later marry. Cindy was an extremely attractive, highly intelligent, twenty two year old brunette. Time had healed my unrequited love experience with Bronwen and I had now fallen deeply in love with Cindy. Bronwen had become just a distant memory. Another episode in my love life.

My relationship with Cindy began January 1976 after a Saturday night out in Newport with an old college friend, Geoff. Following a bit of a pub-crawl, we ended up in one of the ubiquitous, burgeoning discos and the term used for clubs in the seventies. Images of the white suited John Travolta, the Bee Gees and all that. During this particular evening, a gorgeous five feet four brunette smiled and waved at Geoff. At that instant, I was smitten. If there is such a thing as love at first sight, well as far as I was concerned, this was it.

'Do you know her?' I asked Geoff, uncertain if she was someone who just happened to be smiling at him.

'Yes that's Cindy, an acquaintance from one of the coffee bars I used to frequent in Newport.'

I dreaded asking the next question.

'Is she an old girlfriend?'

'I wish!' he replied with more than a hint of regret in his voice, then, adding as an afterthought, 'No, we were just good friends.'

'Come on, you'll have to introduce me,' I insisted.

'Sure I'll introduce you, but I must tell you now, you stand absolutely no chance whatsoever,' he said with a disarming smile.

We casually walked over to the two females, trying to exude an air of nonchalance, although in reality my heart was beating like a jackhammer. Geoff, true to his word introduced me to Cindy and the other girl Lesley. Playing the battle of the sexes is a game, trying not to show too much enthusiasm. I first began talking to Lesley before indulging in conversation with the gorgeous brunette who attracted me so much. When we did start talking I discovered she lived in Newport with her parents. She turned out to be a ladies' hairdresser and twenty-two. Cindy pleasantly surprised me when she readily agreed to dance with me without any sign of hesitation whatsoever.

We had a few fast dances then the DJ played a slow, smooch record. Again, Cindy surprised me by agreeing to stay on the dance floor. Hesitantly I put my arms around her waist and gently pulled her close to me. As I did so, I felt no resistance on her part. She felt so good with her voluptuous body pressing against mine. Her expensive perfume played havoc with my senses and its wonderful aroma. Now the dreaded time for the question, would she like to go out for a meal or a drink the next night? Unfortunately, she told me she went to her grandmother's house every Sunday to perm her hair and would be unable to accept my proposal. My deflated ego took this to be a rejection. However, Cindy detected the disappointment in my face.

'I am not trying to put you off, I really have to go to my grandmother's tomorrow, but I am free on Monday if the offer still stands?' Then she did something, which made it clear she would definitely like to see me. She pulled away from our clinch, picked up her bag, took out a pen and some paper, then immediately began writing her telephone number down.

'That's my number; shall we meet about eight on Monday?' adding, 'Give me a call about forty five minutes before you want to meet. I've been let down so often. Then we can arrange to meet somewhere in Newport.' I found that statement about being let down incomprehensible. This attractive, intelligent female being stood up.... she was incredible.

My head was spinning. This beautiful, stunning female had agreed to go out on a date with me. Not only that, she had given me her telephone number, girls did not usually do this first, only doing so after they had become acquainted. We finished our dance after which, she informed me she had better get back to Lesley as she had left her alone with Geoff too long and she did not like him and they did not get along.

We returned to our mutual friends and said goodbye to each other, after I kissed her on the cheek and whispered I would see her Monday without fail.

'Well?' Geoff enquired, unable to contain his curiosity, 'What happened?'

'I'm taking her out Monday,' I replied with a smug smile of satisfaction on my face.

'You're kidding?' he replied, his tone indicating total incredulity.

The rest of the evening went by as a blur. I could not wait for Monday.

Monday evening eventually came. At the time I was

living with my father, it had now been one year since my mother had died. We tended to live our own lives and not interfere with each other, my father had now developed friendships with various women who seemed besotted with him, but he did not intend to get too involved, relishing his newly found bachelor status.

My father did not believe in phones, being a sort of middle aged Luddite. Therefore, we had no telephone in the house. That night I had to call Cindy from a phone box while travelling down to Newport from Ebbw Vale. Leaving the house at seven o'clock, I estimating it would take forty-five minutes to get to Newport, leaving me fifteen minutes spare.

Unfortunately, the first telephone booth I came to in it was a guy in it and he seemed to be talking forever. The reader must realize we are talking about 1976, when the idea of everyone owning their own personal mobile phone, at that time, seemed like pure science fiction. I spent ten minutes outside before giving up. Travelling down the valley, I discovered the next telephone booth vandalized. The third was not working. It was the ultimately the fourth telephone booth I came to before I was able to phone Cindy. By this time due to all the waiting and stoppages, the time was approaching eight o'clock and I was still some miles from Newport. This beautiful woman would be angry and I would never see her again. Eventually the phone rang and an elderly sounding woman answered.

'Oh shit!' I thought, 'she's got fed up of waiting and has gone out to visit a friend.'

'May I speak to Cindy please?' I asked nervously.

'Who shall I say is calling?' The voice at the other end enquired.

'Could you tell her it's Vinson?'

There was a pause on the silence on the other end after the person told me to hang on. Eventually a voice

I recognized came on the line. Thank God, it was Cindy; at least, she had not gone out or refused to talk to me.

She did however sound slightly angry, or could it be just my imagination?

'Hello,' she said, 'I'd given up on you. Don't tell me you can't make it?' I detected a slight hint of belligerence and anger in her voice.

'No, far from it,' I blurted out hastily before she could slam the phone down on me. 'I'm terribly sorry I couldn't find a telephone booth. Are we still okay for tonight? I'll explain later.'

'Yes, sure,' she replied, her voice mellowing somewhat.

With that, we agreed to meet outside the Queens in Newport at eight thirty.

I arrived outside the pub at eight thirty. There appeared this beautiful girl in an expensive fur coat walking towards me. Her walk exuded pure seduction and femininity and as she approached, I could see had a broad smile on her face.

'We meet again at last,' she said, referring to the night's events.

I took her to my car, and had progressed by this time to driving around in a sports car, a Triumph Spitfire mark IV to be precise, as the old Mini Countryman had given up the ghost. We drove to a pub called the Commodore in Cwmbran for a quiet drink and chat, discovering we hit it off straight away. During the evening, Cindy confessed she had waved to Geoff intentionally in the hope he would ultimately introduce us. So in fact, it was Cindy who picked me up. She even told me she had seen me chatting to a blonde girl for ages earlier in that evening, believing her to be my girlfriend, and had been pleasantly surprised to see I was not with her later in the evening. As I recall I had simply been talking to a girl.

After that first night, our relationship developed and blossomed. I had had a few casual girlfriends following my experience with Bronwen, but nothing too serious. This was the real thing and I could not wait to see her every time we went out. Cindy was constantly in my thoughts. I was absolutely smitten and in love.

Being a normal, young, healthy, sexually active heterosexual, couple and the fact we were deeply in love, Wendy and I had a normal, happy, physical, sexual relationship, a fact which her sexually repressed, conservative, prudish mother would have been utterly mortified to discover. Her mother still believes, to this day, that Cindy and I only had a physical relationship following our marriage, some two years later.

Therefore, it was during the early stages of our relationship, I had been carrying out some laboratory experiments which required the using bromine gas. They had been under way for about two weeks, but after the first week. Unfortunately, I discovered the minute traces of chemical appeared to be exhibiting disastrous effects upon my libido. Despite an overwhelming desire to make passionate love to Cindy, the girl I loved, the most important part of my anatomy required for the act was unable to perform and react in the normal way, despite Cindy's wonderful dexterous, erotic and usually extremely arousing administrations. Every time Cindy and I met, we ended up just kissing and cuddling, with this state of affairs continuing during the duration of the analysis procedures. In all fairness, Cindy exhibited a large amount of patience even though her sexual desires must have been at a peak. She made it obvious she would be relieved when these experiments were at an end, we could resume our passionate lovemaking, and also hoping this would not be a permanent condition, a thought that caused me a bit of consternation as well.

The thought had also occurred to me this condition could be psychosomatic and purely in my mind, believing, perhaps erroneously, the bromine was having this undesired effect. A case of, *'I have heard it does this, so therefore it is affecting me. I hope that my temporary impotence actually being self-induced.'* This proved not to be the case, as I later discovered.

One day, Colin Hudson came into the laboratory, while I was approximately two to three weeks into the experiments. During an analysis, copious amounts of bromine gas tended to be generated, most of it being extracted through the exhaust of the fume cupboard, though some still managed to seep into the laboratory. The instant he came into the laboratory, his inquisitive nature exhibited itself. An endearing, although sometimes exasperating trait, most Valley's Welsh people possess. I include myself in this statement.

'What is that slight odour?' he enquired, in a slightly belligerent manner.

'Bromine gas,' I replied, nonchalantly.

'Is that the same as Bromide?' he continued, not willing to desist in his questioning.

In an effort to baffle him with science, I replied, 'Well it's the same chemical just a different form, gas instead of a solid compound.'

'But does it have the same effect?' he persisted.

'In all honesty I don't know' was my answer, which was the truth, for in reality I was unsure my unwanted impotence was indeed due to the bromine gas, or because of the psychosomatic factors previously mentioned.

'How long have you been doing this?' he continued.

'About two and a half weeks.'

Colin then began explaining this smell had actually been permeating into his small office, which unfortunately happened to be located on the same side of the building as the fume cupboard exhaust and most importantly, generally upwind of the venting, foul smelling, and odious toxic brown gas. Colin, up until that instant, had no idea where the smell had been coming from, believing perhaps it was being generated in the refinery, where any permutation of differing concoctions and smells were being conceived. Hence, his unremitting cross-questioning concerning the subject. Colin further elucidated concerning the subject and the bromine gas, for it appeared he too had been experiencing difficulties in the sexual department and unable *'to rise to the occasion*,' unable to perform his marital duty. Both Colin and his wife apparently, had an above average, healthy, sexual appetite. Now suddenly, Colin could no longer function sexually as normal. Suspicion and recriminations began exhibiting themselves in his marriage. His wife fully convinced herself he had been indulging in extra-marital affairs, leaving him little or no energy and vitality for her excessive carnal requirements.

I now realised my symptoms could only be fact physically taking place within my body and not psychologically as first suspected. I explained to Colin my sexual difficulties, believed to be psychological, but now convinced the bromine had indeed been affecting me.

Colin stormed out of the laboratory, heading straight for the Plant Manager's Office. He complained quite vociferously about the mad chemists in the laboratory, performing irresponsible experiments with toxic chemicals and worst of all chemicals with disastrous effects upon his sexual activity. Dave terminated my experiments shortly afterwards, following Colin's discussion with Gary Yandle, the Plant Manager. Fortuitously, I had acquired enough data to reach a tentative conclusion in the project. I cannot say I was too upset at the termination of the project.

Within a week of terminating my acquaintance with the bromine gas and ending the analytical procedure, my sexual performance and libido returned to normal, much to Cindy's and certainly my relief.

With normal sexual activity resumed, it can only be assumed Colin's sexual difficulties also resolved themselves, for he never mentioned the subject again and is still married to this day, some thirty years later.

The years passed, I became more involved in project work, as Dave had originally intended, utilizing my Chemical Engineering experience for which I had trained. My original duties of Process Chemist and Quality Control being taken over by a new chemist named Gerald Charters who joined WMO. About two years after I joined the company. Gerald had a slightly camp mannerism, despite being married. There were more pressing matters. The project work began taking more and more of my time and I became more deeply immersed and obsessively absorbed with them. One of the first major projects being the objective of removing the minute traces of water globules from the reprocessed oils this exhibited a phenomena known as '*chilling*' in the trade. Whereby the oil, because of the minute traces of water being left in it, at concentrations in the region of approximately 200 parts per million, exhibited a dull, hazy appearance once the oil cooled to ambient temperature and not the sparkling, clear appearance, which should have been the desired appearance. This '*chilling*' had the effect of reacting with the additives, causing them to precipitate out.

Following much research on the subject, particularly by Dr. Williams from the University Of Manchester evaluating discovered the most effective way of removing the last traces of water was to blow dry air through the hot oil through a column with counter current flow. By doing this, the water content could be reduced anywhere from one thousand parts per million down to less than five parts per million. Five parts per million was the acceptable and desired level. This would eliminate all the problems associated with the chilling effect.

The task fell upon me to get a small pilot plant erected in the refinery to carry out an evaluation with one of the process oils renowned for exhibiting this chilling effect. The pilot plant consisted of a cylindrical tower, six feet high, and two feet diameter. Stainless steel Pall rings packed onto a perforated plate. To a Chemical Engineer it was a packed desorption column, to an ordinary person it was a packed metal pipe.

The process system basically consisted of blowing dry, clean compressed air through the base of the column whilst the hot, oil was fed into the top of the column, it then percolated through the Pall rings inside, giving good contact between the oil and the air. Chemical Engineers always talk about heat and mass transfer, and large transfer areas. This column was designed for high surface area and hence good mass transfer with intimate contact between the oil and the compressed air. The hot, wet, air vented through the top of the column after extracting the water from the oil. The dry oil would then percolate through the column, exiting through an outlet, gravitating into a large blending tank. That was the theory at any rate but as is the usual case with life, the actual implementation and practicalities proved a quite a different proposition and the whole project proved not to be as straightforward as it seemed.

Following weeks of scrounging, begging and borrowing from numerous magnanimous suppliers, gradually the desorption column began taking shape.

Cedric Hughes, the Maintenance Engineer on the plant, helped me in my endeavours with the column, his help proving invaluable. Cedric was an irascible forty-something, possessing an extremely low temper threshold and liable to go into a rage for at the slightest reason. He was superb at his job, but boy! Did he let you know it, and never let you forget how good and knowledgeable he was? Modesty and being self-deprecating were not Cedric's failings. He could also be quite lecherous. Often I caught him leering at both Beth and Anne in the laboratory.

For the project, pipelines had to be broken into, extra valves installed, directing the oil into the desorption column as and when required. Following weeks of this upheaval, the column neared completion and we were almost ready for the evaluation.

As usual the process operators exhibited their usual scepticism when it came to anything new or some sort of scientific evaluation involving me. Unfortunately, it proved their misgivings were correct in this particular instance.

The day arrived for the first trial. The production department helped with the trial, everyone being as keen like myself to eradicate and eliminate this '*chilling*' problem. Everything was in place and the oil chosen on which to perform the trial, actually one of the worst oils for the chilling effect. The oil began its tortuous flow, out of the heated process vessel, through the filter press then heading in the direction of the blending tanks. I must admit, I was confident this pilot plant would work. As the oil was finding its way through the maze of pipes, I began opening the valve slightly, allowing the compressed air into the column. Unfortunately, this was a gate valve, giving little or virtually no control over the air flow. We were unable to acquire the more expensive needle valve, which would have been the specified valve for controlling the air flow. This decision to use the incorrect valve would have near disastrous consequences.

Once the task of getting the air flowing into the column had been completed, I turned my attention to the oil line, opening and closing valves, re-directing the oil into my much prized desorption column. The oil now could only flow in one direction through my column, its flow being cut off through its normal route directly to the blending tank. For a few seconds nothing seemed to be happening. I increased the air flow, then, all of a sudden, to my utter horror and consternation, there was a giant fountain of the straw-coloured, slightly viscous, slippery oil, effusing at a tremendously high volumetric rate from the top of the column. The oil rose in a spectacular, yet strangely majestic fashion above the column, before deciding to return to earth, cascading over the miniature edifice which was my column, running in rivulets down the side of column finding the least restricted route. While I stared open mouthed at my experimental fiasco and disaster, the process operators watching nearby were more decisive in their actions, making a hasty retreat from the vicinity of this debacle, running in every direction to escape this mini Vesuvius. The direction not mattering, just anywhere away from this hot, angry, viscous, straw-coloured material which at its maximum temperature would be in the region of one hundred and ten degrees Celsius.

My duty was clear. I had to stop the flow of air into the column and re-direct the flow of oil through the route it would have normally taken, re-directing the oil into the blending tank, without it having to detour through the desorption column. Mustering all the courage within me, I ran under the never ending torrent of the hot, viscous material. I began closing the gate valve which was obviously allowing too much air in, forcing the oil out of the vent at the top of the edifice, having restricted its flow down the column. Unfortunately, there had obviously been a considerable pressure build-up within the confines of the column and unfortunately, turning the flow of air off having no immediate discernible effect. The oil continued disobediently erupting out of the vent at the top of the column then cascading down, drenching anyone and anything in the vicinity. That anyone, being myself, with everyone else observing from a safe distance.

Once the initial task of closing the gate valve had been performed, the next task on the agenda was the re-directing of the oil flow away from the column, directly into the blending tank. I began opening the valve allowing the oil to flow, unrestricted, directly into the blender. As this task was being performed, I could feel the oil getting warm then hot. My plastic safety helmet prevented the oil from contaminating my hippy long hair. However there was nothing to prevent my overalls becoming saturated with the cascading, straw coloured material. I was fully cognizant of the fact that this oil was getting hotter and hotter, and it was only a matter of time before it reached the maximum process temperature of two hundred and thirty degrees Fahrenheit, or one hundred and ten degrees Celsius, ten degrees above the boiling point of water. Fortuitously for me, the oil had to travel through a considerable length of cold metal pipe-work which had cooled the initial flow down quite considerably, but I knew it was only a matter of time before the torrent above me reached the scalding process temperature. After what appeared to be an interminable amount of time, the valve allowing the oil to flow directly into the blender was at last fully open. That successfully completed, the final task was to close the valve allowing the oil to flow into the desorption column. As I began performing this third and final task, the torrential flow began almost immediately to abate, the cascade visibly becoming a trickle then ceasing immediately, the only flow now being the remnants of the oil as it flowed down the side of the column also dripping from my safety helmet and saturated overalls. Had the cascade of oil continued for another minute, then the outcome would have been very different.

I experienced a strong sense of relief, after re-directing the flow, as I looked at my catastrophic experiment, as the oil dripped from the edifice in tandem with the oil dripping from my safety helmet. Of course I received a good ribbing from the process operators as they all surveyed the spectacle in front of them.

'Was that supposed to happen?' being one of the sarcastic comments I recall, and 'That was quite impressive!' being another.

With my ego well and truly battered, I headed for the showers in the changing rooms, as I did so, the swarfega incident came racing into my mind. I remained in the shower for a considerable period of time, happy in my solitude away from the comments I knew would be directed at me. The cascading fluid different to the one I had just experienced that of warm water and soap and pleasant. Eventually all the mineral oil was extirpated from my whole body. I felt clean again.

Following the removal of the offending organic mineral oil from my body, I changed my clothing. Fortunately, experience had taught me to always keep a spare change of clothing, particularly when working in the oil industry. The oil saturated clothing now superfluous to requirements was unceremoniously binned.

As I had thought, upon my return to the process landing, the jokes and ribbing flew thick and fast concerning the utter debacle which they had all witnessed. The process operators considered the whole incident thoroughly amusing. It is my considered belief process operators are direct descendants of the Luddites, having little or no confidence in technical innovation or change. Unfortunately, my little fiasco with the cascading oil only confirmed their beliefs. The incident had also convinced them I was completely mad, particularly the way in which I had run the gauntlet of the cascading hot oil without any consideration for self-preservation. Also in addition to the amusement which the incident had caused, my credibility as a Chemical Engineer had also received a considerable setback.

My credibility as a Chemical Engineer became mercifully restored somewhat, when after about a week, modifications to the desorption column were carried out, with Cedric's assistance. By fitting a needle valve, a far better control of the air flow from the compressor into the tower was attained.

Other modifications required carrying out, such as fitting a pressure gauge to the side of the column, pre-empting any pressure build-up inside the column, eradicating any repetition of the first run.

With these simple modifications in place, I was able to perform a number of successful evaluations without any further mishaps. The results proving beyond any doubt, by counter current blowing air through the hot oil, any '*chilling*' effect within the oils could be eradicated, bringing the water content down to an acceptable level.

# CHAPTER 9

As mentioned, I met Cindy, my first wife, almost one year after having started work at West Mercian Oil. Cindy still lived with her parents on the outskirts of Newport; ironically, the town I had just left after terminating my employment with Birchwater Containers. Her home was located approximately twenty-five miles from where I now lived with my father. By this time, the old, blue Mini Countryman had given up the ghost and had to be scrapped. However, with the money bequeathed to me by my mother, I progressed to driving around in a soft top, yellow Triumph Spitfire mark IV sports car, invariably cruising around, mostly with the hood down during the long, extremely hot, dry, arid summer of 1976. I must admit to probably looking quite the poseur, with my long hair, beard, and baseball cap and Polaroid sunglasses. What a summer 1976 turned out to be with the hot, sunny weather seeming to be never-ending. I purchased the Spitfire from a certain Sir Andrew Chandrok Hulsey the future 9th Baronet of Shirebrook Vale, who, despite his upbringing and title, exhibited the characteristics, tendencies of a complete charlatan, rogue, and crook, a complete contradiction to his elevated title. In truth he possessed no class or morals whatsoever. You had to count your fingers left after shaking hands with him. Unfortunately, the 9th Baronet of Newton would, periodically keep appearing in my life causing total mayhem and upheaval.

Cindy and I enjoyed seeing each other as much as possible, which necessitated driving quite a bit and clocking up the miles on the spitfire. We were in love or probably lust would be a more apt description. Making use of the hot long summer evenings of 1976, frequently indulge in passionate lovemaking in the limited confines of the Spitfire and sometimes outside the sports car for variety. During one lovemaking session inside the confines of the vehicle, down a secluded country lane, a driver approached us, knocked on the driver's window to ask directions. Fortuitously, as well as other things, that night we had the soft top up. Both Cindy and I heard the vehicle stop and its driver approaching, compelling us both to desist in our mutual carnal pleasure before he arrived at the side of the car. We both just managed to make ourselves presentable before the unwanted intruder tapped on the steamed up window. I only wound the window down a couple of inches before giving him some brief garbled directions, trying to limit his view as much as possible concerning both our states of undress.

Yes, Cindy and I wanted to be with each other with each other as much as possibly, which entailed a fair amount of travelling by car. However, with all this travelling, the inevitable happened and the little sports car succumbed to mechanical difficulties and defects, exacerbated somewhat by Sir Andrew's wife, Lady Cynthia, the previous driver and owner. I later discovered Lady Cynthia happened to be a notoriously bad driver, particularly in the way she abused her automobiles.

Whilst driving Cindy home one evening after having consumed an expensive Italian meal in Cardiff, the Spitfire broke down. The incident happened at the Llandaff roundabout located on the outskirts of the Welsh capital city. During a long break in the traffic, approaching from the right hand side, I lifted my left foot off the clutch, anticipating a quick getaway. The little car barely moved. Fortuitously, there were no cars approaching from the right, otherwise, there could have been a vehicular contretemps. Panic began to consume my whole body, as I desperately tried to achieve more power by depressing the accelerator pedal. This produced no difference whatsoever; the Spitfire not wishing to accelerate one iota, only moving by its original inertia. My depression of the accelerator caused an excruciating and seemingly painful whining of the engine as I desperately tried to propel it forward in a somewhat futile attempt to move the car away from the roundabout and the approaching traffic. The tachometer needle swung wildly into the red as I pressed the accelerator pedal, an indication I was pushing the engine beyond its design capabilities and all acceptable limits. The car barely moved despite all this excessive use of the accelerator and clutch, it should have been propelling itself forward in a racing start and burning rubber. The car moved slowly towards the safe haven of the kerb side on the opposite side of the roundabout. The full realisation hit me, the clutch had become worn due to excessive use, and this had the deleterious effect of reducing the transmission of the engine crankshaft movement to the rotational movement of the spitfire's rear drive wheels by not generating enough torque on the rear wheels, thus reducing velocity and forward momentum... Alternatively, putting it another way, the clutch was knackered.

'What's the matter?' enquired Cindy, her voice quivering with apprehension.

'I think the clutch has gone. I'll have to phone the RAC.'

I eventually located a telephone booth and made a phone call to the RAC we had a half an hour wait, before the man from the RAC van eventually arrived at the scene, confirming my amateur diagnosis. The clutch of the Spitfire Mark IV had indeed given up the ghost. The RAC man, informing me the car would necessitate going to a garage for repair and worse, my membership precluded the availability of a tow all the way home to Ebbw Vale. He did however offer to tow the car to Cindy's house in Rogerstone a suburb of Newport. To my relief, I discovered the towing by the RAC not as formidable a task as I had originally believed, finding it no difficulty at all, and the rigid tow-bar making it relatively easy. This lulled me into a false sense of security, a circumstance I would regret a few days later.

After being towed to Cindy's house and leaving the car there, she then drove me home in her ancient Ford Prefect, before returning to Newport. Cindy did not have to go to work the next day which allowed her the luxury of a late lie in. Her mother, upon seeing my car parked outside the house, immediately jumped to the wrong conclusion, namely that I had spent the night with her young, beautiful, innocent, daughter. Eva, Cindy's mother was such a prude and a prig, as explained, not believing in pre-marital sex, or for that matter probably post-marital sex, considering it the work of the devil. She fully expected a showdown with both of us, but experienced total relief when her daughter emerged from her room alone, explaining to her mother the circumstances as to why my car remained parked outside the house.

Meanwhile the next day at West Mercian Oil, I approached the vehicle Foreman Fitter, Peter Parker, asking him if he would be kind enough to tow the Spitfire from Cindy's home to my father's garage. After talking to him in what must have been a sickening and obsequious manner all day, he finally agreed, whether out of pity or because he tired of me continually pestering and badgering him, I do not know. I was just grateful he had finally agreed to do it.

Leaving at six o'clock in the evening, we drove to Newport, arriving there at about six thirty and after travelling at breakneck speed. To my horror, astonishment and utter disbelief, Peter stopped the company van just in front of my beloved sports car and immediately began attaching, what I considered to be, and an extremely and inadequate short piece of nylon rope to the towing hook located on the van. Once he completed that task, Peter then attached the other end to the tow connection at the front of my Spitfire Mark IV.

'What about the towing bar?' I enquired, exhibiting a distinct nervousness as the somewhat rhetorical question quivered out of my larynx. I then heard the reply containing words I did not wish to hear.

'What towing bar?'

A mild to extreme panic now began exhibiting itself throughout my body and the pressure began exerting itself via my bladder. Inspecting the six feet of flimsy, oil smeared, nylon rope, the umbilical connection between the company vehicle and my spitfire, did nothing whatsoever to allay my fears.

Little voices began speaking in my head, trying to re-assure me. *The man from the RAC drove fairly slowly, I'm certain Peter will do the same thing, probably. He will drive quite slowly due to the fact he is using a towing rope and because it is so short.'*

Eventually, he finished connecting the rope to the two vehicles, indicating he was ready to get under way, but firstly issuing his final instructions before commencing.

'Keep the engine running and the gears in neutral, your brakes are servo assisted and won't work if the engine is not running. It will also keep you warm. Keep your headlights on dip and don't brake too violently!'

Peter walked towards the van, adding one final addendum, which really put the fear of God into me.

'One more thing, keep your eyes glued to my brake lights and don't forget to release the handbrake before we move off. Okay, let's get the show on the road.'

Both of us entered our respective vehicles, after switching on the engine, lights and releasing the handbrake as instructed, I waited for the sudden jolt, indicating the journey had begun.

Almost at once, I experienced the sudden expected jolt, accompanied by the groaning and creaking of the nylon rope as it elongated and strained between the two vehicles, groaning as if in excruciating pain. The Spitfire began slowly accelerating, with the tension becoming less as the rope began to slacken. While Peter's vehicle slowed down as he changed gear, the van lost its momentum while the Spitfire maintaining the same speed, and the rope then became taught once again as he accelerated. So far so good, indeed we appeared to be travelling at a sedate, reasonable and sensible speed. The vehicles had not yet left the housing estate with numerous small junctions requiring negotiating before reaching the main valley road. At each junction, Peter barely slowed down for fear of losing the vehicle's momentum, only slowing down to observe briefly any movement of other traffic on the road. Fortunately, it being a cold winter's night, not many vehicles appeared to be travelling the roads that night thus allowing us to reach the main road in a very short space of time.

Now the junction at the main road happened to be another story. Peter braked gently, easing his van towards the white lines, allowing me plenty of warning and time to brake in a gentle and relatively serene manner. My mind began contemplating the journey ahead as he waited for a gap in the traffic, considering, so far it had been quite easy. The little voices in my head spoke once again.

*'This is not too bad at all. A piece of cake in fact, not as bad as you feared.'*

My experience of life should have told me not to be so blasé about things, the above statement being a classic 'Murray Walker' moment, completely contradicting my thoughts. For shortly following the germination of this thought in my mind, the nylon rope once more began to creak and groan with the appearance of pain at the increasing tension and strain as both vehicles began pulling away. We now reached the main valley trunk road between Newport and Ebbw Vale, heading north. Our velocity seemed to be increasing. We were no longer travelling at the sedate speeds required on the estate roads, with my eyes now firmly fixed on the brake lights ahead of me. When I did take my eyes off the brake lights for no more than a millisecond to glance at the odometer, I could not believe the speed we had attained, travelling at fifty-five miles per hour, with barely six feet of rope between the two vehicles.

I was, by now, absolutely terrified, my eyes transfixed on the brake lights ahead of me, now not averting them for even a nanosecond. During that journey, we attained speeds well in excess of the mandatory national speed limits and well in excess of the speeds. I normally travelled those particular valley roads. Houses, parked vehicles and pedestrians all hurtled passed my field of vision with the distinctive whizzing sound in my right ear of two bodies passing at speed.

After what seemed like an eternity and much to my relief, Peter began slowing his vehicle down as we approached my father's house. Despite it being a cold winter's evening, my shirt absorbed all my perspiration, generated entirely due to the abject fear and terror I had experienced and been subjected to, and absolutely nothing to with the ambient temperature. A journey which normally took me an hour was completed in less than forty minutes, albeit without any mishaps. God only knows how!

Ever since that January night, I have had a pathological fear of anyone towing me, unsurprising really. What is surprising is that I have not experienced flashback nightmares of that horrendous evening. It is not surprising I never asked Peter to tow me again.

Those early days of WMO are still memorable and I recollect them with affection, one of those periods in one's life when everything is running smoothly. Dave Jarvis could be unpredictable on occasions. I remember once telling me I should have adjusted a particular batch of refined oil when it was within normal spec and never been previously adjusted, then doing again what he had instructed a few weeks later and being told off. He must have had mental aberration that particular day.

I was now engaged to a beautiful, intelligent, sophisticated woman, Cindy, and life appeared to be going to plan. The personnel at WMO even had a social side, challenging local teams to football and cricket matches. Cindy would frequently drive up the valley to watch if I happened to be playing. Ah! The blossoming of a new love, *l'amour*, is a wonderful thing to behold. One particular cricket match happened to be between WMO and a local Police team. Cindy was on the side lines watching while WMO happened to be fielding. The police team in nineteen overs had scored one hundred and twenty five runs. Someone passing by asked the question to one of the Police team, who were sitting down awaiting their turn to bat.

'Who are you playing this evening?'

One of them pointed to the score on the board, and sarcastically replied, 'The Blind School.'

Wendy told me this story and had quite a chuckle at that now politically incorrect remark.

I believe the final score finally ended up something

like the Police team one hundred and thirty for one wicket... in twenty overs. WMO thirty-five all out after ten overs. I think we used to put the fear of God into all opposing teams, well, in our fantasies anyway.

Those were memorable days, with everyone pulling together and the company thriving. All appeared to be well with the world and my work was enjoyable.

After a couple of years at the Refinery, I was given the task of commissioning a new plant for the recovery of chlorinated solvents, which at that time were used extensively for degreasing components, particularly in the automotive and electronic industries. The solvents are no longer in use in the new millennium and banned due their impact in exacerbating the greenhouse effect, and causing adverse health effects. But at that time in the seventies, these solvents were used in large quantities, their adverse and detrimental effects only being discovered and coming to light in the eighties.

Craig Theake and Phil Meredith both conceived the solvent recovery project. They both possessed the foresight and business acumen to see the potential for a solvent recovery plant, buying used waste chlorinated solvents for a few pence per gallon, re-distilling and then selling the re-distilled solvent for a few pounds per gallon. The new project eventually generated quite a substantial profit margin even after deducting the re-processing costs and overheads, making it a very lucrative venture indeed.

Following the solvent recovery plant's installation, I had the task of operating and running the recovery plant for a couple of months, aided by two volunteer operators. My remit was to evaluate and resolve all the teething problems before eventually handing the plant over to the Production Department, a Chemical Engineer's dream. A completely new process plant to play around with for at least a whole month, with the added bonus of no pressure with production commitments nor requirements with production deadlines having to be met, just getting acquainted with the new equipment. I truly felt as though I had died and gone to heaven. During that time, the wiped film evaporator went through its paces re-distilling waste non-flammable chlorinated solvents, in particular 1.1.1 trichloroethane, a solvent extensively used during the seventies, particularly in the electronics industry, but later phased out because of the adverse effects upon the ozone layer and safety issues and later discovered to have deleterious effects upon unborn children in the womb and thus later banned.

The solvent recovery plant, in particular the wiped (Luwa) film evaporator, went through its paces. Upon discovering a problem, remedies and solutions were found. If this remedial action required spending some money, as long as it was not too much, then so be it. At that time, spending extra money appeared to be no problem for WMO, which happened to be a rare and gratifying experience for me. However, I did discover one major problem which would be expensive to resolve.

After six weeks, the plant became part of the Production Department's inventory, leaving me to do the quality control aspect of the process. A few mishaps occurred during those early days. On one occasion whilst opening a drum of waste solvent which had no ullage and filled to the brim, upon turning the drum bung and releasing the pressure, in an instant, there was a sudden and violent effusion of the solvent. Contaminated with oil occurred, erupting like a huge fountain. I had insufficient time to get out of the way and the solvent and oil went into my eyes through the side of my safety glasses and got into my eyes. This necessitated a wild, blind dash to the toilets to extirpate the offending, vile, obnoxious smelling fluid from my eyes and giving them a thorough eye wash. Following that experience, I wore a full-face visor and not safety glasses every time I sampled the drums, the experience indicating safety glasses offered insufficient protection.

It may appear to the reader that I was the only person experiencing mishaps and catastrophes during my time at WMO, not so. During my vacations, Dave Jarvis would often cover for me, taking over my duties. This particular day, the process operators experienced technical production problems, requiring Dave's assistance with his technical expertise. The distillate appeared to be of inferior quality, which necessitated Dave going over to the solvent recovery plant and inspect the distillate. The distillate from the wiped film evaporator was stored in galvanized tanks, stored on a platform approximately two metres off the ground. To inspect the product inside the tanks required climbing a metal ladder and walking along the platform adjacent to the tanks. Dave ascended performed all those tasks without any difficulty, upon reaching the offending storage tank and product, he opened the manhole lid on top of the tank beginning to inspect and scrutinize the solvent which lay within.

For those acquainted with the dangers and hazards associated with solvents, it is a well-documented fact; never inhale highly concentrated solvent fumes. Dave peered into the product tank. The next instant, much to his confusion and bemusement, he found himself sitting on the bund wall outside the solvent building with Doug, the senior operator, gently slapping his face in an effort to revive him.

It transpired that the cause of this aberration to Dave's mental faculties occurred at almost the instant he peered inside the storage tank, immediately turning pale, his eyes rolled in his head, and finally he gently slid down the side of the tank, lying comatose on the metal platform. Doug and John, the other operator, wisely thought it prudent to get Dave outside the building into the fresh air as quickly as possible, the task sounding easier than the actual implementation.

They manhandled Dave Jarvis across the platform and down the two-metre high, vertical metal ladder, which necessitated the implementation of the fire fighter's lift. Following this manoeuvre Dave had to be man handled once again outside the building. To their credit, both Doug and John performed these operations resolutely, sitting Dave on the bund wall, allowing the fresh, invigorating, relatively pure cold air to perform its duty reviving the comatose Chief Chemist.

Gradually, Dave revived, regaining consciousness. Explaining the incident a few days later, following my return to work, after my break, Dave insisted he had not inhaled any fumes whilst peering into the storage tank, and found it incomprehensible why he had passed out.

Dave was utterly embarrassed and mortified that such an incident should have happened to him, of all people. He always gave the appearance and persona of having omniscient and unlimited knowledge of Chemistry. The incident had proving he was as fallible as the rest of us. Ironically, because of that particular incident, my liking for Dave increased, discovering he was human like the rest of us mere mortals after all.

In all, my employment with WMO lasted almost five years, but as the universe and cosmos is in a constant state of flux, turmoil and unpredictability, so is my life, requiring adaptation and adjustment as I journey through life; such was the case with MOR.

Prior to my appointment, Phil Meredith had made the executive decision, with the full agreement of the other directors, to sell West Mercian Oil to a much larger international company, Peshco, the sale being necessary in order to obtain the much needed and necessary finance for the acquisition of land and the building of the Refinery. Take-overs, acquisitions and mergers come at a price. With the take-over, Phil lost his complete autonomy of the company, relinquishing it to the board of Peshco. He had taken his independence for granted, but it no longer existed. Every extra penny, any projects, any extra expenditure, cash or any improvisation required written justification, appealing to the main board for their necessary approbation and approval.

As the years progressed, Phil Meredith hankered for his autonomy and independence and being his own boss once again. Towards the later part of the decade, he sold all his remaining personal shares in West Mercian Oil Ltd., and for quite a substantial amount. My last encounter with Phil Meredith happened during one of my infrequent visits to the Dudley Refinery, following his resignation from the company. Phil, together with his wife, had called into the refinery in order to tie up a few loose ends and to say goodbye to everyone. They were both just about to drive away into the sunset in his expensive looking, immaculate, gleaming white, superbly impressive, brand new Lotus Europa, fortuitously, the instant I arrived at the site. It was a touch of the déjà vu, reminiscent of our first meeting in the laboratory. He came over to me exchanging a few farewell words. We wished each other well and all the best for the future. Both he and his wife then drove away, as they say, into the sunset.

It is rumoured he made over one and a half million pounds from the sale of his remaining shares in West Mercian Oil, which was not an insubstantial amount in the late seventies, having come a long way from the early days of owning a few old, rusty, obsolete railway tankers together with an old boiler. His was a rags to riches story and well-deserved. Phil was one of nature's gentlemen, and everyone was sad to see him leave.

Craig Theake assumed the mantle of Managing Director and, as with everything, Craig put his heart and soul into it with enthusiasm and gusto, giving it one hundred per cent of his ability and his *'best shot.'* I personally believe he did an admirable and exemplary job.

Unfortunately, the main board of Peshco took a different viewpoint, appointing their own man as Managing Director of West Mercian Oil some six months following Phil Meredith's departure. The board gave Craig the consolation prize of Marketing Director.

This was too much for Craig, who felt affronted and betrayed, after having devoted so much time, effort and energy to the company. His pride and ego had taken a huge battering and because of this, he informed Peshco in no-uncertain terms to stuff their job, then promptly resigned. Yet another person I felt sad to see leaving the company, believing it was more their loss than his.

From that point onwards, the whole ethos and character of the company altered beyond recognition. There was no longer any foresight and imagination at the helm instilled by Phil and Craig. Both men lived, ate, and breathed West Mercian Oil. Both developing and nurturing it through the good and bad times. While they were there, both considered the workforce as part of the company and always looked out for our welfare.

The new Managing Director had no such altruistic ideals. Phil Meredith and Craig possessed a certain charisma and charm, together with superb man-management skills; the new Managing Director had no such endearing qualities and on the very few occasions I met him, he exhibited no personality or charisma whatsoever.

Gradually, the halcyon days dissipated, becoming

ephemeral and transitory, the days of everyone pulling together also gradually disappearing, they too becoming ephemeral. Dissension began to grow between union and management, with both sides becoming more intransigent in their ways.

Cindy and I tied the knot August the nineteenth 1978, after first buying a brand new house, incurring the obligatory mortgage that went with it. Unfortunately, for us, the new regime at West Mercian Oil deemed it necessary to keep my pay increases low. I discovered personnel joining the company and working in the laboratory were actually getting more pay and as versatile or as knowledgeable as myself concerning the processes, not being involved in as many areas as myself. Upon expressing my concerns to the plant management, he replied bluntly, 'Take it or leave it.'

My problems stemmed from the solvent recovery plant. During my period evaluating the plant, it came to my attention that excessive amounts of water was usually brought in with the waste solvent, distilled over with the 1.1.1 trichloroethane during the evaporation process. The solvent is an azeotropic mixture, that is to say they did not separate during the distillation process. The water and 1.1.1. Trichloroethane reacted with the mild steel pipe work, corroding it and generating hydrochloric acid. This then caused a chain reaction causing more corrosion, generating more acid. In my many recommendations concerning the plant operation, I stated in my extensive report that the pipe work required replacing and should be stainless steel not the mild steel presently in place, incurring vast expense. I could not win whatever I did, for if I had ignored the fact. I would have later been criticised for not detecting the problem and being incompetent. Alternatively, if I mentioned it, the persons involved in designing the plant would take offence, and my life would be hell. This is exactly what happened.

The two main people heavily involved in the design of the plant were Shaun Michaels, the plant Manager from Dudley and Gary Yandle, the Plant Manager from Ebbw Vale. Both took offence at the criticism and became instrumental in not giving me the pay increase which others had received. They kept my salary at the same level as the previous year... pay back.

Now, my ego and confidence took a huge knock, as it seemed obvious to me my services and commitment to the company did not receive any form of appreciation.

The interest rate on my mortgage had increased. With my pay increasing at a far slower rate than I had anticipated, I decided perhaps the time had come to move on and to leave WMO. I had no option, having gone to the limit on my borrowing for the mortgage, finding it difficult to survive. The repayments were now astronomical because of the soaring interest rates.

During the latter part of 1979, I began applying for jobs advertised in the local newspapers, fully realizing the experience gained at WMO would now stand me in good stead when applying for the technical jobs in industry, particularly connected with Chemical Engineering. This would be completely different from when I applied for the position at WMO a few years earlier.

I felt no disloyalty in applying for alternative employment. The person who had originally employed me had himself quit the company in acrimonious circumstance. Having asked for fair treatment and receive a salary equivalent to people who had joined the company after me and who had less experience of the processes, I had the distinct impression I seemed inconsequential. Dave Jarvis had not backed me one iota concerning my pay rise, apparently afraid of confronting Shaun Michaels and Gary Yandle.

Within a couple of months of my 'take it or leave' ultimatum, I was taking another step in my career path. Once again circumstances had been imposed upon me over, which I appeared to have no control.

# CHAPTER 10

I had applied for numerous jobs advertised in the local newspaper, one of which happened to be the position of Shift Supervisor with a company called Cox & Sons, an old, well established company manufacturing inks and paints. The position was based at the production facility located near a small village on the outskirts of Cardiff, although the Cox & Sons Head Office was actually based in London. It was about thirty miles from my newly acquired semi-detached home in Abergavenny and quite a commuting distance. Because of this distance, it came as quite a surprise to be invited to attend a preliminary interview.

My first interview was with Jim Gunn, The Production Manager for the Litho Plates Division and held shortly after my CV had been posted. Within a few weeks of attending that preliminary interview, I received an invitation to attend a second interview. This time the interview was with the Divisional General Manager, Jack Houseman and Gary Hudson the Personnel Manager. During my interview with Jim Gunn, all indications were the salary on offer would be quite substantial.

I was fairly relaxed during both interviews, again convincing myself, as with WMO, I stood very little chance of getting this particular position of shift Supervisor, primarily because of my limited managerial and man management skills. On reflection, how I ever obtained employment throughout my life with this negative attitude and lack of confidence is beyond comprehension. However at the time I felt the interview would, help me brush up on my interview technique, a bit of practice in effect. My impression was the interview went quite well, but still convinced in my own mind that lack of supervisory skills would eventually let me down, coupled with the long commuting distance involved.

Following the interview, the days became weeks which then became months, with no news from Cox & Sons. Both Cindy and I became convinced the interview had been unsuccessful and a bit miffed Cox & Sons had not even exhibited the courtesy of sending me a rejection letter. Then at least I would know where I stood.

Then, unexpectedly, one Wednesday evening, I received a telephone call, from a certain Joanne Meredith. Cindy took the phone call, on the one phone we had, located in the hallway. Which necessitated my wife coming back into the living room and informing me the telephone call was actually for me, at the same time giving me a filthy look.

'There's a Joanne Meredith on the phone for you, she wouldn't tell me what it was about, insisting on talking to you personally!' Cindy's evil expression implying there was something secretive between me and the secretive Joanne. It was the look of the dreaded *Green Eyed Monster* and insinuated we were indulging in some nefarious relationship. I was completely bemused, not having the foggiest idea who Joanne Meredith could be. By this time I had virtually forgotten about Cox & Sons and the two interviews. Upon answering the phone, Joanne firstly apologized for phoning so late in that evening and went on to explain she was phoning on behalf Of Gary Hudson, the Personnel manager from Cox & Sons and was his personal secretary. Cox & Sons was offering me the position of Shift Supervisor, Litho Plates Division and asked whether I was still interested in the position. She went through the salary remuneration and additional benefits previously discussed during the second interview. My mouth began drooling as she reeled off the financial facts and figures. Everything on offer beat my current situation with WMO hands down; better pay, overtime, shift allowance, more holidays, better pension allowance, sick pay. The whole nine yards. The only problem being, Gary Hudson wanted an answer within two days, requiring me to hand my notice in as soon as possible. In truth I was ready to accept the position there and there, but felt it only fair to discuss it with Cindy first as it would mean a tremendous upheaval to our life, with shift work being involved and the large commuting distance. After first thanking Joanne for her phone call, I informed her Cox & Sons would get my answer the following morning, but I needed the letter of acceptance before I handed in my month's notice. With that we wished each other a good night and terminated our conversation.

Returning to the living room, I discovered Cindy pretending to be watching the television, which now appeared to be at a much lower volume from when I left the room to take the phone call.

'Who was that?' enquired Cindy, without even averting her eyes from the television screen, desperately trying to exhibit an air of complete indifference and distinct lack of curiosity. However, I knew that outward impression was the complete antithesis of what she was really feeling. Inside she was a seething cauldron of unbridled feminine curiosity, with a need to know who I had been talking to and what the conversation had been about.

Partly because it was impossible to contain my excitement, and partly because it seemed prudent not to antagonize my hormonal wife, I immediately began imparting the required information without any form of procrastination and most certainly no prevarication began telling her the facts straight away.

'That was Joanne Meredith, the Personnel Manager's secretary from Cox & Sons. They're offering me the Shift Supervisor's position which they interviewed me for weeks ago. I thought I had not got the job to be quite honest.' At this juncture I paused, awaiting some sort of response from her, and I was not to be disappointed.

'Are you going to accept?' she asked, by now having abandoned any pretence of being interested in the programme being transmitted on the television and had turned it off to emphasise this fact.

'Yes,' I replied emphatically. 'They've just made me an offer which I can't possibly refuse, more money, better holidays, overtime, the whole works, the only drawback being it does mean I will have to work shifts. But it is too good an opportunity to miss and the way they consider me at WMO and the disenchantment I feel, it's definitely time for a change!'

To my complete and utter astonishment, she was in complete agreement. Knowing full well how hurt and humiliated I felt about the *'Take it or leave,'* remark from the WMO Plant Manager, her reply was succinct and straight to the point, 'If that's what you want, I won't stand in your way. I think it may be a good move.' The look on her face indicates she was completely and utterly sincere in the statement she had just made, even sealing it with an affectionate peck on my left cheek to emphasise the point. I think were both excited about the new path our lives were about to lead and that excitement culminated into an evening of passionate lovemaking.

The next day, secretly phoning from work, I informed Joanne Meredith of my decision to accept the position offered, also informing her of my contractual obligation to give one month's notice with my current employer. She informed me Gary Hudson was cognizant of the fact concerning the one month's notice and it would not pose a problem. The official letter of acceptance would be sent that morning, laying out the conditions with a commencement date for the first of October, 1979.

Within an hour of the secret telephone call, my letter of resignation was on Dave's desk, but only after first experiencing the last minute doubts and misgivings about leaving a relatively secure job, with its familiarity and regular routine. Ahead lay uncertainty and the unknown, my mind contemplating a bleak, pessimistic and dismal future, with various scenarios presenting themselves.

*'What if it doesn't work out? Am I doing the right thing?'* The usual last minute doubts we all experience when leaving our familiar and safe surroundings, ones I had already experienced.

At last with the dirty deed done was there was no request from WMO management for me to reconsider my decision without a possible increase in salary which did not surprise me in the slightest. It would have been nice to have been asked to stay, but my resignation was accepted without any comment whatsoever. This did, however, help mitigate any feelings of guilt about leaving on my part.

The final weeks of my employment passed fairly quickly, mainly involved in showing Gerald Charters all the duties I had to perform with the solvent recovery plant, for which I had been given full QC control.

When my final day at WMO finally arrived, I was quite touched to receive leaving gifts, one of which was a silver tankard, duly inscribed. The gifts were accompanied with the obligatory farewell speeches. One of the most surprising aspects was how affected the two laboratory assistants appeared to be, shedding copious amounts of tears during my short,

159

embarrassing speech. Well at least, I thought, some people would miss me. As I left the refinery gates, there was the emotion of slight regret, recalling my first time on the site and that unforgettable interview with Craig Theake. My thoughts were, '*This would be my last time ever be at the plant*?' Years later, events would prove me completely incorrect in that erroneous assumption.

So this was to be yet another move on my, so far, short, unspectacular career but I was determined this time this would be my final move, come hell or high water. It appeared to be a caring company with a paternalistic attitude towards its workforce. Being a family company having been established well over one hundred years seemed to instil this ideology. My immediate boss, Jim Gunn appeared to be firm but fair in his man management style.

That first day was a typical first day for anyone, filled with trepidation, apprehension and dread as I entered the main gates of this large industrial conurbation, the smell of processed resin and solvents permeated the atmosphere as they hung in the air. Doubts began to re-assert themselves. However following an extensive chat with Jim Gunn in his office for well over an hour, the fear and trepidation gradually abated and I began to feel more at ease and welcomed into the fold. Jim was in his mid-thirties, tall and lanky at about six feet two with a rapidly receding hairline, the diminishing remains of fair hair evident on either side of his head. He also smiled quite a lot giving him a warm, friendly appearance. He did, however, go over the top somewhat, '*bullshitting quite a bit*' to use the Americanism the British term would be the antiquated expression '*flannelling*', extolling the virtues and attributes of Cox & Sons. Jim was unashamedly, and unapologetically, a company man, stating there were unlimited opportunities for those willing to work and pull their weight. Jim also took great pains to explain the reason for the vacancy as Shift Supervisor. Dave Parry, the person being replaced, had been promoted to Assistant Production Manager at Litho Chemicals, another section of Litho Plates. I was to be Dave's replacement. To use the term 'bullshitting.' concerning Jim Gunn is actually grossly unfair. For Jim was obviously enthusiastic and exuberant about the whole set-up and the company, having been with them for a number of years and having worked his way up. He obviously thought a lot of the company with this feeling being reciprocated by the company, who obviously though a lot of Jim. This enthusiasm and exuberance about the company set-up was actually contagious. Jim fully believed in everything he said about the company and could be described as company zealot. Not since the early days of WMO had I been subjected to such ebullience and total commitment verging on fanaticism towards the company ideals. The more Jim spoke, the more my misgivings evaporated about accepting the position. He went into detail about the company, giving the company history, explaining how it had started off in the last quarter of the nineteenth century manufacturing inks for the printing industry based in the east end of London. Over the years the company had expanded and had diversified into making resins and paints, establishing manufacturing plants throughout Britain and then throughout the old British Empire. Promotion could mean being based at any of these plants located on the pink locations of the world atlas.

Jim then went into details about the Litho plates, explaining it was a relatively new division within the Cox & Sons Empire having only been established about ten years. The litho plates were used in the off-set Litho printing industry, the company philosophy being, the company manufactured the inks to print, why not go another step and manufacture the Litho plates, used on the giant rollers as well? This was a completely new industry, involving electroplating copper and chrome and photosensitive coatings. Still, it would be another string to my bow.

My only doubts now concerned my ability to perform the job required of me and living up to their expectations as Jim went into details about the processes involved. This was completely different to the oil industry. He could probably see the doubts being generated in my mind by the furrows presenting themselves on my brow. He smiled in a sort of patriarchal, re-assuring way, which assured me I would not be thrown into the lion's den immediately and would have four weeks training, giving me time to become acquainted with all aspects of litho plates, spending time in each of the departments. Following this initial four weeks training period, I would then spend time on my shift, which had the designation 'C' Shift. This meant spending a fair amount of time with the incumbent supervisor, Dave Parry. Becoming acquainted with the personnel, the quality controls required, the operation of the shift, setting up the line programming. The list just seemed to be endless, as Jim explained them in detail. My head began to swim with all this detail, and I was beginning to experience information overload. This training would be another four weeks, after which time, it was hoped I would be able to fly solo and Dave Parry could begin his duties as Assistant Production Manager Litho Chemicals.

That first day I was broken in gently, being taken around the facility with Charles Sharpe, the Assistant Production Manager Litho Plates. The day was a blur as Charles introduced me to personnel throughout the facility. Introductions were made and names quickly forgotten, as the next person was introduced. My brain was a jigsaw puzzle of information, facts, figures, names titles, jobs which, hopefully, would gradually piece together over the weeks as everything slotted into place with the overall picture becoming clearer.

Over the coming weeks my training began in earnest, with a tremendous amount of facts and figures being thrown at me whilst I made copious notes. Also other information came to light, particularly about the position I was being employed for.

Poor, unfortunate Dave. He had originally been promised his promotion well over a year ago. It transpired I was not the first person employed to replace him. A certain Haydn Powell had been in my job six months previously. Another person had been given the job a few weeks earlier but had not showed up on his agreed first week. Hence the phone calls from Joanne Meredith.

Dave told me about Haydn who had returned to the United Kingdom, having spent a number of years in Iran being employed by one of the multi-national oil companies. Unfortunately his well-paid, utopian, ephemeral and somewhat transitory existence came to an abrupt termination, following the rise to power of the religious fanatic, the infamous Ayatollah Khomeini. Being awoken from this dreamlike existence, like most Europeans, Haydn considered it a wise and prudent move to return to his native control in the wake of the religious extremism pervading Iran, believing the Ayatollah had him singled out for incarceration and imprisonment. Haydn believed he had to escape the clutches of the Ayatollah and his henchmen. His first position of employment upon returning to good ole' blighty happened to be with Cox & Sons Ltd., doing the very job I was now training for.

During my first few weeks of training, my tutor, educator and pedagogue was Ian James, the Plant Chemist. Ian appeared to be an exact clone physically of Alan Whicker. He possessed the same dark, luxuriant, highly visible, dark moustache, and even the same spectacles. The only discernible difference being their ages was Ian being a good two score years younger, with far fewer creases and wrinkles to his youthful facial features, coupled with the fact the Plant Chemist had the distinctive South Wales accent instead of the highly refined journalistic accent possessed by the celebrity. Otherwise, Ian was an exact copy of the famous television journalist. Every time I saw Ian James, I kept thinking Alan Whicker. Another idiosyncrasy Ian had in common with his famous clone was his ability to relate and impart a story, for Ian was yet another wonderful raconteur and storyteller, which I must admit does seem to be a trait of the Welsh. He had a wonderful, colourful, expressive manner of bestowal and delivery. He took great delight imparting information concerning my predecessor, for whom I believe he held in secret esteem, veneration and admiration. Probably living some form of vicarious existence by relating Haydn's story.

Through Ian, a picture of the ex-patriot began to emerge and present itself,

Haydn terminated his job as Litho Plate Shift Supervisor after only two months, discovering, according to Ian, he was expected to lead by example, with a certain amount of hands-on supervision, an aspect necessary in the job for efficacious and smooth running of the shift. He cynically suggested Haydn had been presented with such an easy life and existence whilst working in Iran, he experienced difficulty in acclimatising to working conditions in Britain, where managers were now being expected to roll up their sleeves and get stuck in, which appeared to be a complete anathema to Haydn.

Ian extolled another hypothesis as to why Haydn had terminated his position so early. Somehow, so management believed, Haydn had become bitter and twisted through having received insufficient training and guidance during his short time at Litho plates, causing him to become a malcontent and disgruntled with his lot, hence the reason for my extensive period of training. However, Ian did not subscribe to this last train of thought, being fully convinced Haydn was totally mentally ill-equipped for hard work, having led a thoroughly spoiled and pampered existence during his sojourn in Iran. Basically he was just a lazy sod who found the work load just too much to deal with. Jim Gunn did not subscribe to this latter theory and it was due to his belief in Haydn being unhappy at the amount of training he received, the four week training period came into existence, plus extra tuition whilst on the shift. I was not complaining, being a great believer in getting as much training as possible. Jim's aim was to prevent me from becoming a malcontent like Haydn because of insufficient training.

During my long discussions with Ian James, other events gradually came to light, which answered a lot of questions and filled in a lot of parts to the puzzle. It transpired another person had actually been offered the position in preference to me between the time Haydn terminating his employment and the evening phone call from Joanne Meredith. Unfortunately for poor Dave Parry, his designated and appointed successor failed to appear on the first day or the second day, hence the phone call from Joanne Meredith. It appeared I was the substitute. Needless to say, my ego received a body blow upon being privy to this piece of information, thoroughly convinced I had been the first choice. Still,

165

it did explain why Cox & Sons took an interminable amount of time in approaching me; they had simply been hedging their bets, the cunning devils. Well at least thanks to Haydn, I now had the luxury of being employed for a full month without any hassle or responsibility whatsoever of a fully-fledged Shift Supervisor. It was my intention of grasping the opportunity and enjoying it, yet at the same time still learn the intricacies of the job and all it entailed, or at least as much as I possibly could. As I have since discovered throughout my career, it was an extravagance and indulgence never to be repeated. This training period initially meant having to spend a considerable amount of time in the company of Ian, who, in addition to being the Plant Chemist, had, in his time, also been a Shift Supervisor, so he knew all about the plant, how it worked and the job of Supervisor itself.

Like Jim Gunn, he was enthusiastic and exuberant about Cox & Sons and the Litho Plates Division. As I was to discover, was the psychological atmosphere of the place. It was the early days of WMO again, with its 'esprit de corps' when I first joined it. Most everyone enjoyed working for the Litho Plates Division. There were a few who didn't, but then again, they were the type who would not enjoy working anywhere. Ian was totally unselfish and avid when it came to imparting his technical knowledge concerning the facility and the process, unlike a number lot of people encountered in previous jobs and since, also acquiring a great deal of knowledge about electroplating.

Ian was good company and an excellent raconteur. In between explaining the process, he took immense delight and pleasure in relating stories, stories which had become folklore in the annals of Cox & Sons' illustrious history. After hearing some of the stories divulged by Ian, with near disasters and catastrophes, I began wondering, 'Had I made the right decision?'

My emotions had a strange feeling of ambivalence. On the one hand, with Ian's tales of near disasters and misfortunes which had beset previous Shift Supervisors my mind had a feeling of impending doom and trepidation. On the other hand, the thought of being in complete charge of a shift with autonomy frightened, yet at the same time strangely exhilarated and exciting me, causing the adrenaline to surge through my veins.

# CHAPTER 11

One of the legends, folklore, myths, call it what you like, which Ian often related with relish concerned one of my predecessors, a certain Andrew Morgan. The story, which Ian frequently told with his unabated enthusiasm, shows how things can go horribly wrong in a short space of time mainly revolving around Andrew, the shift supervisor in charge of 'A' Shift. The incident in question occurred quite a few years before my time with Cox & Sons, taking place late one winter's evening, at approximately ten thirty.

For the particular evening in question, we must first flashback about twenty minutes prior to the actual incident, when an electrical blackout took place, affecting the whole valley. The Cox & Sons facility, being extremely large, covered at least three hundred acres, with the Litho plates Division occupying a very small area of the huge site and located at the back right-hand corner of the plant, well away from the front of the facility and about as far back as you could possibly get from the main entrance, the aforementioned being the only authorised access and egress to the site.

At approximately ten thirty a huge voluminous cloud of a potentially toxic gas, comprising mostly of a material called maleic anhydride, an additive used extensively in the manufacture of paints, formed. The toxic maleic anhydride cloud generated from one of the main resin process vessels. The main resin plant happened to be located exactly in the centre of the huge, industrial site, which meant the toxic cloud also formed slap bang in the centre of the industrial conurbation, the cloud having been formed as a direct result of the electrical power failure some twenty minutes earlier as previously mentioned. It happened to be a one in a million chances and just pure misfortune or bad karma. The maleic anhydride powder had been added just prior to the power failure. The addition of the maleic anhydride powder was a standard operational procedure and normal practice and part of the manufacturing process for this particular resin. The power failure happened almost at the instant the addition of the maleic anhydride had been made into the process vessel. All the electrical power went off, with the exception of the emergency lighting. There being no other electrical power source to fall back on, the giant stirrers, and extracts pumps together with other ancillary process equipment shut off almost immediately. As a consequence, the whole facility shutdown with the plant become as silent as the grave, all machinery ceasing to function, with their only source of energy having been denied them. An eerie, unusual silence descended on the plant which generally hummed and buzzed with the cacophony of various machinery noises associated with a large industrial site.

The whole scenario for the incident had now been set in motion, with the giant paddles no longer performing their duty as required and not producing the angular momentum or torque. The heat and mass transfer of the maleic anhydride in the resin was not being gently mixed in a controlled manner as it should have been, that is to say, slowly and gently homogenizing the maleic anhydride into the resin. Inexorably the particulate of the powder settled gently into the resin, eventually lying at the bottom of the process reaction vessel. There it remained like some malicious creature and it waited, slowly festering generating an exothermic reaction within the resin, the heat and mass of the anhydride not gently dissipated by the giant stirrers which would have occurred in the normal process when the stirrers functioned normally.

At approximately ten thirty, the electrical power to the whole area was restored just as suddenly and surprisingly as it had been terminated. With their source of energy restored, the giant paddles in the process vessels suddenly sprang violently into action, awakening like some giant prehistoric creature. They began revolving in their angular, circular motion. This sudden expending of energy by the giant motors and the attached paddles caused a giant vortex within the resinous liquid. The exothermic reaction taking place at the bottom of the vessel had generated extremely high temperatures, causing the reacting chemicals to become gaseous. The sudden agitation and vortex assisted in helping this angry bubble of toxic gas to rise through the resin, before eventually reaching the surface of the viscous liquid. The immense bubble of gas then emitted and expelled at a high volumetric rate into the atmosphere via the extraction fans perched on the top of the process vessels. They too had also been revived into action by the immediate surge of electrical power.

Following its tortuous journey through the extraction system, the toxic maleic anhydride vapour vented into the cool, clear, still air of a moonlit winter's night. The first indication there was anything amiss came when the sensors at the top of the building picked up the rapid decrease in the oxygen level, usually at nineteen per cent but now well below that figure because of the very high concentration of the toxic maleic gas.

Almost immediately, claxons, sirens and alarms began their haunting, wailing sounds. The plant, because of its location the basin of a river valley and the stillness of that winter's night, seemed to enhance the ghostly, reverberating, and wailing sounds of the alarms. The sides of the valley also increased the volume, escalating the acoustics as the sound waves reflected from its sides, back and forth. With this cacophony of noise, wailing banshees and orchestra of alarms, the residents of the nearby village must have thought World War III had just erupted.

Andrew thought it prudent to contact the Site Shift Manager for the whole facility and find out the reason for this shattering of the winter's evening silence and this noise pollution taking place. The site Shift Manager, someone in the resin division, informed Andrew of the reason for all this noise which had now spoiled his evening, namely the giant maleic anhydride cloud belching into the night air, and now expanding into a giant mushroom cloud above the manufacturing facility. The manager also imparted more bad news; a very slight breeze helped exacerbate the situation by inexorably pushing the giant cloud in the general direction of the Litho Plates building. The Litho Plates building, by now, to all intents, cut off from the rest of the site making evacuation through the front entrance impossibility. The twenty five men from the Litho Plates section were unable to make their escape through the plant, as it would mean them having to pass directly below and possibly through the toxic cloud. They would just have to sit tight and wait until a rescue plan could be put into place.

Andrew called the men together for a communication meeting during which he informed them of their predicament and how they were cut off from their only means of escape, the front entrance to the facility. He also told them they would just have to sit tight and wait. Following a wait of twenty minutes, which seemed more like twenty hours, there appeared to be no sign of any assistance. Through the still night air, in the distance, they could hear the distinctive wailing of the sirens of ambulances, fire engines and police vehicles. Also, because of the clear moonlit

171

night, they could see the outline of the cloud as it continued heading inexorably in their direction. Andrew had not been idle during this time of extreme consternation, but rather was ceaselessly trying to locate self-contained breathing apparatus in order to expedite an escape, searching everywhere. Eventually, he found what he had been looking in the Litho plates storeroom, albeit one self-contained BA unit. The unit fortuitously had a small amount of oxygen in it, only sufficient for one person to escape. He called another communication meeting with the workforce, informing them as he was the only person with the proper BA training, he would have to go and get help, and assist the emergency services and lead them to his besieged workforce. It was truly a magnanimous, altruistic and generous sacrifice on his part; well that's what he tried to convince them, although to a man they all believed the exact opposite was probably nearer the truth.

Following the departure of their illustrious leader, another ten minutes elapsed with still no signs of a rescue. Still the cloud drew inexorably closer and closer to the besieged workforce who by now had become more than slightly worried, possibly bordering on panic stricken concerning the situation.

The men had a discussion amongst themselves deciding to evacuate through the back perimeter fence in the opposite direction to the slowly approaching cloud of doom and disaster. Unfortunately, Andrew had taken the only available large torch with him causing the workforce to experience great difficulty in negotiating their way to the perimeter fence, mainly due to a distinct lack of illumination. Upon eventually reaching the fence, they discovered, to their dismay and chagrin, the fence had a height of well over eight feet, with barbed wire at the top and no means of exit. This meant someone retracing their steps back to the Litho plates building and locate some wire cutters or snips in order to expedite their escape.

Finally, after locating some wire cutters, the beleaguered workforce cut a rather large hole in the fence allowing an exit to be made from the impending cloud of toxic gas. Unfortunately for our intrepid escapees, there happened to be a fairly deep trench on the other side of the fence containing a couple of inches of foul smelling, putrid, rancid, stagnant, marsh water, which, because of the distinct lack of illumination, the workforce did not perceive. One by one, lemming-like, they fell into this rancid marsh water. Apparently the only sounds which could be heard were the cries, followed by a slight splash as one by one the escapees slithered into the rotting trench. They all climbed back onto the narrow earth ledge alongside the fence and between it and the muddy trench making their exodus alongside the fence, clinging desperately to the wire fence. Fate had once more conspired against the workforce, for unfortunately, there had been excessively high rainfall that previous week, saturating the thin section of earth, virtually transforming it into a heavy sludge. The thin section of earth was unable to sustain the combined weight of the twenty five or so men, some of whom were in excess of sixteen stone, ultimately, succumbed to the excessive weight, eventually collapsing, causing the mass of men to cascade and hurtle yet again into the stagnant, distinctly cold quagmire beneath them. Deciding it prudent to stay in the stagnant trench and not chance walking on the unpredictable ledge, the workforce followed the shallow trench as best they could on the dark, murky and what they now began to consider a thoroughly miserable and horrendous night.

While this fiasco transpired at the back of the Litho Plates, another one occurred on the opposite side by the

173

main entrance. The Cox & Sons facility had always been a high profile site with the media bearing down on it, a fact the site management wished did not exist. This state of affairs existed because of the plethora of chemicals stored and manufactured on site. This high profile, mainly instigated by a local, stereotypical, ambitious, sleazy councillor, was forever in contact with the media via the local press, radio or television. Unfortunately for the company, his comments were usually derogatory, with a fair degree of negative bias, hence the concomitant result that Cox & Sons was always being portrayed in a bad light to the local public. The councillor's somewhat limited knowledge of chemicals and chemistry added to the confusion generating a complete misrepresentation of the facts. Of course, all this was lapped up by the media and press as being *'good copy.'*

Thus, with the alarm raised and the emergency services informed, it is not difficult to imagine the *'knee jerk'* reaction generated by everyone. Within half an hour, the site played host to most of the emergency services from the local area and beyond after having been virtually invaded by them. There must have been at least ten fire engines, thirty ambulances, and indeterminable amount of police with other emergency vehicles in attendance. There were people from every emergency service imaginable and, of course, the press, as if by magic, appeared in force. All in all, it was quite an eventful night, with people being rudely awakened and disturbed from their slumbers, or whatever nocturnal activities they happened to be indulging in at the time, then quickly evacuated to what was considered to be a safe distance from the incident.

The emergency services did go slightly over the top for by the time they converged on the normally sleepy hamlet, most of the maleic anhydride cloud had dispersed and had been no danger to the nearby village.

Andrew did nothing to alleviate the emergency services fears and concerns, appearing at the main gate, modelling his chemical suit, together with the self-contained breathing apparatus. He further exacerbated their concerns, upon informing them there twenty five men trapped at the back of the facility. At this news, the firemen donned their breathing apparatus and took spare equipment for the poor unfortunate souls, ostensibly still trapped at the back of the facility. What they did not know at that instant in time, those poor unfortunate individuals were they entering the doorway to a very different building, a secluded public house on the side of Rudry Mountain, which, because of its very seclusion, managed to stay open long after the legal and statutory licensing hours of the time. The hour now approached eleven forty five p.m. with the pub in full swing with after hour's revellers, mostly local farmers and the local residents with the traditional rural lock in. The cold, wet, bedraggled, tired, and somewhat '*ripe*' escapees joined the regular after hours drinkers and law breakers with unabated enthusiasm following their rather traumatic ordeal. The escapees imbibed in various forms of alcohol, purely for medicinal purposes, the taste being all the sweeter, being as it was being consumed in company time. After consuming quite a few drinks, the 'couldn't give a damn' mentality gradually began to take effect as the alcohol coursed through their veins, distinctly impairing their abilities.

Meanwhile back at the plant, the Chief Fire officer immediately assumed the worst scenario when his men discovered the Litho Plates building completely deserted like the Mary Celeste. He immediately began co-ordinating the other emergency services in attempt to search the entire Cox & Sons facility to find the missing men, his pessimism automatically assuming the

175

worse possible outcome fully expecting to discover twenty five corpses, possibly huddled together in some dark, dank cellar in their efforts to escape the toxic fumes. Despite the fact that by this time the toxic chemical cloud had abated and completely dispersed. A helicopter scoured and hovered over the mountains using searchlights to search the mountain for the missing workforce.

After some time, the mutilated back fence and hole through which the workforce had made their desperate exit was discovered. The trail was followed, this time without the same mishaps experienced by the original pathfinders. By the early hours of the morning, the 'poor unfortunates' were located in the public house on the side of Rudry Mountain, most were slightly the worse due to the various intoxicating beverages they had consumed.

Following all of these events, during which it must be stated no-one was injured apart, that is, for a black, arthritic, cat knocked down by a speeding fire engine, because of his infirmity, was unable to get out of the way of the speeding fire engine fast enough. Although some of the Litho plate's workforce did incur some minor cuts and bruises during their involuntary descent into the stagnant trench.

The local councillor took great delight during the next week in going around telling everyone, 'I told you so!' spending more time on television than he had done during the previous five years. According to Andy Warhol's philosophy he experienced his fifteen minutes of television fame, a number of times over, which boosted his already over inflated ego, the trait of most local councillors. The villagers also had another topic of conversation to discuss besides the weather during their visits to the local shops.

Despite, or perhaps because of Ian's recounting of

this story, I felt my decision to accept the position of Shift supervisor had been the right and correct one to make. My training period was gradually drawing to a close and I began to look forward to my initial baptism of fire, albeit with mixed feelings, to my actual time on the shift. I would actually be responsible for running the shift, which was a daunting thought.

The final weeks of training involved shadowing Dave Parry. He was an amiable character, although a bit quieter than Alan, which wasn't too difficult. Dave had a good knowledge as far as Litho Plates was concerned, with what could be termed a good pedigree at the site. He was a local lad, actually living locally, having been born and bred there. Dave had played scrum half for one of the local teams and had been considered to be quite an athlete and talented player in his younger days. That is, until injury forced him to retire from the game. He had joined Cox & Sons when he was about eighteen after gaining his ' A' Levels in chemistry having joined the Litho Plates division during its early inception. He was one of the most experienced people there and knew the process inside out also extremely popular and a tough act to follow.

He enjoyed winding up the local councillor who caused the facility so much grief. One night while Dave was having a quiet pint in the rugby club, the chlorine alarm went off in the Litho Plates effluent plant. Dave knew the alarm was so sensitive and the slightest gust of wind could trigger it, there were also high winds at the time. The councillor, who happened to be in the club at the same time heard the alarm and asked Dave what it was. Dave casually told him it was the chlorine alarm. Now this occurred shortly after an incident in America where a train carrying chlorine in tanks had derailed causing the nearby town to be evacuated. Dave knew the councillor would use the opportunity for self-publicity. As Dave thought off the councillor went to stir things up. He had egg on his face when the facts came to light about the alarm being set off by the high winds at the time.

Unfortunately for Dave, there existed a personality clash between himself and Jack Houseman the General Manager, which had curtailed Dave's promotion somewhat, allowing people such as Jim Gunn, who had joined the company after Dave, to leap frog over him in the hierarchy. I could never fathom out why this personality conflict between Dave and Jack existed. Both appeared to me to be decent blokes with easy going temperaments. I had a good working relationship with both Jack and Dave and liked each of them, yet there existed this antipathy between them. I tried to stay neutral in this conflict, not taking either side and that's the way it remained on my part. This promotion for Dave was long overdue, and a lot of the workforce was concerned, with circumstances appearing to conspire against him such as with Haydn to restrict his career enhancement. The shift held Dave in tremendous respect and he was going to be an extremely difficult act to follow, which also added somewhat to my consternation and trepidation at taking over 'C' shift.

Dave, for his part, wanted nothing to go wrong this time and was willing to impart everything and anything he knew about Litho Plates, teaching me all about the process, personnel, any little trick, nuance or hint which would help eliminate any chances of him having to revert once again to the position of Shift Supervisor, and determined the incident with Haydn would not be allowed to occur again.

Because of Dave's openness in teaching me the job, we became good friends and working colleagues. Towards the end of our month together, Dave allowed me to virtually run the shift, taking a back seat, only getting involved if he thought I needed help, or guidance. He didn't mind it was an easy time for him as well, I would run the shift, while he relaxed in the office drinking copious amounts of coffee and reading the newspaper. It felt comfortable, knowing if any major problems arose, Dave could be called upon to advise and possibly assist.

Finally, crunch time arrived and it was time for me to fly solo. The first week happened to be afternoon shifts, which in itself was quite a good thing, as there were the other managers around for most of the shift such as Ian James, Charles Sharpe and even Jim Gunn to consult if should things go horribly wrong and *'tits up.'* They were around until six or seven in the evening. It was the night or *'graveyard shift,'* which caused me the most concern, working between eleven p.m. and seven a.m. in the Morning. Those were the shifts when I was completely in charge, with no one to refer to, although that is not entirely true as I did have Gordon, the Lead Hand to back me up and refer to if things were not going as they should.

I suspected Gordon to be in his early sixties, although one of those characters who probably always appeared old, even in his younger days. Hence his true age was very difficult to ascertain, and I never asked at that time. He had a generally surly temperament and could be quite irascible on occasions. He was forever rolled his own cigarettes or *'rolly's,'* which he smoked down to the last millimetre, resulting in a nasty smoker's cough and heavily nicotine stained, brown fingers. Notwithstanding his temperament and despite his disposition, it must be stated, Gordon helped me a great deal and was extremely helpful in times of crisis. He was an invaluable asset in the running the shift. I could not have done it without him.

The electroplating process itself comprised mostly

two lines running parallel to each other, both as automated as the technology of the day would allow for the late seventies, although by today's standards, they would be considered pretty archaic. The first or number one line electroplated copper onto oblong steel sheets about four feet high by three feet wide and a couple of millimetres thick. The second or number two lines then electroplated matt chrome onto the previously electroplated copper.

The sheets were attached to metal frames or jigs, clamped at the top, with suckers at the bottom to keep them steady. The jigs moved along the line, being immersed for specific times in cleaning agents, degreasers, water baths, sprays, and electrolytes then dipped and sprayed once again.

After off-loading, following the copper electroplating process, the plates were buffed and washed prior to being put on the jigs which went down the chrome line and then electroplated. With matt chrome, which was a similar set-up to the copper plating, with the jigs moving in the opposite direction to that of number one line. The only manual part of the operation involved the loading and off-loading the plates with the jigs and the buffing operation.

The operation may sound simple and basic. However, in addition to running the line and maintaining discipline, my other duties included quality control checks with the process, ensuring the metal thickness was within certain parameters. These could be maintained by adjusting immersion times of the plates the solutions. It was also necessary to keep the solutions within certain concentrations and calculating additions when required. All these checks helped maintain the integrity of the product. After the electroplating process, there was a further application by means of a curtain coater, of light sensitive coating, which was put on top of the chrome. This was so images could be etched prior to them putting onto the printing presses. Selwyn, the coating operator, was in sole charge of that. I left him to it. My main concern was the electroplating lines.

During the early weeks of working nights, the electroplating lines inexplicably kept stopping resulting in lost production. Each stoppage requiring at least a minimum of twenty minutes

Re-setting the electroplating lines coupled with scrap product, caused by too much immersion times of the plates in the solutions. Because of my inexperience, I put these stoppages down to electrical or mechanical malfunctions which did not show up on the computer board. It never occurred to me that the stoppages were deliberate and premeditated, instigated by one or two of the workforce sabotage.

It was Ian who put me in the picture concerning the stoppages during the following week when I was on the afternoon shift. He was uncompromising and utterly forthright in his allegations.

'The bastards are testing you!!' he angrily informed me.

Apparently this seemed to happen with the new Supervisors, and was considered to be a form of initiation by the indigenous workforce, in particular the more disruptive, lazy elements who enjoyed this little sport and entertainment at the new supervisor's expense.

'Well, how are they doing it?' I enquired, slightly bemused and innocently

'By pushing the emergency buttons and then pulling it back out quickly, the line will stop the instant the button is pressed in!.' Ian replied with a thorough, complete knowledge of the process. He then gave me a large piece of white chalk which he magically exhumed from his laboratory coat pocket. 'But I have the answer!' he stated with a knowing smile on his Alan Whicker-like face. Ian hated disruptive elements or shirkers in the workforce. As I previously mentioned, he was a company man through and through and hated anything which was detrimental to the working of the facility.

'How does that work?' I asked innocently.

'You go around at the start of the shift and mark the emergency buttons with white chalk marks, when the press the button, the chalk comes off and if you're lucky, you may even see some of the chalk on the perpetrator .'

Jim Gunn was also concerned about these incidents, having read about them in my shift logs. There had been a fair amount of downtime together with the concomitant result of increased scrap rates and because of these effects it was incumbent upon me to mention these stoppages.

After a few of these incidents, and while I was on the afternoon shift, Jim told me in no uncertain terms, I had to resolve the situation with the workforce, insisting I confront them after the break that evening. He even allowed me an hour of downtime for my 'discussion,' with the shift.

That evening, was one of the most nerve-wracking moments of my career. I was alone, confronting twenty two men, by now, a hostile workforce. They tried to give the impression of indignation and outrage at being accused of sabotage and interfering with the process. I tried to be as diplomatic about it as I could, want to discuss the problem and endeavour in coming to an amicable agreement and understanding. We all knew there were only one or two perpetrators of this sabotage with most of the crew being innocent bystanders. I also stated they were putting their colleagues at risk, from a

Health and Safety aspect, also with the viability of the facility they were putting people at risk by indulging in this type of action.

Overall, the meeting went reasonably well, with some sort of mutual understanding and dare I say it, respect between ourselves. Not bad for someone, who up until that time had received no man management training. Whether it was the discussion or the chalk marks or perhaps a combination of both, the incidents of line stoppages dropped marked. There were still some stoppages, but they were due to legitimate reasons such as plates getting buckled as the jigs dropped but they could be explained.

Discipline for the shift was ultimately my responsible. One of the team members, Alex Reynolds, had a bad time keeping record on the early shifts, and was forever late. Jim Gunn told me in no uncertain terms, the next time Alex was late, it was necessary for me to call him into the office and warn him about his proclivity for spending extra time in his warm bed when he should be in work. So the next time he was late, I called him into the office to have a word with him. Now here I was, a fresh youngster about twenty eight years of age, giving a man in his sixties, someone old enough to be my grandfather, a bollocking about his timekeeping. Embarrassment does not even come close to describing how I felt.

Alex was very quiet and apologetic and contrite. At the end of my little chat with him and after informing him of the consequences should he persist, he looked at me disarmingly and said, 'I'm sorry Mr. Chard. I know I'm a 'bad un', I'll try not to be late again.'

He was so docile, meek and apologetic it was hard chastising him. I think I would have preferred him to be belligerent. After he left, I could not help but have a small chuckle to myself at his, 'bad un' remark. In all fairness to Alex, he was as good as his word and his timekeeping did improve with no further need of more one-to-one discussions in the office.

Within a short space of time, the Christmas period had arrived. Those early weeks at Cox & Sons had come a gone so fast, and time appeared to have speeded up. We had two weeks shutdown, and I desperately needed the rest and recuperation to recover from the stresses and strains of the new job. During that two week period, the weather turned decidedly inclement with a higher than normal rainfall. Nobody was around to keep an eye on the Litho Plate's facility.

Unfortunately, the deluge of rainfall had quite a disastrous effect on the nearby river, which rose to record depth at that time. This dramatic rise in the river level had caused the water to breach the embankments, flowing into the facility. The sunken effluent plant systems was totally immersed and swamped by the river water. The solutions in the sump became mixed together forming an extraordinary chemical cocktail. Heaven only knows which reaction occurred first, dependant on which tanks were flooded first. There were some horrendous chemicals in that effluent system, sulphuric acid, hydrochloric acid, chromic acid, alkaline soap solutions, sodium hydroxide, potassium cyanide, hypochlorite solution, chromium sludge. The system was sealed from the river, but no one could foresee at that time how the river level would rise so dramatically and totally swamp it. When the extent of this pollution was realised by the security guards at the main gate, Jim had to inform the Welsh Water Authority who did not prosecute, mainly because the pollution had been caused by a "natural event".

When the solutions overflowed, they all became mixed together. No-one knows which reactions occurred, for example, in no way should cyanide come into contact with concentrated acids, as the highly toxic gas hydrocyanic gas is generated. In all probability, by the time the solutions mixed together, the dilution factor had taken effect with no extremely dangerous chemical reaction taking place. Fortunately, nobody was in close proximity to test this hypothesis. I would like to believe the chemicals neutralised each other; as I recall my reason for studying chemical engineering had been to protect the environment not to pollute it with some of the most dangerous chemicals used in industry. Upon returning after the holidays, we discovered the effluent tanks contained only dirty water with a neutral pH. Ian James carried out chemical analysis only to discover, there were no chemicals left in the tanks. The Litho plates lost two days production before able to return to normal working. Following this incident, it was decided for prolonged periods, all chemicals in the effluent had to be neutralized before the facility was shut down.

Following the higher than normal rainfall, January turned even more inclement with sub-zero temperatures. The ambient temperature dropping well below zero degrees Celsius reaching as low as minus fifteen to twenty degrees. Today these temperatures are very rare, but in the late sixties, seventies and early eighties during the winter months, the icy cold nights were quite common from November to March, with global warming, such low temperatures are at the beginning of the new millennium now very rare indeed. I recall these low temperatures for personal reasons.

One of my final duties at the end of the Friday night shift necessitated closing the main water valve which was about three quarters of a metre in diameter and unfortunately located at the bottom of five thousand gallon header water. The main problem being, the header tank was located about forty feet up in the air, perched on top of a giant metal frame. The giant valve was located just at the base of the Braithwaite tank. To close the valve required climbing a metal ladder, which at 4:30 am in cold January and February Mornings happened, unfortunately, usually to be coated in a thin layer of freshly acquired ice. The valve was not close to the rungs of the ladder, and so closing the valve required a superhuman feat of reaching out and laboriously closing the valve by turning it clockwise with one hand, whilst precariously clinging onto the ladder with the other hand. This was not an easy task whilst trying to balance forty feet up in the air. On particular night shift, I was in the middle of performing this highly dangerous manoeuvre, when my footing slipped on the dangerously icy rung of the ladder. My only lifeline was now my frozen, virtually lifeless, left hand which was clinging desperately to the rung of the ladder. My mind contemplated the thirty or forty foot drop to the frozen ground below, which concentrated my mind somewhat, causing the adrenaline to surge through my frozen body. Fortunately, I was able to regain my footing on the ladder and complete the necessary task. The ordeal caused me to shake uncontrollably with fear, as I stealthily descended the ladder reaching terra firma without any more mishaps.

It was because of this cold and rather inclement weather over that weekend, all the pipe work surrounding and feeding the effluent plant froze quite solid. The temperatures reached as low as minus twenty degrees Celsius. Upon arriving in work on the Monday afternoon, I discovered the all the management team including Jim Gunn and Charles Sharpe desperately trying to thaw out the pipe work of the effluent plant using steam lances. There were hose bags everywhere and a permanent haze of condensing steam. Whilst the management team, which also included Ian James,

Andy Morris, the other Supervisor and Dave Parry, tried to defrost the effluent plant. The workforce was busily trying to get the electroplating line set up for running the production. The whole scenario reminded me of West Mercian Oil during its early inception, with everyone pulling together in an attempt to overcome obstacles and adversity. It was a heart-warming sight to observe and take part in.

At last, at about five in the afternoon, the effluent plant finally relented and all the frozen water within the labyrinth of pipe work finally turned to liquid. This meant it was now possible to actually run the electroplating lines. All brought about by hard work and a team effort.

The weeks inexorably and slowly began to slip by; winter gradually turning into spring and accompanying the change in the seasons, there was the associated improvement in the weather conditions, which obviated any need to thaw out any frozen pipe work. I began settling into my role as Shift Supervisor and was on the final section of my learning curve. My confidence improved with each passing day. Cindy had accepted the shift system without too much difficulty and actually no longer minded being on her own during the night shifts. The men on the shift also began slowly to accept me and there were no more incidents, stunts or tricks, call them what you will of the emergency stop buttons being pushed.

There was, however, a fly in the ointment, namely one of the Shift Supervisors, Gary Bishop. Altogether, there were three Shift Supervisors, including myself, the other two being Andy Morris and Gary Bishop. Andy Morris was an amiable, friendly, garrulous happy go lucky sort of individual, slightly older than me, in his early to mid-thirties. Andy's main problem, like Myfanwy, whom I worked with many years before, was he smoked far too many cigarettes for the good of his health.

Due to the shift setup pattern, rota, call it what you will, 'C' shift, my shift, always followed Andy's shift. It was during these shift change-over, he always had a lot to say for himself and what had transpired during his shift. In all fairness, he always gave me a thorough changeover briefing. I got to know Andy reasonably well, as well as it is possible during a twenty minute changeover five days a week. We got on well together and had a good rapport. Having said that, Andy was the type of person it was hard to take a disliking to because of his happy, chatty disposition and nature, as a result, he got on well with most people.

Gary Bishop was the total opposite of Andy, virtually his Doppelganger. He was surly, unsmiling, with an almost non-existent sense of humour. Unfortunately for me, Gary's shift always followed mine in the rota. As well as writing in the log, I always tried to impart as much information as I could verbally informing Gary what had transpired during my shift and what was required of his shift. During my hand-over, call it paranoia, but I had the distinct impression Gary Bishop took a disinterested in what I had to say. The vibes were most definitely there, he did not like me one iota. On more than one occasion he would give the curt, abrupt and dismissive and what I considered ignorant retort, 'I'll read it in the log!' There was most definitely no rapport or love lost between Gary and myself. I must confess to experiencing a feeling of intimidation from Gary.

Gradually over the weeks, it became evident; Gary was trying to gain brownie points at my expense. The new kid on the block was ripe for exploitation. His comments in the log were usually vitriolic and at my shift's expense. Criticizing it for one thing or another, knowing full well Jim Gunn always read the shift log book religiously and without fail every Morning. I was not used to this constant insidious attacking and sniping by a fellow work colleague, and I must admit it was beginning to affect me mentally, causing a crisis of confidence. Jim Gunn was not the only one who read the log book, Ian James also read it as his duties included troubleshooting with the process, he always like to be pro-active rather than reactive so he too used to read the log to ascertain whether there was a potential process problem looming on the horizon which needed rectifying or resolving. Ian also noticed the damming, harmful reports in the log written at my expense criticizing my shift for some misdemeanour or other.

Ian's hours were nine until five, although he usually stayed on until about six or so after reading the book and all of Gary's uncomplimentary remarks concerning my shift. Ian took me aside and gave me some advice, explaining in great detail the areas of the plant Gary spent a lot of his time inspecting and which he was quite *'au fait,'* with. He advised me on what things had to be done and inspected regularly to reduce or even eliminate criticism from *'Peter Perfect,'* a derogatory term he to describe Gary.

I had no way of fighting back, for Gary's shift always followed 'C' Shift due to the vagaries of our shift pattern. This is where Andy came to the rescue, as he began a campaign of criticising Gary's shift and all the mistakes made on it, checks not adhered to or just a simple case of bad housekeeping, similar to all the things Gary took great delight in pointing out in his log report when writing about my shift.

Andy and I came to a gentleman's agreement. I never wrote derogatory remarks about his shift in the log if there were problems. Whenever possible, and I would discuss it with him face to face during the next shift changeover. This eliminated bringing other people into the equation such as Jim and Charles, which could result in something trivial being blown out of all proportion. It also obviated any chance of there being an acrimonious working relationship between Andy and me which was the situation between Gary and me. There were more than enough conflicts in my life. It was precisely because of our good working relationship and communication that Andy was always more than obliging when it came to assisting me in my altercation, conflict and somewhat acrimonious relationship with Gary. In fact, on occasions, Andy's comments could be quite cutting when describing Gary's shift shortcomings or failures.

Eventually, the comments and remarks in the rose to such a pitch and crescendo, Jim Gunn was forced to insist, during one of our departmental meetings, for all derogatory and scathing remarks in the log book to desist, telling us all to work together as more of a team. Jim's pep talk must have worked, for subsequently, Gary's comments in the log book became more conciliatory. He realised no brownie points could be achieved by being so aggressive towards my shift, which in effect meant me and in fact they could even be detrimental to his promotional ambitions. Andy also followed suit.

Gradually things began to settle down and production began to run smoothly, and when it actually does become boring, I was not complaining. My life had gone through quite a few upheavals during previous years. Monotone, set routines and boredom had their appeal at that time. We all began to pull together as a team. My demeanour became much more relaxed and I began to take much more of an interest in the people I worked with.

My right hand man on the shift was Gordon. My initial impression of Gordon was that of a surly belligerent individual, with very little sense of humour. However as our working relationship grew and nurtured, I began to realise there was much, much more to Gordon than the person I have just described. Gordon had, what can only be described as, a wicked, dry sense of humour and I never knew if he was being serious or joking whenever he made comments.

At about the same time as I began working for Cox & Sons, another person began her employment, Janet. She was a State Registered nurse who had been taken on permanently to work in the Medical Centre based on site. At that time Cox & Sons was a caring, paternalistic, altruistic company. With the welfare of its workforce being one of its main priorities, hence a fully qualified nurse permanently based on site. I first met Janet during my first week of employment, when she gave me my mini-medical; taking my blood pressure, weight, height, urine sample, asking me about my medical history; the usual medical stuff. Janet was thirty-something, slim, petite, with short natural blonde hair, extremely attractive with a friendly disposition. As if these attributes weren't enough, she became even more captivating, alluring and enticing by the fact she always wore a crisply ironed and starched uniform which rustled as she walked, this did no end to enhance her already numerous and prolific attributes.

For the first few months of her employment, Janet much like me was becoming acquainted with her duties and responsibilities, together with the facility and the personnel on site.

Janet was very conscientious, taking her duties and responsibilities extremely seriously indeed, but still this was not enough for her. Janet thought it prudent to add to her, already extensive undisputed medical skills, capabilities, and experience by acquiring a thorough background and working knowledge of the chemicals handled at the facility and their inherent dangers, in preparation for any incidents which could befall the site, the maleic anhydride incident being a classic example of this, her philosophy and ethos being "forewarned is forearmed".

Following some time being spent in the other departments on site, Janet eventually arrived at the Litho plates building. Fortunately for me this happened to be during an afternoon shift. Being the incumbent Supervisor, meant she would have to spend some time in my company, acquiring a knowledge of the processes, chemicals and the attendant dangers associated with the whole operation the fact she would be spending some time in my company caused me no unhappiness at all; in fact the exact opposite was the case.

When Janet arrived, I showed her around the Litho Plates section, describing to her the operations, why certain chemicals were used, what their main function or purpose was and the inherent dangers associated with them. As we walked around, Janet would ask pertinent, intelligent questions about the operation, and the chemicals.

'What would you consider to be the most dangerous chemical handled in the Litho Plates Division?'

'Well,' I thoughtfully replied, 'it depends upon your point of view. We have chromic acid which gives off fumes which can cause chromic ulcers of the nose and possible tumours. We have sulphuric, nitric and hydrochloric acids which are all highly corrosive. There is chlorine gas which is toxic and corrosive. Finally, there is potassium cyanide which is highly toxic.... take your pick.'

'Tell me about potassium cyanide,' Janet replied. 'In

what way does it attack the body?'

'Different ways,' I replied. 'Ingestion, skin absorption, inhalation when it reacts with acids to form hydrocyanic gas or as a dust.'

We continued our tour of the Litho Plates facility buildings, with Janet pursuing her cross questioning. She was really getting the bit between her teeth, finding the whole process quite fascinating and also quite horrific and frightening with all the inherent danger associated with the electroplating industry. She had now become totally concentrated on the subject of potassium cyanide. 'Tell me more about potassium cyanide. Is it fatal at low concentrations?'

'I suppose the simple answer is yes, there are a lot of factors such as the metabolism of the person who has taken a dose, the form in which the cyanide has been taken, the short answer being, a couple of grams could kill you.'

At this juncture of the tour, Gordon was standing next to me, quiet as a church mouse, not uttering a word, keeping his own counsel,

Janet was, meanwhile, writing copious amounts of notes, on her A4 note pad securely attached to a clipboard, with each answer I gave her.

'Who mainly handles the cyanide during the shift?' she continued relentlessly and unremittingly.

'On a Monday Morning or afternoon shift, it could be any of the workforces when they are cleaning out the cyanide filters on the re-circ. system. During the week when the electrolyte needs replenishing, Gordon, my right hand man here, does it.' As I said this, I immediately pointed towards Gordon.

Janet turned to him and asked him rhetorically,

'You obviously wear the full protective clothing when making the cyanide additions?'

'Of course!' Gordon replied, indignantly and in a

somewhat belligerent manner, giving the appearance of being distinctly annoyed at being asked such a stupid question. He even looked Janet straight in the eyes, almost daring her to doubt him, and pursue the point. Janet appeared completely satisfied with Gordon's answer, pressing the point no further. She then asked if she could continue to reconnoitre the facility on her own. I reluctantly agreed and she went on her merry way still making copious notes as she went.

Gordon and I watched for a short time while Janet walked away. Her hips swivelling unintentionally and I believe, unbeknownst to her, quite sexually seductive as she walked away from us. The instant she was out of hearing distance, I turned to Gordon.

'You lying, old bastard,' I said, in a good natured way, with a slight grin on my face, 'I've lost count the amount of times I have told you about wearing the full safety kit when making the cyanide additions, PVC gauntlets are just not enough protection when making those additions!'

Gordon just looked at me with a distinct mischievous glint in his eye and a slight grin on his wrinkled old features with the unapologetic reply,

'What she doesn't know won't hurt her.' And with that, he walked away, whistling merrily to himself.

Every time Gordon made the cyanide additions, he had a form of ritual. After having performed the titration and calculated the amount of the toxic white powder to add, I would inform Gordon, he would then put on a pair of PVC gauntlets, pick up the medium sized plastic scoop and the shovel out the potassium cyanide powder from a 25 Kg drum and weigh out into a specifically designated plastic drum allocated for that chemical only, which zeroed tarred on an electronic scales. Gordon always carefully weighed out the calculated addition and once that task had been performed put it into the mixing vessel which pumped it into the electrolytic solution in the bath. The PVC gauntlets were the only protective equipment which Gordon deemed necessary for his safety. Following completion of this task, Gordon customarily smoked a *'roll your own' outside* the building and as far as I believe and recollect, probably without even washing his hands, having lost count of how many occasions Gordon had been informed about the dangers of cyanide by me, Dave Parry, Ian James, even Jim Gunn, all of us resigning ourselves to the fact Gordon would never listen and would continue to do the job in his own inimitable way, having his own philosophy concerning the subject.

For me to castigate, chastise or even reprimand Gordon would have been, to say the least, more than slightly hypocritical. For I too, on occasions, had been guilty of distinctly flouting the rules of personal health and safety whilst working in the Litho plates division. Many times during my time as Shift Supervisor working in the Litho plates, it had become necessary to extricate twisted plates from the jigs after they had become entangled during the descent of the jig into the baths of solution. Usually and unfortunately for me, this happened to be the baths containing the potassium cyanide solution.

After firstly turning off the line, then isolating the electrical power to the anodes, I would put on a pair of PVC gauntlets and make my way to the electrolytic bath and then walk gingerly and very carefully and deliberately along the top of the buzz bars like some high wire artiste to remove the offending, partly electroplated sheet of metal. Beneath me was 9,000 litres of potassium cyanide solution to slip into the solution which would result in certain death as cyanide does not have to be ingested. Absorption through the skin is another means of receiving cyanide poisoning. After extricating the offending plate, I would carry the plate and return gingerly the way I had just come along the tops of the buzz bars. This operation was performed a number of times during my time at the Litho plates section. I also only wore gauntlets for the whole exercise, fortunately for me without any incidents. I never asked Gordon to perform the task, because of his age and lack of agility.

I suppose the cyanide was the most dangerous chemical at the facility, although the other chemicals had their dangers also. It was a chemical responsible for a number of incidents at the Litho plates section.

The antidote at the time widely used for any ingestion of cyanide was a two part solution, which required mixing, the first part was a chloride solution and the second was barium carbonate solution, upon mixing the two together, a dark green, vile, obnoxious looking green sludge was generated. This sludge had to be swallowed in one quick gulp, there was no other way, this solution was most indefatigably not the type you could drink in stages ... it was a distinct case of all or nothing. The way it worked as an emetic, that is to say, once ingested it caused you to vomit, taking the poison with it. Looking at it however was enough to make one sick, never mind the ingestion. During one of the shifts, not 'C' shift, I hasten to add, one of the workforce believed he had received a splash of cyanide solution on his lips and immediately informed his colleagues. Without any delay, they virtually frog-marched him to the First Aid Room to give him the required cyanide antidote. The solutions were hastily mixed to form the slightly gelatinous, green obnoxious slime, resembling something akin to the green slime found on the surface of stagnant ponds. The victim looked on in abject horror, disgust and revulsion as the gelatinous green slime began to generate within the confines of the Perspex vessel. A final stirring was carried out to homogenise the mix.

The victim decided it was time to state his point of view and make his opinions known at having to ingest the vile looking solution, 'I'll take my chances with the cyanide!' he said, almost pleading and whimpering as the words came out of his mouth. He was also slowly trying to exit through the door, hoping nobody would notice as he surreptitiously tried to make his escape through the door of the small room.

'No you don't!' exclaimed the person leading the medical team 'Grab hold of him boys!' And with that, two a man, they pounced on the poor victim. As if getting poisoned by cyanide was not enough, he was now being violently assaulted by his work colleagues. In all there were five of them; one on each leg, one on each arm. The fifth person and the one leading this team trying to save the victim's life, was physically prying open the victim's unwilling mouth and trying to pour the obnoxious fluid down his gullet. This despite the victim's protestations.

With all the grappling and struggling taking place, quite a large amount of the green slime managed to find its way onto the victim's face and clothing, with only a small amount actually making its way into his gullet. Once they were happy he had ingested enough, the victim's assailants released him, as he coughed and spluttered, having almost been choked in the affray.

The victim stood up and almost immediately, his face began to turn green, nearly the same colour as the liquid he had just ingested. He put his hand over his mouth and ran out of the room quickly seeking the toilet, where he immediately began regurgitating the liquid he had just drunk in a loud and distinctly voluble manner, evident to all around was happening within the confines of the toilet cubicle. This was how the vile liquid it was an emetic. Probably if the actual liquid, itself didn't make you vomit, the sight of it would... The poor victim then spent the remainder of the shift, indulging in projectile vomiting. With the antidote obviously doing its intended job, the victim survived his ordeal and lived for a number of years following his experience. In truth, had he received a sufficient dose of cyanide, he would have died long before reaching the first aid room and his assessment of 'taking his chances with the cyanide' probably would have been the correct one. Still hindsight is a wonderful thing. The correct thing to do at the time was to administer the antidote and that's what was done.

# CHAPTER 12

Research and Development was also carried out at the Litho Plates Division, in addition to the main production. The research mainly concentrated upon improving the electroplating process and developing better light sensitive coatings. The two main industrial chemists involved in this research were two PhD's having their Doctorates in pure Chemistry. They were Dr. Silas Holmes, and Dr. Herbert Voss. These two doctors were characters in their own right, having the attributes of being oddball and slightly mad, eccentric scientists. Both were extremely intelligent and knowledgeable in the field of chemistry, but totally impracticable when it came to dealing with the real world, despite possessing IQ's which were virtually off the scale. Both were the stereotypical nutty professors, with a dishevelled appearance, completely eccentric with their hair usually long, unkempt and protruding in all directions from the top of their craniums. Allocating time for such incidentals as having their hair cut never came into their time management regime. Also in keeping with this stereotypical image of a mad scientist, both Doctors wore thick rimmed spectacles which were normally damaged, through one mishap or other and held together by a strip of sellotape or similar adhesive in an attempt to keep the damaged frames together.

Silas was the more senior of the two, in his mid-fifties, having transferred after working at the main production site in Orpington Kent for a number of years. Jack Houseman, the General Manager informed me, during one social event, Silas had been a biker in his early days, always commuting to work on his seven fifty Triumph motorbike, suitably attired with leather jacket, flying helmet and goggles. Silas would often hurtle into the Orpington car park, at high speed, only stopping just in time and terrorising other workers on the site with his high speed machine...

Herbert Voss, the other half of this eccentric duo was also extremely knowledgeable when it came to the Litho Plate operation. Having been born locally, Dr. Voss also had another passion local history of the area and was a member of the local historical society, his hobby bordering on obsession and almost fanaticism. He was totally mad in a nice way.

Of the two, Silas appeared to be the more accident prone, and misfortune always seemed to happen to Silas, who seemed to attract calamity as a magnet attracts iron filings. One particular day, Silas had been allocated the task of showing some very important customers around the Litho plate's facility. For the visit, Silas had pulled out all the stops, having invested in an expensive suit especially for the occasion, determined to impress the important customers, even resorting to getting his hair cut. As I recall, Andy Morris happened to be the Shift Supervisor at the time. These mishaps appeared to happen to Silas, usually through no fault of his own. This particular incident was one in a million, occurring while Silas happened to be in the vicinity. He was showing the important customers around the site and explaining in great detail the operation and answering their questions. Silas was walking past a two inch plastic re-circulating pipe which carried a weak solution, thankfully, of potassium cyanide solution. At the exact instant Silas was walking by and in the middle of explaining the intricacies of the operation, the plastic re-circulating line sheared and because of the pressure, spewed voluminous amounts of the toxic liquid all over Silas who caught the full blast of it over his lower torso. In all the time the electroplating line had been in existence that particular section of pipe had never caused any maintenance problems and ironically, it chose that particular time to malfunction and fail. One of the quicker thinking and fast-acting workforce instantaneously pushed the emergency stop button for the re-circulating pump which immediately stemmed the massive effusion and haemorrhaging of the toxic liquid.

All the operators had been fully trained in the actions to perform in such an incident and immediately fulfilled the required task which involved physically hurling and projecting Silas into the safety shower unit. The shower was activated by a pressure plate, which meant as soon as a person stood on the plate, water cascaded down onto the poor unfortunate below. Now this particular unit had never been used in anger. The instant Silas's weight was on the plate, water began to flow from the shower head. The term flow is a totally inadequate description of what actually happened. The deluge of water completely saturated poor Silas, who was lying horizontal and prostrate on the pressure plate of the safety shower. His suit had completely absorbed the water quickly becoming saturated. The noise was unbelievable as gallons of water effused, cascaded and deluged down upon the coughing and spluttering Silas, was, by now, totally bemused and shocked by the whole experience. The torrent of water from the shower head forming a solid block as it descended upon poor Silas, as he was entombed in this curtain of water. Because of the volume of water being generated, the drainage system could barely cope with this sudden down-pour of water, resulting in the area flooding. Meanwhile, the toxic liquid, namely the potassium cyanide which had contaminated Silas's clothing, causing all this mayhem, had by now been forcibly and physically expunged from his clothing.

Silas, who, a few moments earlier had been in danger of cyanide poisoning as the toxic chemical was slowly absorbed into his skin, was now in danger of drowning from this torrent of water. This fact was not realized immediately by his colleagues. The bemused V.I.P. customers stared in complete horror and astonishment at the scene being enacted before their very eyes. The sheer volume and force of water left Silas gasping and spluttering, curtailing his ability to shout and tell his audience to turn the shower off and restricting his escape from the horrendous downpour.

At last, Silas's rescuers thought it prudent to get their charge from the shower, but finding it almost impossible to drag him from the pressure plate because of the water and the fact that Silas was unable to assist them in their endeavours to get him off the plate, being unable to move due to the force of the water. Meanwhile, the water inexorably poured down onto the poor unfortunate Silas below who was still coughing and spluttering.

Andy Morris heard the commotion and left the confines of the Supervisor's office to investigate what was happening. Upon reaching the scene Andy quickly did an appraisal of the situation and being quick thinking and level headed, quickly turned the valve off on the line feeding the shower unit.

The instant the cascading water desisted, Silas was quickly manhandled from the unit, still coughing and spluttering, gasping desperately for precious oxygen to replenish his exhausted lungs. Fortunately, he had not been in there long enough to become unconscious and recovered from his ordeal fairly quickly. The same, however, could not be said for his new suit, which had not only become saturated but ripped and torn beyond repair during the whole incident, never to be worn again.

Another incident concerning the accident prone Silas, occurred while he was doing some experiments and involved a machine called using a Triple Roll Milling Machine. Basically a machine which has three large roller used for printing, each roller exerts a tremendous pressure on the other as they exude whatever is to be printed. During his evaluation, one of his sleeves got caught between the rollers dragging the sleeve inexorably between them and hence his arm slowly approached the rollers. Silas was unable to reach the emergency stop button, his movements, by now being limited by his accidental entrapment. Being a perfect gentleman and of the old school, Silas never or rarely swore. Now if anyone else had been in the same predicament, myself for example I would have been shouting and screaming at the top of my voice, words to the effect, 'Someone turn the fucking machine off!' Not Silas, apparently he was barely audible with his very polite and stiff upper lip request.

'Would someone please kindly turn off the rolling machine, I appear to be caught in it?'

The feeble request was barely audible above the noise of the machinery. So it was a short while before Silas' pathetic cry for help was heard. Meanwhile, his arm was being pulled ever nearer to the rollers. Eventually his stiff upper lip composure did falter and Silas did allow himself the luxury of shouting a few decibels higher to stop his arm being mangled in the machine. Fortuitously, someone happened to be walking by and upon hearing Silas's ever so polite request, turned the Triple Roll machine off in the nick of time saving Silas's arm. He was undoubtedly one of life's eccentrics.

My days at Litho Plates were turning into weeks, which themselves turned into months. I now began to enjoy my job as Shift Supervisor, as I became more acquainted with the duties and overcame new problems as they arose, ably assisted by Gordon whose help was invaluable. My confidence was growing and my demeanour more relaxed. As the Americans would say "I approached the top of my learning curve". Even my nemesis, Gary Bishop, appeared more reasonable, even pleasant. My shift had accepted me and had stopped playing silly buggers and trying to wind me up. Obviously I had passed my initiation.

The winter months and the attendant inclement weather gradually disappeared. There were no freezing pipes or trying to thaw out the effluent plant. The long winter nights were gradually turning into long summer days, which meant driving to the facility during light hours, which made it more enjoyable particularly as the facility was located in a rural part of the world, 'out in the sticks.' My marriage was good and Cindy was accepting and even embracing the shift working pattern; all was well with the world. Unfortunately it is the very time when life hits you from behind with a sledge hammer, as I was about to discover.

There had even been the dubious privilege of running the electroplating line faster than it had ever run before and since, unknowingly, contravening an agreement, virtually running a horse and trap through the time and motion agreements between unions and management. A fact which Ian James had took great pleasure when informing me. He thought it great I had my shift working harder than they had ever worked before, a situation which came about when we ran plates thicker than normal, which meant the line could be run faster as the plates did not flap or move about so much as they were immersed in the solutions.

My instructions had been to increase the process speed as much as possible, with no upper limits being specified. So I followed my instructions and ran the line as fast as possible, which, as it transpired was much faster than the upper agreed limit with the union. It was quite funny to watch the men loading and unloading the plates on to the jigs. With the normal rate, they had times to roll their own cigarettes, read a paragraph of a book, while the line was going through its sequence and before loading or unloading the plates, dependent upon which end of the line they were working. I watched one of the guys, Roger, trying to roll his cigarette, but could never quite make it before the jig dropped ready to be loaded with a steel plate.

This went on for quite a while before he was able to eventually complete the task. It was indicative of the speed of the line, his inability to roll the cigarette, the frustration becoming evident on his face. It was only when I did a timing did it become evident how fast the lines were working. Of course the first time, I was unaware that the agreement between management and unions was being broken concerning the maximum rate of running the plating line. Yes, things were looking good.

As the months passed, Andy and I became good friends, but he was a bit highly strung and chain smoked his way through the shifts. His addiction was such that during our twenty minute shift changeover, he usually smoked two cigarettes. Andy's addiction to cigarettes was highlighted during, or rather following an incident.

I had arrived for the afternoon shift in the office at about two forty five in the afternoon ready for our discussion about his shift and for him to highlight the problems and to tell me the scheduling intended for my shift. The office was deserted when I arrived and so I thought I would read the shift log, only to discover the page was completely blank. The shift, date and time had been underlined at the top but that's as far as it went, nothing had actually been written down about the shift. I sat down and waited. Five minutes passed, then ten minutes, fifteen and still no sign of Andy. Eventually, he appeared about ten minutes into my shift, his face bright red he was coughing and spluttering quite heavily.

'Jesus Andy! Andy, what's happened to you?' I asked, concerned at his condition.

He tried to explain the reason why he was in this condition, desperately trying to explain between the coughs and splutters, while at the same time desperately gasping for air.

'Had....' cough..... cough..... splutter..... cough, 'a whiff,'..... gasp ....... cough... splutter, 'of chlorine gas .... hadn't tightened down the nut,'.... cough... splutter, 'enough.' cough.... splutter.... 'on the gas bottle!' cough... splutter.

Then incredulously, he began searching for his cigarettes and once finding them, lightening up, his face by now bright red and the coughing continued unrelentingly. 'For fuck's sake Andy, you're coughing your lungs up and decide to smoke a cigarette. Perhaps you should go to the infirmary?! I said, castigating him for what I considered to be an irresponsible action.

'I need....' cough.... cough 'It....' cough.... cough... 'To calm....' cough.... cough ...'my nerves' he replied in response to my remark totally unconcerned about my statement and tone. I asked him what had happened during the shift, apart from him nearly gassing himself with chlorine. In between coughs, he told me it had been a quiet shift and for me to continue plating a particular size of plate. With that he left, still smoking his cigarette and still coughing, not bothering to write anything in the log book.

Apart from his smoking, Andy was slightly gullible and could be easily misled. Cindy and I had been married about eighteen months and we were still in our 'honeymoon period.'

This particular week I had been working the early shift from seven in the morning until three in the afternoon. Cindy had been on a hairdressing course in London and had been away for a week and returning late on the Thursday evening. I collected her from Abergavenny railway station, stopping on the way home, to pick up a Chinese take-away, together with a bottle of wine. We had a romantic meal, caught up on the week's events, finished the bottle of wine and as we were still in the early years of our marriage, a night of passionate lovemaking to complete the scene, indicating how much we had missed each other. Eventually, I had some much needed sleep at about two in the morning. I am still uncertain whether the alarm clock sounded and I turned it off in a stupor, or if it just did not go off. Whatever the reason, the result was I slept late, awaking at about seven thirty when I should have been in work by seven at the latest. To add to my misery the journey normally took about an hour. So upon awakening I was in a complete state of panic and totally disorientated.

Before embarking on my journey, I woke Cindy, after first dressing as quickly as I could, requesting she phone the facility and inform them I would be late but that I was on my way. I then rushed out, still completing my attire as I left the house and got into my car.

Meanwhile, imagine the scene back at the Litho plate section seven arrives and there is still no sign of myself. Up until that point, I my time keeping had been exemplary and so this was completely out of character. Andy now began to panic.

'Vinson has not shown up, what should I do?' he foolishly asked one of the more experienced guys on his shift. Unfortunately for Andy, the operator also happened to be the shift practical joker and prone to winding people up. With a serious facial expression, he then informed Andy that Abergavenny, where I lived had had about a two foot of snow and that it was very unlikely I would be in work that day. The fact that it was late April and the weather was quite mild, completely escaped Andy. Andy, instead of phoning me at this juncture which was about ten past seven, phoned Dave Parry who had been covering Gary Bishop and had been working the previous evening and would be in that afternoon. He was not amused at being awoken so early, fully expecting to have a ' *lie in.*' Next on Andy's call list was Jim Gunn, Charles Sharpe, Ian James, all and sundry except the person who really counted.... me.

Andy was told to go home by Jim and someone would cover the shift.

Eventually, I arrived in work about eight thirty only to discover Jim reading the log book. He gave me a bollocking for being late, but was secretly amused at the reason for my being so late, namely my nocturnal activities and also at Andy's reactions. The next time I saw Andy, he was so embarrassed about what had happened and about being duped by his workforce.

The month of May arrived. The weather was warm and sunny which added to my feelings of wellbeing. The journeys to work were enjoyable, being light most times with long daylight hours, the sun shone constantly, skies were blue, and driving with the radio playing on a nice sunny day, which, as far as I am concerned, is one of life's enjoyable experiences. Life was now becoming good and I enjoyed working in the Litho plates, as I reached the top of my learning curve, a terminology I picked up during the years. All was well with the world, life was coming together. I was employed in a job I enjoyed, and the pay was pretty good.

During my week of day shifts, I had not seen Jim Gunn, who would religiously come down at about eight thirty and read the shift logs. I was not concerned about Jim not making appearance, assuming he had a higher than normal workload and had no time for reading the log book and things were going well, so there was no real need for him to come down.

However, what did concern me was the fact it was evidently becoming more difficult to find storage space for the completed Litho Plates, which was indicative the plates were not selling, but our production runs had been good with very few problems or rejects and high yields, so I just assumed we were just too efficient for the sales department and more pressure would be exerted upon them to sell the product. During April, I approached Jim about the amount of stock we held. Jim, forever the optimist, told me not to worry and that during his many years at Litho Plates he had seen it far worse.

During the early part of May I had been on the back shifts and so again I did not see Jim Gunn, which was not all that unusual, however, it was Andy Morris who began the alarm bells ringing when he asked me towards the end of one week when I last saw Jim. Andy had been on the early, day shift, and I was on the afternoon shift. He began explaining to me he had not seen Jim all week. I replied that perhaps he had been on holiday. Andy replied by saying he had not been on holiday and had been actually in work all week, but had not been down to the electroplating lines.

Once again fates had interfered and were about to mess up in my life, kicking me in the bollocks. During a night shift towards the end of that May, Jim Gunn phoned me about midnight. Now I was concerned, Jim had never ever phoned me late at night during the shift. After a few embarrassing pleasantries on his part, Jim informed me there was to be a meeting in the canteen for all of Litho plates staff at twelve noon the next day, he thought it best if I attend, but fully understood if I couldn't. By the time I arrived home it would be about eight in the morning, then I would have to be up at ten thirty and drive back to the facility. I pressed him about the meeting, but ever the professional, he told me he was not at liberty to tell me. I knew it was serious, but to what extent I would have to wait. Since that day, during my working life, there have been a few meetings in the canteen, invariably it has been bad news. I now have a compulsive phobia about attending meetings in canteens.

I did not attend the meeting, knowing I could phone Andy who would inform me of the bad news that Friday afternoon. Upon phoning, discovering to my consternation, the news was far, far worse than I thought, Litho plates was to close within the month, there would be some, and redundancies, but not everyone, and some would be transferred to other departments. Litho chemicals would continue for about six months. Bloody typical! Just as I was enjoying the job this had to happen. Cindy was devastated when I told her, that weekend we both got well and truly plastered to drown our sorrows.

The following weeks, there was not much enthusiasm for work and moral reached an all-time low. I was to see the effect of redundancy once again, having seen it for the first time in Birchwater. People congregated in huddles discussing events, everyone concerned how it would affect them personally. Meetings were held with Gary Hudson in Personnel to discuss the possible alternatives and even possible relocation. Also this time it was also different for me.

The last time, I wanted to go for various reasons, this time I had a wife, mortgage and financial commitments - the whole nine yards. I could not afford to be made redundant and become unemployed. Cox & Sons, although paternalistic, were realistic and took the opportunity to weed out the undesirables keeping on the ones they considered to be good employees.

I was offered employment in 'The Finishes Division Research' which would be at a new site in Whitney, Oxfordshire. I took Wendy to the place, but she had no intention of relocating, thoroughly enjoying living in Abergavenny, with friends, family and acquaintances nearby. So I had to decline that offer. They even offered me a chance to relocate overseas together with a promotion and substantial pay rise in South Africa. Once again, Cindy would not contemplate a move, particularly to another country, even refusing to discuss it. I thought that would be it, Cox & Sons had offered me alternatives, but having declined twice, thought it would be the end of the road with me having to seek alternative employment with another company which I thought would be difficult at my age.

As the time was approached for the closure of the facility, I began to become concerned as it looked as if there was no job for me with redundancy looming. At the eleventh hour, Jim Gunn informed me there was a vacancy in the Finishes Division, where they made specialized paints and lacquers. Firstly, I would have to undergo a colour blindness test.

The test was arranged the fear being I would not pass. Fortuitously, I just managed to have an acceptable level of colour recognition. Jim informed me the job was mine and I would be transferring within the month. So yet another change in my career loomed on the horizon and once again, through no fault of my own.

# CHAPTER 13

Being located on the same industrial site as Litho Plates made relocation for my new wife and me unnecessary. My new employment hours now changed, from a shift pattern to a normal working day from eight in the morning until five in the evening with one hour for lunch. It would be a normal working week Monday to Friday with no weekend working. The major concern for Cindy and me revolved around the reduction in salary due to the loss in shift allowance and unsociable hour's payment. This amounted to nearly twenty per cent reduction in my monthly salary with no overtime payments. Life for the foreseeable future would have to be a little more austere. But at least I had a job, unlike some of the others in the Litho Plates Division. Unfortunately Dave Parry happened to be one of those casualties and was made redundant after twenty five years of service, Cox & Sons being the only company he had ever worked for, having joined them straight from school. Apparently, there had always been some sort of personality conflict between him and Jack Houseman, which explained why Dave's promotion within Litho Plates had not been as fast as the others such as Jim Gunn and Charles Sharpe for example. This personality conflict finally culminated in a heated argument during the re-deployment negotiations between Dave and Jack. The argument between the two of them became so acrimonious it ended Dave's career with Cox & Sons, with Jack deciding he no longer wanted Dave working for the company. It was, however, probably based on his personal feelings for Dave. I was sad at hearing the news. Dave who had been with Cox & Sons far longer than me and had taught me a considerable amount about the Litho Plates

Operation during my training and because of our time together, we had become friends. Now he was now out of work, admittedly with a substantial redundancy package, but nevertheless he was out of a job. Later I discovered Dave had found employment with a large fairly local company making internal lacquers and external paints for the canning industry. He was to become their new Plant Manager, a highly paid position complete with company car. So in fact Dave came out of the situation well with his substantial redundancy and a new highly paid job. Dave's good fortune helped mitigate any feelings of guilt on my part at still being employed by Cox & Sons.

At sixty three years of age, my second in command, Gordon, opted for early retirement, deciding perhaps it was an ideal time to spend his declining years with his grandchildren.

Ian James re-deployed to St. Helens Lancashire, together with most of the laboratory personnel, including Silas Holmes and Herbert Voss.

Gary Bishop, my nemesis, opted for the job in South Africa.

Charles Sharpe went to work in the Resin Division. The shift operatives were either re-deployed and scattered throughout the facility or made redundant, the latter group being all the undesirables. Cox & Sons took the opportunity of closure to get rid of the flotsam and undesirable personnel.

Andy Morris, Jim Gunn and I were all transferred to the Finishes Division. Andy and I were allocated to work in the QC Laboratory. Jim became Finishes Division General Manager designate, taking over from the current General Manager prior to the incumbent General Manager taking early his retirement within six months.

My first few weeks were spent working in the QC

Laboratory reporting to Allan Williams the Laboratory Manager and getting acquainted with the products. However after this short period of time, I would be sent to the facility at Sidcup in Kent for training. The facility at Sidcup was being closed and most of the people were to be transferred to the new facility at Whitney which would become the main Research and Development laboratories for the Finishes Division, with all the Finishes products being manufactured. All the manufacturing currently being carried out at Sidcup site transferred to the site. My brief being to become acquainted with these products and the manufacturing, although some of the personnel would be relocated at Orpington or possibly made redundant, the decisions were being made as to who would actually be moved and those to be made redundant.

I told Cindy the instant I knew about this change in plans concerning my training period at Sidcup. She was not at all pleased at this news, but could not say a lot. After all, Cox & Sons had gone out of their way to re-deploy me. She was even less enamoured upon discovering it would in all probability be for about three months, with me coming home every weekend, the latter part sweetened the bitter pill somewhat.

My little remaining time was spent being instructed by Allan Williams in what to look out for and the information vital for the transfer concerning the production and the Quality assurance techniques with the specialized products which at that present time were not being manufactured at the site. Basically it was, simplified it was take note of everything. The Cox & Sons management were quite flexible concerning the travelling times. I was allowed to leave home at the normal leaving time on the Monday, which meant not arriving at the Sidcup facility until lunchtime or early afternoon on the Monday. On the Friday, I was allowed to leave lunchtime to arrive home a reasonable time that evening. When they put all this to me, it didn't sound so bad.

The first week of my extensive training period, there had been a mix up in arranging my accommodation, the consequence of this oversight, necessitated me staying at a swish, luxurious, expensive hotel in Kent.

Later, I discovered the hotel to be one of the hotels where Cynthia Payne, the well-known madam, used to sell her luncheon vouchers for sex. I must confess to not being unduly upset about this oversight on Cox & Sons part in billeting me in the hotel, as the rooms were plush and extremely comfortable with all the amenities a five star hotel. Pity I had forgotten to pack my bathing trunks, otherwise I could have availed myself of the indoor swimming pool. Despite it being the middle of summer, the weather for my first week's stay was absolutely horrendous, raining quite heavily. The usually, stereotypical British summer in fact. I had travelled to Sidcup using public transport, train all the way from Abergavenny to Sidcup and not taking my car.

Having no way of travelling around independently and because of the rather inclement weather, I decided to spend the evenings in the hotel eating at the 'a la carte' restaurant, accompanied by a few alcoholic drinks to help wash the food down. I had not been instructed to eat out and believed this was quite acceptable as the weather was quite deplorable. I did not see the hotel bill for my week's stay as it was sent straight to Head Office at Easton Street. I discovered by accident quite a few weeks later, whilst spending an evening out with Jim Gunn in London. Jim was training at the Orpington facility he also spent his first week. However his instructions were explicit, on no account was he to eat in the hotel restaurant and was to use a much cheaper local eating establishment. No-one actually reprimanded me for eating at the expensive restaurant. So I guess the financial department was not too pleased at receiving the horrendous hotel bill which they were forced to pay for one of their more menial staff. Poor Jim was unable to avail himself of the wonderful restaurant facilities and service, which I can recall, even to this day were absolutely wonderful. My evening meal bills were in the region of twenty five pounds every night which was extravagant for the late seventies early eighties.

My first weeks at the Sidcup site were really enjoyable, getting to know and acquainted with the personnel; Elliot Hill, the Plant Manager, Phil Hedges, Martin Sheehan and Tommy from the shop floor. I began to find out about their foibles and the animosities, together with the politics which exist in any working environment. For once, it was nice to be an outsider, knowing I would not be there for a long period of time. This was to be a transient employment with me returning to the Welsh facility. The tension and differences between the staff became evident after a very short period of time.

I spent a large amount of time with Martin Sheehan the Quality Control Chemist who taught me the required tests to be done on the various products, such as viscosities, mostly using Ford Cups, Specific Gravities, drying times coating thicknesses by running bars over various metals. I acquired knowledge about the formulations and the functions of the various components within those formulations, quickly discovering it was imperative to learn as much as much as possible before lunch. Phil Hedges one of the managers had taken a liking to me and began inviting me down the pub at lunchtime with some of his mates. It became evident, 'lunch' comprised mostly of an alcoholic, liquid lunch with perhaps a sandwich comprising the solid part of the meal. As Phil usually met two of his mates from other places of work, everyone bought a round during the hour we were allowed. Four pints were usually consumed in that time, with Phil driving back to our place of work. All this was a complete culture shock to me, as Gwent had one of the highest rates for drink driving convictions in the United Kingdom. Motorists in Gwent were, and still are very wary of drinking and driving, whereas in the Home Counties drink driving in the early eighties appeared to be the norm.

Phil appeared to be so relaxed about consuming four pints of lager within the space of an hour and then casually driving back to the site without the slightest fear of losing his license. I could not comprehend this cavalier attitude towards the drink driving laws. Besides this flouting of the drink driving laws, there were other ramifications to all these liquid lunch sessions, one being the fact I was totally incapable of acquiring any knowledge upon my return to work during the afternoon. The alcohol consumed, combined with the solvent fumes permeating the laboratory completely suppressed my somewhat limited ability to assimilate any information imparted to me. I quickly learned to acquire as much information before lunch as anything after two in the afternoon was a complete waste of time. I may as well have gone back to my digs. The second ramification to these lunches spent at a local pub were more basic, that of my physique. Up until this time in my life, I had been fairly slim, with a reasonably flat stomach. However, a happy marriage, coupled with a rich diet aided and abetted by this increased intake of alcohol soon put paid to my lithe figure. Soon, I began acquiring a beer belly or paunch. After a few weeks of being away, my wife started to comment about this dramatic change in my physical shape.

'What the hell are you eating up there?' she enquired one day. After looking in the full sized mirror, it struck home how my physique had deteriorated and had begun to acquire the shape of a seven month pregnant woman.

There was another reason for this sudden explosion in my weight, namely my new accommodation with Mrs Hornsby. After my first week spent in luxury and opulence of the hotel, the accommodation became more basic, with my stay being transferred to a B & B at PettsWood, owned and run by Mr & Mrs Hornsby. The arrangements included a generous full English breakfast and substantial evening meal. Circumstances were conspiring against me to mutilate my lithe shape.

Mr & Mrs Hornsby had a somewhat bizarre relationship. He was a few years younger than her; she was forty five, he was probably in his mid-thirties. But that was not the reason for it appearing bizarre. Also staying at the house was another Cox & Sons employee, Bruce, who was training at the Orpington facility. Bruce was an Australian. He had been at the house for well over a year. He was in his mid-twenties. Mrs Hornsby openly flirted with him in front of her husband, who appeared to be totally and utterly unconcerned with the attention his wife was proffering upon this young man from the antipodes, even allowing his wife to accompany Bruce around the United Kingdom for a week's holiday.

Indeed, Mrs Hornsby even propositioned me one Friday Morning during breakfast when she asked quite innocently what I had planned that Friday evening upon getting home. I replied in a blasé sort of way.

'Well my wife and I will probably have a Chinese take-away, buy a nice bottle of wine and then we will probably be in bed by half eight.'

Mrs Hornsby's reply completely had me non-plussed and left me open mouthed,

'Well if you come up to the bed room I can sort that little problem out for you right now!' What took me aback was the fact her husband was in the room and taking no notice whatsoever of her suggestive comment, continuing to read his newspaper while at the same time consuming his large breakfast. Either pretending to ignore the comment, or not caring. I quickly left the table and rushed off to work as fast as I could. Mrs Hornsby was quite rotund and not what could be described as beautiful. After our little discussion, I made a point of not discussing sex or making any form of double entendre in her presence. She frightened me to death and it was with some relief when I eventually left the B & B run by Mr & Mrs Hornsby. I think I can safely say Mrs Hornsby was a *'maneater'*. Perhaps her husband was glad to have a rest from her overwhelming, demanding sexual appetite, who knows? Whatever, she certainly put the fear of God into me. I was deeply in love with Cindy and could never be unfaithful to her, and certainly not with Mrs Hornsby.

The Sidcup site certainly had a lot of character and a lot of characters. Spending a lot of time with Martin Sheehan, it became evident he lived in a sort of Walter Mitty world. He was in his mid to late twenties and lived near Biggin Hill, telling myself and everyone else he held a pilot's license, having learned to fly at the Biggin Hill aerodrome, forever informing everyone how he had once taken over the controls of a passenger aircraft after the pilot feinted or passed out for some reason. It was only through Martin's heroic assistance, all the people on the aircraft were saved. By taking the controls, he had prevented the aircraft from flying into a mountain, after which he then landing it safely. Martin would recount other heroic feats which he had performed, but that one was the most heroic episode. Phil and Martin had no time for each other, constantly criticising each other, or slagging each other off. I tried to stay out of it in an effort to once again remain neutral. I like both of them, each had their individual foibles and peculiarities but neither had done any harm to me and both were helpful in '*showing me the ropes.*'

I felt sorry for Martin. He was unmarried, had no girlfriends that he spoke of, and could in no way be described as a ladies' man or womaniser. From what I was able to glean he had no real close friends, male or female. However he was good at his job teaching me all he knew concerning the different formulations and products. Phil on the other hand basically taught me how to drink excessive amounts of alcohol in a short period of time. A lesson he taught mainly during the lunch hours.

I also befriended Tommy, the senior operator, he had ragged features and spoke with a typical London accent, which being Welsh and 'provincial' I always closely link with a Cockney accent. Although I realise a true Cockney has to be born within the sounds of Bow Bells, nevertheless Tommy had the distinctive London twang as indeed did Phil and Elliot Hill, the Plant Manager, but Tommy's was much more pronounced and evident. I talked to everyone at the plant. One of the operators in his twenties spoke with a very educated accent indeed and when I asked Tommy about him, he informed me the person in question had graduated with a Degree in Ancient History, which he obtained at one of the red brick universities. Not having the right connections, he was unable to get a job in research with the BBC or some other large public organization concerned with Ancient History studies. Tommy also added in his London accent, 'He's a fucking idiot!'

Upon enquiring why Tommy considered the graduate in such a manner, I was told in no uncertain terms. 'He keeps writing the fuckin' batch numbers on the containers in those fuckin' Roman numerals, we can never find batches of stuff to go out to the fuckin' customers!' I had to turn away to hide my amusement at something which Tommy obviously considered to be a major problem, firmly convinced the graduate did it to wind up his works colleagues to help pass the time in what was evidently a mundane, boring and soul destroying job for someone with such intellect. When I asked the operator in question why he did not go into teaching, he said it was a profession and career he had no interest in taking up.

I could relate to that, trying to teach a load of 'in your face', spotty-faced, self-opinionated, arrogant youths with absolutely no interest in learning, which would in my case be something like maths or chemistry, two of the worst subjects to teach as far as students are concerned. The graduate corroborated what Tommy had said, informing me it was virtually impossible to get employment in research with the old established employers unless you were part of the old-boy network, having gone to Eaton or Harrow and graduating from Oxford or Cambridge. If you had gone to a grammar school and then graduated from a red brick university, then forget it as far as the classical subjects were concerned. Upon hearing this I was glad I had taken the scientific route, at least there was and always has been more opportunity within industry for a Chemical Engineer. So in order to pay the bills, this highly qualified graduate was reduced to working as packer in a paint factory. He was still there when I left so heaven knows what he ended up doing.

My time at Sidcup fortunately coincided with the

summer months, with the extended, warm, light, balmy summer days and evenings. Phil Hedges, Elliot Hill and Tommy took me out on a number of occasions to play golf at the local municipal golf course at Lullingstone. They would collect me from the lab at four in the afternoon, one hour before my proper finishing time, enabling us to get a nice early start on the course before the other office workers arrived. I enjoyed these excursions immensely, with the friendly banter and joking between my works colleagues. As one would have expected never having played the game before, I was totally useless, usually coming last, but I enjoyed the social aspect ending with a drink at the nineteenth hole at the end of the evening in convivial and pleasant surroundings.

Other nights I amused myself by going to the cinema or arranging to meet Jim Gunn and Andy Morris who were at one of the offices in Easton Street the centre of London, arranging to meet them for a drink 'in town,' catching a train from Petts Wood, anything which would keep me out of the amorous advances of the rotund, buxom, and obviously sexually frustrated, Mrs Hornsby.

It was during one of these social evenings Jim, after imbibing in a few taverns, inns, pubs and clubs he becoming slightly maudlin told me the whole story concerning the sad demise of The Litho Plates Division.

Cox & Sons had begun its life in East End of London. In 1870, manufacturing inks initially, for the printing industry, expanded and then diversified into resins and paints. In 1968, Gary Cox, the incumbent chairman at the time, had the idea of producing Litho plates. The company already manufactured inks for the printing industry; why not manufacture the disposable off-set Litho plates used for putting the inks onto the paper as well? Hence the Litho Plates Division came into being and became well-established due to the large amount of land available on the Welsh site. All this happened about 1969, all at the behest of Gary Cox. At the time of this discussion in July 1980, I had joined the company the previous October, just about the time Gary Cox happened to be retiring.

The Litho Plates division had never made a profit in all the eleven years since its inception, being propped up and supported financially by the other more profitable sections of the business. Gary Cox always insisted in keeping Litho Plates running, confident it would hold its own and one day eventually make a profit. The instant Gary retired from the business and during the first board meeting without him, the momentous decision was taken to close the facility. With its mentor and chief supporter now gone, the motion was unanimously taken to close the Litho Plates section the following June. The decision to close the Division been taken November 1979. One month following my employment with the company, Jim was eventually informed of this decision May 1980.

The way Jim told it, he locked himself in the office the day he was informed of the closure and spent the rest of the day staring blankly at the wall, completely stunned and shocked. Somehow he felt responsible for the decision, although in reality it was completely out of his hands. The facility never made a profit during its ten years in existence and the Board of Directors had decided enough was enough. When pressed by me about his absence from the production area, Jim admitted he had locked himself in his office during the weeks prior to the general meeting in the canteen, unable to talk to people for fear of being asked a direct question concerning the possible closure of Litho Plates. He could not lie about it, but he had also been instructed not to inform anyone of the demise of the facility so there was the moral dichotomy. If pressed, he would tell, but had orders not to. In order to alleviate this dilemma, Jim locked himself away from everyone until the meeting.

I was probably one of the few people he actually conversed with prior to the meeting when he phoned me that night shift. Jim was still experiencing feelings of guilt concerning the closure. That night he related the whole unfortunate saga. I have no feelings of hatred or recriminations towards Cox & Sons, Jim Gunn or Jack Houseman. It was simply a number of unfortunate circumstance coming together and being at the wrong place at the wrong time. However this experience as a supervisor would later help me further down the line in my career, so it was not entirely a waste of time.

My stint at Cox & Sons Sidcup gradually came to a close. Due to being led astray by Phil Hedges; I gained very little knowledge following my liquid lunches.

Phil Hedges and Elliot Hill relocated to Witney in Oxfordshire. Martin Sheehan did not wish to relocate, opting for voluntary redundancy instead. Tommy did the same.

It was now time for me to head back to working in South Wales and because of my hedonistic tendencies, with very little acquired technical knowledge.

# CHAPTER 14

The imminent closure of the Sidcup site loomed on the horizon. With the closure, and my training considered complete, it was time for me to return to the Finishes laboratory in South Wales. More importantly, from my point of view, it meant resuming a normal married life. Ah, the joy of once again being able to live at home and sleep in my own bed with my wife, her warm, naked, voluptuous body alongside mine.

Within a week of my return, however, higher management decided to send me on an induction course, a form of welcoming for new starters to the company. I considered this to be a complete waste of time and money. By this time, Cox & Sons had employed me almost a year, now they intended sending me on a tour of other sites within the company. My private thoughts considered that particular training would have been more beneficial within the first few weeks of joining the company, not one year later. Still, it would mean a few days away on a jolly. I had begun experiencing feelings of self-doubt about my ability to perform the job without Martin Sheehan's guidance and experience. The induction course would delay the inevitable just that little bit longer.

When all the manufacturing equipment from Sidcup finally arrived on site, all my insecurities and concerns really began shooting to the surface. If only I had not spent so much time in the pub with Phil Hedges during the lunch breaks, consuming copious amounts of beer, rendering me incapable of assimilating any information during the afternoons. If I had not spent so much time in the pub, then I would have acquired more knowledge concerning polyester resins, road-marking paints, specialized internal lacquers and external paints for cans and especially the mysterious, somewhat enigmatic, magical and what I considered almost mystical techniques involving colour-matching.

Another person from the facility would also attend the induction course, Andrew Wynter. He also worked in the Finishes laboratory. Andrew was a surly, morose, twenty-something and a person rarely given to exercising his facial muscles with a smile. Thus, the few days spent on the course would not exactly be enjoyable in Andrew's company.

Meanwhile, back home, Cindy experienced incredulity and like a certain Queen Victoria, was not amused at the prospect of her itinerant husband about to return to '*the big smoke*' for yet another week.

Andrew and I caught the train from Newport to Paddington then travelled by underground to the Head Office at Easton Street; soon to be relocated in the Orpington manufacturing facility in Kent.

The train journey from Newport to Paddington turned out to be uneventful. Andrew revealed himself to be less of a conversationalist than I had originally thought. He indeed proved to be a young man of few words, the completely opposite of Martin Sheehan who suffered from verbal diarrhoea and virtually impossible to shut up. Andrew was undoubtedly the antithesis, the other end of the spectrum with his monosyllabic conversation. When Andrew did condescend to hold a small conversation, he droned on monotonously in a depressing voice, continually complaining about virtually everyone and everything. He protested that he did not want to be on the induction course and imparted various reasons as to why not. He reminded me of Marvin the paranoid android from that wonderful book, *The Hitch Hiker's Guide to the Galaxy* by Douglas Adams. By the time we arrived in London, he was not the only one depressed. One *Leonard Cohen* record and

I would almost certainly have ended up topping myself, then and there.

Fortuitously, the next day, it became evident there happened to be quite a few others on this induction course who were certainly more affable, friendly and easier to hold a conversation with than my colleague. I managed to team up with a couple of lads in their late twenties, and nearer my age. They both worked at the facility in Stallingborough near Grimsby. Matthew was an easy-going Mancunian and Steve, his colleague, a Geordie from Newcastle. Steve possessed a broad Geordie accent and the temperament associated with people from the north-east. No nonsense, speak your mind attitude. The two of them turned out to be far better company than my taciturn, morose colleague.

The next few days became a series of hectic tours involving visits to various facilities belonging to Cox & Sons located throughout London and the Home Counties. The penultimate day of the course involved a coach trip to the photocopying ink manufacturing site based at Midsummer Norton, Somerset, and then back to London.

The hotel used as accommodation during this induction course happened to be located near the Mount Pleasant Post Office sorting office. By the end of the week, I began experiencing feelings of exhaustion. The Mount Pleasant Office operated twenty-four hours a day, with the incessant cacophony of sounds keeping me awake and preventing a restful night's sleep. Luckily the course, (although it could not in reality, be put into the category of a course) but simply a guided tour of some of the Cox & Son's facilities meant very little concentration was required during the day, unlike other courses, which usually included some sort of exam at the end and necessitated a fair amount of paying attention.

On the final evening of the 'course,' my colleagues decided to have good blowout and go on the razz, ending up with a tour of the fleshpots of London, which, as I recall, was probably instigated by myself. The debauched itinerary included a tour of the pubs, around the West End and possibly the seedier spots of Soho. It turned out to be an interesting evening. One of the local London lads in his late teens continually bragged about his drinking prowess. He had two pints of beer and had to go home, feeling the worse for wear, some drinker!

One of the other people on the course had not long been married and spent most of the evening continually looking for telephone booths and phoning his new bride and often returned to his hotel room quite early in the evening, probably to indulge in some romantic chat with her.

So that last night ended up with Matthew, Steve, Andrew and myself intent on visiting a strip club ... well it's not often one is in the centre of London and after all, it's virtually compulsory to visit these dens of iniquity, particularly when it's a gang of males on the razz. Andrew continually complained about how he had no intention of paying money to gangsters. However, Steve, Matthew and myself realized we would probably be ripped off, but willing, you could say, almost happy, to go along for the ride.

We chose one of the seedy strip clubs at random, located in the Soho area. After a brief discussion, the four of us decided to give it a try. At this point Andrew informed us he had no intention of being ripped off by the mob and would be going back to the hotel. He believed all three of us would go back with him, well at the least, I would.... not a bit of it. We intended having a good time, and about to make the most of what remained of the evening. Once again, Andrew asked if I was going back with him. I told him the night was still young and I would be going into the strip joint with my newfound drinking friends. With that, Andrew returned to the hotel. I followed Matthew and Steve into this den of iniquity, which beckoned seductively, with its flashing, gaudy neon lights. I must confess to being filled with trepidation, although the amount of alcohol coursing through my veins went some way to reduce and alleviate those feelings slightly.

Upon walking in, we observed two intimidating and extremely large bouncers. The attractive girl in the foyer asked each of us for ten pounds, quite a large amount of money for 1980. Still, we all paid up willingly, anticipating an evening of erotic sexual performances, full of debauchery. The three of us walked sheepishly through a narrow dark corridor, which opened, into a darkened room, darkened because of the dim lighting used in the room. We could just make out numerous, rather flimsy, circular tables around which the audience sat. On small stage, an extremely attractive, well-endowed, blonde girl performed. I can testify to her being a natural blonde, by certain bodily hairs. The collar and cuffs matched as they say.

The attractive blonde-haired girl pulled a scarf between her open, bare thighs in an extremely erotic, provocative and sexual manner. I was quite surprised at the amount of men, mostly middle aged, who actually inside the dimly lit room. We experienced difficulty negotiating our way around, the tables due to the dim lighting, in the room, to which our eyes had not yet become accustomed, making it extremely difficult in finding a place to sit. Eventually we managed to locate a table with three vacant seats, and three women seated around it. I assumed they were women and did a double take at seeing the opposite sex frequenting a strip club.

I nervously sat down next to a red-haired woman, with extremely large protuberances, wearing a low cut dress and exhibiting her cleavage to good effect. She was drinking champagne from an old-fashioned champagne glass. I began watching the spectacle-taking place on the stage.

All of a sudden, the girl on stage stopped her erotic performance, departed from the small stage, to be replaced by yet another blonde-haired woman, this time accompanied by a brunette. The two of them immediately began indulging in a lesbian performance on the small stage. Whilst everyone concentrated on this spectacle, a waiter approached our table and handed each of us a large card with the prices printed on it. In between looking at the girls on stage, I had a brief look at the drinks menu.

My mouth gapped open upon noting the prices; three pounds for a small glass of coke, five pounds for a pint of lager, four pounds fifty for a pint of beer. The exorbitant prices went on, quite extortionate for the declining years of the seventies. I decided not to buy a drink but instead concentrate on the erotic show-taking place in front of me. Well it would be rude not to sit quietly and watch the two artistes giving it their all….in more ways than one. Besides, I had consumed more than enough alcoholic beverages for that evening. After all the girls were good enough to go through this rather arousing act, the least I could do was sit and watch.

The waiter returned. He then approached Steve enquiring which drink he would like to order. Steve replied in his loud, somewhat inebriated Geordie voice.

'Wha man, I d'ana want a drink ... look at these prices for fuck's sake besides I paid enough to get in the place!' Disgruntled, the waiter went away and quickly returned. Meanwhile, I continued watching the two girls on stage, admiring their superb feminine bodies.

The waiter whispered something into Steve's ear. Steve was however not so quiet in his response with distinctive Geordie accent.

'Why do we have to buy a drink man, besides, he hasn't got a drink, he hasn't got a drink…. neither as he?' Steve voiced his opinion quite vociferously, at the same time pointing to numerous different customers in this den of iniquity. As he pointed in the various directions, each man in line of the accusing finger looked decidedly embarrassed, and immediately looked away in alternative directions, hoping to avoid further attention.

Meanwhile, I desperately tried to concentrate on watching the two girls on stage while this contretemps between Steve and the waiter continued, unabated. Once again, the waiter went away and then approached each man whom Steve had pointed out. Yet again, he returned, this time he too shouted his reply, in a cockney accent, a complete contrast to Steve's extremely broad Geordie accent.

'Look mate, each of those men has been here for ages and each one of them has bought a couple of drinks; you have to buy a drink or leave!'

Steve once again retorted, 'I d'ana want a drink man!' the waiter once again went away. I sighed with relief, still trying to concentrate on the show. However, unfortunately, Steve refused to remain quiet and now began criticising the lesbian performance-taking place on stage. The two nubile, beautiful girls had superb figures and knew how to erotically gyrate them to good effect.

'Wha' up man they're faking it, they're not enjoying that!' Shouted Steve, his voice raised so that virtually everyone in the place could hear him, I could tell by the stares he got, even from the two performers who gave him filthy looks. Matthew and I sank slowly into our seats, hoping to become invisible and trying to pretend this loud Geordie had nothing to do with us and had just happened to walk in to the premises at the same time we did. The waiter returned yet again, this time accompanied by the two intimidating, huge gorillas, who I assumed to be bouncers. Also, there was a third person, almost normal looking, dressed in what looked like an expensive mohair suit. I began wishing I had made a will. I began visualising my body supporting one of the new fly-overs proliferating throughout the country, wearing a concrete overcoat and Cindy assuming the mantle of a young, desirable widow in her thirties. The waiter and two bouncers glared down at the three of us as their companion spoke.

'Look lads,' he said in an appealing, calm, almost paternalistic voice. 'We don't want any trouble, so we're going to ask you to leave and we will give you all your money back. Now that's fair isn't it?'

Once again, Steve chirped in with his broad Geordie accent, 'But man I h'ana seen all of the show yet man!'

With that, Matthew spoke up. 'Come on Steve, let's call it a day, we'll get our money back.'

Steve had a look around and suddenly had second thoughts about staying after observing the Neanderthals surrounding us. 'Waha man, perhaps you're right.'

I spoke as well, almost pleading with him, 'Yeah let's go we've seen a bit of the show.' With that, we all got up to leave. Before I went for some inexplicable, self-destructive reason, I spoke to a red-headed woman sitting next to me. Well, I assume she was a woman, 'How much do you charge by the way?' She looked at the bouncers and a horrified expression appeared on her face... she then muttered something then turned away, desperately attempting to ignore me. Steve, Matthew and I walked out slowly convinced we were all going about to get a knuckle sandwich. However true to his word the spokesman took us to the pay booth and told the girl to refund our monies, which she then did, in full.

I wished the spokesman and the two bouncers a good night, only to be on the receiving end of cold stares from three pairs of eyes. Once out of the premises, the three of us walked quickly away from the seedy strip joint. After that, we called it an evening and returned to the hotel and the safe havens of our individual rooms.

When I thought about it the next day, we came out of it ahead, we had seen part of a strip show free, and had not paid an extortionate amount for any drinks. Andrew was green with envy when we broke the news to him over breakfast the next morning concerning the previous night's events. That afternoon we all parted company, heading to our various destinations. Andrew and I caught the train from Paddington back to Newport. Cindy and I had an early night and the usual passionate lovemaking following our enforced celibacy. I never told her about my little excursion into the Soho strip club. Somehow, I do not think she would have appreciated it.

Life began settling into a routine in the laboratory at The Finishes Division, now slightly boring when compared with my previous lives in the Steelworks, Birchwater, West Mercian Oil and Litho Plates. There was also a lot of animosity towards us from the other laboratory personnel, antipathy with which I could sympathise. Both Andy Morris and I were doing the same jobs as the other staff, but receiving more remuneration. We had been quite highly paid in the Litho Plates division because of our status. As an incentive for us both to stay with the company, Cox & Sons paid us over-inflated salaries. The only person I could relate to in the laboratory besides Andy was a

233

person called Mike Dicks. He appeared to be in his late forties and possessing a wicked sense of humour. He had suffered a nervous breakdown some years earlier and a young lad called Allan Williams became his boss, whereas previously, it had been vice versa. Still, Mike had a certain pragmatic stoicism concerning his change in circumstances. We got on well together.

Mike and Jim Gunn never saw eye to eye. One of Mike's duties also involved showing visitors around the site. During one of his tours of the Litho Plates, one day, he saw Jim Gunn, immediately informing the visitors, deliberately within earshot of Jim so he could hear. 'This is Jim Gunn,' adding, with a pun, 'He's the big shot around here!'

Jim never really forgave Mike after making a joke of his surname. Now Jim had progressed to becoming General Manager of the Division and Mike's boss. As previously mentioned, it pays to be very careful what you say in the workplace.

I also had a good rapport with another person named Daryl, the Assistant Production Manager. Daryl happened to be quite young, in his early twenties and in the throes of getting over a long-term relationship with his girlfriend, which she had ended.

As Mike kept telling me, 'Since Daryl split up with his girlfriend, he has found out what his prick is for, and I don't mean for pissing through. He is experiencing as many females as he possibly can, the lucky bastard!'

Daryl, to his credit, did not brag too much about his numerous female conquests and in fact appeared quite reserved on the subject. However, one day he came into work in a foul mood. Calling people with CB radios everything under the sun and they were most definitely not terms of endearment. I should perhaps explain at that, time owning a CB (Citizen Band) radio the authorities deemed it to be illegal. Of course, the fact that they were illegal and the police were unable to enforce the law made owning the forbidden fruits that much sweeter, more appealing and exciting. Therefore, in the late seventies a proliferation of CB radios took place. The law later changed and CB radios became accepted and legal. With the concomitant result, they also became less popular, making it an extremely wise move on the government's part. I pressed Daryl as to why he hated CB radio enthusiasts so much.

After much persuasion, he began relating the circumstances of the previous, night's events, which, evidently, had annoyed him so much. He and his girlfriend of the moment happened to be on top of a secluded mountain in his car and about to indulge in carnal knowledge with each other. Being a hot summer's evening, both he and his female companion eventually ended up as naked as they day they were born. While they indulged in what came naturally, someone in a car with a CB radio had spotted them. Being an unselfish sort of individual, he then contacted other CB enthusiasts in the vicinity, informing them of events taking place in Phil's car.

Within a short space of time, other vehicles appeared on the scene, all with their headlights off, and surrounded Daryl's car. At a given signal, all the participants turned their headlights on, full beam, illuminating his car in a flood of artificial light. Apparently, he was actually on the point of reaching a climax. All systems full speed ahead as they say. Suddenly, both Daryl and his female partner discovered themselves totally enveloped in blinding white light. At first, Daryl believed it to be a close encounter with an alien spacecraft, before suddenly realising, there were a number of cars surrounding him. Coitus with his willing female partner was immediately forgotten. He emerged from his car and started running towards the source of the light, completely naked, ranting and raving at the voyeurs, hurtling like a demon towards them.

Suddenly, he remembered his naked state and the cool night air reducing his aroused state quite considerably and doing nothing to enhance his manhood. One of the guys mocked him as he drove away, shouting. 'You ought to get a CB radio mate ...then you wouldn't get caught out,' adding the final insult. 'You little prick!' whilst at the same time, pointing to Daryl's nether regions.

After making that statement, they all drove away laughing leaving Daryl standing naked and shivering on top of Rudry Mountain. He never had much truck with CB enthusiasts after that, following his experience. I can't blame him.

There also happened to be one young lad of about seventeen working in the laboratory with whom I talked to on occasions. One day he seemed to be very depressed. I Began talking to him and enquired why he was so glum, as he appeared to have all the worries of the world on his shoulders.

'It's my father,' he replied rather despondently.

'We just don't seem able to get on with each other.'

'Well,' I replied, trying to help and give what advice I could, 'There has always been a difference between the ages and generations; it's a fact of life... how old is he?'

My mouth dropped open when this fresh lad of seventeen told me. 'Eighty five,' he replied.

I was speechless and my mouth gaped open. I resembled a giant carp which had just been hooked and landed. He broke the embarrassing silence, looking at me and smiled disarmingly.

'I know what you're thinking,' he said. At that

instant, my powers of speech, thankfully, just about returned.

'What am I thinking?' I croaked in reply.

'That my father's a dirty old man!' The smile increased on his face, as he observed my embarrassment. He looked at me questioningly. 'Am I right?'

I nodded my head, confirming he was correct. The actual thoughts generating in my head went something like '*Lucky, randy, old, bastard, still able to have his end away when well into his sixties, obviously, with a much younger woman*!' My mind had quickly worked out the arithmetic. It now became obvious why he and his father had a communication problem. I never talked to the young lad much after that. I thought he may have been winding me up, but others told me he had indeed been telling me the truth.

The summer came and went, turning into autumn. A lot had happened in the year, with me now doing a very different job from the one I had been doing at the start of the year, discovering I had become the proverbial square peg in the round hole. I wish I had paid more attention whilst at Sidcup, instead of listening to Martin Sheehan, going off at a tangent and continually talking about his life as an amateur pilot and also refrained from getting pissed at lunchtime with Phil Hedges.

As the process equipment began arriving from Sidcup, I began the task of doing the quality tests and rectifying any quality problems, and the worst of all colour matching. Which, I still consider to this day to be an art form, not a science, having to assess which colour to add, particularly to the polyester resin to get the colour back, an art form at which I was absolutely rubbish. There is a definite technique to it and paint sprayers working on car re-sprays for example have my admiration at being able to get a complete colour

237

match. I would put in completely the wrong colour or amount. Attempting to get the colour correct, it would go completely haywire. One of the lads from the Finishes lab would invariably have to come and bale me out on a number of occasions. It amazed me how they were able to correct the colours with relative ease, add a bit of red a bit of black, a bit of white bit of yellow etc. They instinctively knew which colours to add. A task which had taken me ages and which I had inevitably made a debacle. Unfortunately, this happened quite a few times and my confidence began taking a battering. I could also sense resentment from a young man called Hugh. He had instructions from Allan Williams to assist me whenever I had trouble with colour matching. I was earning much more than he was and I was completely inept at the job. Other tasks such as measurement of viscosity, pH I could handle and correct easily. Getting colours right I could not handle or comprehend, having not the faintest idea which colour to add in order to get the correct colour match with the standard. I knew I should not have dropped art so early on in Grammar School. This alternative job was just not right for me. I could not do the colour matching which was an extremely important part of my duties.

I began to get depressed at being unable to perform the tasks and do my job properly, relying on other people, and requiring support from other members of the staff. Andy Morris also had trouble with the colour matching, so I was not alone in that respect, which was a small comfort. Cindy too began to notice a change in my demeanour and began asking why I had become sullen and quiet during the evenings on my return from work. After talking it through, we decided I should look for yet another job. So, every Thursday and we began reading the job vacancies in the Western Mail, in attempt to find a suitable opening.

The year drew to a close with the nights becoming longer and the days colder. Our new house slowly began taking shape as we began adding to our meagre belongings. That December saw the assassination of John Lennon... Upon hearing the news that evening, I, like many others, experienced shocked and disbelief, and was totally devastated at the news, news which exacerbated my depression. One of the leading icons of the sixties and seventies, cut down in his prime.

The new decade began and 1981 now replaced, 1980, with a right wing Conservative government firmly ensconced in power and destined to be there until May 1997.

One evening, Cindy pointed out a job being advertised in the Western Mail, with a company called Repeat Controls Corporation. The company was advertising for Engineers of all types, including Chemical and Process Engineers needed due to an expansion programme taking place at their facility in Brynmawr, a valley town neighbouring my birthplace of Ebbw Vale and not too far from Abergavenny, and most certainly a lot nearer than the Cox & Sons facility. Repeat Controls Corporation manufactured computer tapes and the new computer discs being used in the mainframe industrial computers. The computer industry had begun expanding exponentially and appeared to be definitely the way forward, with far better prospects.

Cindy began telling me about the advert, convincing me the job was just up my street, and that I should apply as soon as possible. With my CV updated, I immediately posted it to the advertised address. It was now February 1981. Within a short space of time, I received a reply, requesting me to attend an interview with Neil Harries. I had quite a few holidays available, and had no problem in obtaining the time off to attend.

I was now almost thirty years of age, with quite a fair bit of industrial and Chemical Engineering experience under my belt. Because of this acquired knowledge and experience, it was time for a change. I must confess to attending the job interview with a fair amount of self confidence, unusual for me. I desired this job and this happened to be my territory, whereas colour-matching most certainly was not and something I had not picked up easily, and it showed. I had come a long way since Birchwater and West Mercian Oil, having acquired knowledge about different processing equipment and techniques. I had been a Supervisor, albeit for about eight months, my works repertoire had grown in leaps and bounds.

As I entered the gates of the Repeat Control Corporation facility, my nostrils scented a strong, sickly smell of solvent permeating the atmosphere. The solvent I later discovered to be cyclohexanone, used in vast quantities for manufacturing computer tapes.

The interview was with Neil Harries, a heavily built forty-something with receding blonde hair and Head of the Consultancy Department. The interview went very well. After a while, he informed me the vacancy in his department had been filled; however, he also informed me the Process Engineering Department had a position vacant for which he believed I would be eminently suitable. He then asked if I had time to attend another interview that day. I told him I had, having taken a day's holiday off work and it would not be a problem. He then instructed me to wait in the well-provisioned canteen.

Therefore, I attended another interview that day, this time with Tom Evans and Damian Morgan, Managers from the Process Engineering Department. They both gave me a good technical grilling and seemed impressed with my time spent at West Mercian Oil and my supervisory experience gained at Cox & Sons. The interview eventually came to an end. Despite it appearing to have gone well, it was impossible to say whether I had been successful in obtaining employment with the Repeat Control Corporation. I would just have to wait to discover the outcome.

A few days later, a letter came in the post asking me to attend yet another interview, this time with Craig Prosser, the newly appointed Production Manager. The interview had to be held at the Repeat Control facility at seven in the evening. Due to the short notice, I could not get a day off and had to attend the interview after work.

Craig Prosser turned out to be a young looking thirty eight year old year old, with a charismatic personality. He reminded me very much of another Craig, Craig Theake. We had a one to one discussion, Craig asking me question about myself, explaining his current position as the Personnel Manager but he was now in the transition of becoming the new Production Manager and he wanted a new young team under him. He visualised exciting times ahead with an expansion in the site and opportunities for all. His exuberance definitely reminded me of Craig Theake and Jim Gunn. I must admit the facility impressed me immensely, modern buildings and equipment, part of the hi-tech boom which had been generated because of the developing computers. The facility was obviously very new. There appeared to be hundreds of people around. The front offices were carpeted, light and airy, festooned with a tremendous amount of lush, green foliage. Someone had obviously been studying office layouts using Feng Shui to generate such a pleasant working environment.

I had however now become a bit blasé to the 'spin' about companies and how good they were. My experience with Cox & Sons instilling in me a degree of scepticism, after all, Jim Gunn had waxed lyrical about Litho Plates and the bright future, which lay ahead. I was taken in and thoroughly convinced. Look what had happened there! Despite my scepticism, I wanted the job and just wanted to get out of my current position, one I could not do with any proficiency, with a much lower salary than when I first joined. It was not the job for which I had originally joined Cox & Sons and time to leave gracefully.

Craig Prosser began telling me of the discussions he had had with Tom Evans and Damian Morgan and the job was mine as Disc Coating Engineer, working for the Process Engineering Department with a salary of eight thousand pounds per annum, working a normal five day week. It was a decent salary for 1981 and much more than my current salary with Cox & Sons. In addition there would be overtime payments, a generous pension scheme, twenty five days holiday per annum and with salary review in six months which as long as I performed as expected would be in the region of eleven per cent, and a salary review every six months thereafter until I reached the same pay level as my peers.

In addition, there was a four hour call out for any major problems. Otherwise, it involved working regular hour's eight until four thirty in the afternoon with an hour for lunch. He just kept on reeling off the figures and I began to think. '*I have died and gone to heaven*!' even drooling like one of Pavlov's dogs. My God, I was dreaming! This could not be happening. I was going to awake in a moment. However, no, this was really happening, this job did exist. Finally, Craig Prosser stopped talking and asked me if I wanted the job and, if so, when could I start. Unfortunately, I had to give a months' notice, which he told me would be no problem. I asked him if I could have it in writing which he said would be with me before the end of the week.

Upon getting home, I told Cindy immediately, being unable to contain my excitement. She had recently changed hairdressing salons, with her new job being much more highly paid than previous and she enjoyed working for her new employer. Things seemed to be coming together for us. I could not believe how our life appeared to be getting better and better as we now approached the top of the rollercoaster.

Upon receiving confirmation of my position as Disc Coating Engineer, I handed my notice in at The Finishes Division. Allan Williams did not appear to be unduly upset; neither did any of the others in the laboratory personnel, apart from Mike Dicks and Andy Morris. However, I did have to go have a discussion with Gary Hudson, the Personnel Manager. We had a frank discussion, where I explained my unsuitability for the job at the Finishes Division and felt my position in the laboratory unfair on Cox & Sons and upon the staff in the laboratory and unable to do the job justice and not the job I had joined the company for. There were no hard feelings on my part, but I felt it best to leave. Gary told me they were sorry to see me go, and if it was a question of money, perhaps Cox & Sons could match the salary now on offer from Repeat Control.

When I told Gary Hudson the remuneration on offer and with six monthly reviews with pay increases, holidays, hours of work, plus overtime, he just shook his head in disbelief.

'Well we certainly can't match all of that,' he said, with what I perceived was a hint of regret. We ended our discussion, shook hands and he wished me all the best for the future.

A few weeks later, for the very last time as an employee, I walked out of yet another set of gates those of Cox & Sons facility. My departure tinged with a hint of sadness but I knew this was certainly for the best.

Funny how life throws curved balls at you. Had Litho Plates remained open, I would have, in all probability, stayed with Cox & Sons, then who knows where fate would have taken me and which other path I would then have followed?

The next eight years with Repeat Control Corporation contained some of the most memorable and, as it turned out, life-changing events of my life. Most certainly the most financially rewarding, whilst meeting some fascinating and interesting characters. Working for a hi-tech computer company certainly would have its benefits. It was to be another episode in my ever-changing career on this rollercoaster we call life and which we all travel.

The eighties beckoned with a new job. The previous decades had most certainly been quite eventful with my time as a Student, Labourer, Civil Servant, working in sales, Industrial Chemist, Shift Supervisor and yes, Colour Chemist, the latter acting as a catalyst for this new change. My qualifications allowing me into the industrial world and gain experience as a Chemical Engineer. I had married Cindy, acquired my first mortgage, and a new house.

Yes, the seventies had been eventful. What had the eighties to offer I wondered, apart from outrageous fashions? I looked forward to the future decades with eager anticipation. So far, the years had indeed given me a life with a rich mix.